CAT
CLARKE

WE ARE
YOUNG

Quercus

QUERCUS CHILDREN'S BOOKS

First published in Great Britain in 2018 by Hodder and Stoughton
This paperback edition published in 2018 by Hodder and Stoughton

1 3 5 7 9 10 8 6 4 2

Text copyright © Cat Clarke, 2018

The moral rights of the author have been asserted.

A CIP catalogue record for this book
is available from the British Library.

ISBN 978 1 786 54005 8

Typeset in Perpetua 14/17 pt by
Palimpsest Book Production Limited, Falkirk, Stirlingshire

Printed and bound in Great Britain by Clays Ltd, St Ives plc

The paper and board used in this book
are made from wood from responsible sources.

MIX
Paper from
responsible sources
FSC
www.fsc.org   FSC® C013585

Quercus Children's Books
An imprint of
Hachette Children's Group
Part of Hodder and Stoughton
Carmelite House
50 Victoria Embankment
London EC4Y 0DZ

An Hachette UK Company
www.hachette.co.uk

www.hachettechildrens.co.uk

AUTHOR NOTE

If you are affected by any of the issues in this book, you can turn to page 357 for links to advice and support.

This book is for anyone who has ever felt voiceless and hopeless.

'Ambulance service. What's the emergency?'

'Fuck . . . Oh my God. I can't— There's been an accident.'

'Sir, I'm going to need you to calm down. Are you hurt?'

'No, but the people in the car . . .'

'Sir, can you tell me your name?'

'Vincent. Vince.'

'OK, Vince, can you tell me your location?'

'Fairfax Road – the school car park. There's a girl on the ground. She's . . . oh, Christ . . .'

'Tell me what you see, Vince.'

'She's . . . *broken.*'

'Vince, I need you to listen to me. An ambulance is on its way. Can you look at the girl? Is she conscious? Vince? Can you hear me?'

'She's dead.'

'Are you sure she's not breathing?'

1

'Her head isn't . . . yeah, I'm sure. I . . . think I'm going to be sick.'

'Take a deep breath, Vince. Are there other people inside the vehicle?'

'Two . . . no, wait, three. I can't get the door open. If I can just . . . OK, there's a boy.'

'You're doing really well, Vince. The ambulance is a couple of minutes away. Is the boy conscious and breathing?'

'There's blood . . .'

'Where's the blood coming from?'

'I can't fucking see! His arm . . . oh, Christ, his arm . . . Come on! Just breathe, will you? Fucking *breathe!*'

'Talk to me, Vince. What's happening? What's wrong with his arm? Vince? Are you there? Vince? *Vince!*'

ONE

Trying to make sure you're drunk enough to get through your mother's wedding day but not so drunk that she notices is not an easy task. It doesn't help that one of the waiters happens to be a boy from school; he keeps sneaking me top-ups of wine at every opportunity. I've never talked to Marcus Bloom before in my life – unless you count the apology I uttered when *he* bumped into *me* in the cafeteria that one time. Boys who look like him don't tend to bother with girls who look like me.

Mum catches my eye during the speeches and I know I'm busted. A few minutes later, she corners me before I can escape to the loos. I pull her into a hug, hoping to distract her.

'Tim's speech was so good!' The truth is, it was a little over the top. He mentioned Mum's 'beautiful, beautiful soul' so many times it started to get weird.

'Are you drunk?' Mum whispers in my ear.

I accidentally sway a little. 'Are *you* drunk?'

She pulls back and looks at me closely. 'How much have you had?'

I lean in close, peering back at her. On a day-to-day basis my mum is kind of pretty in a dainty way – blonde and pixieish – but today she looks stunning. 'Your make-up is flawless, you know. Nikki is a fucking wizard. I wish I'd got her to do mine. And your hair! I didn't even know hair could *be* that shiny. It's like . . . it's like . . . molten gold.'

Mum rolls her perfectly lined eyes. 'Soft drinks from now on, OK?'

I stand up straight and salute her. 'Aye, aye, Bridezilla.'

'If I really *was* Bridezilla, I wouldn't have let you wear Doc Martens to my wedding.' She laughs, then surprises me with another hug. 'I know this hasn't been easy for you, but I want you to know that I appreciate the effort you've been making – with Tim. And he appreciates it too.'

I shrug as we hug again. I haven't done anything special, unless you count trying not to be a total dick about the wedding. And I'm not sure I've been completely successful at that.

I look over to find Tim deep in conversation with my aunt. She seems to be doing most of the talking,

4

but he's listening like she's the most interesting person in the world. (And my aunt is absolutely not in contention for that title.) It's one of the things that surprises me most about Tim — that he doesn't yabber on all the time. On his radio show, he's all non-stop chatter and enthusiasm for anything and everything. Breakfast Tim is exhausting, but it turns out he's nowhere near as annoying in real life.

I've just about come to terms with the idea of Mum and him being together, but that doesn't mean I'm delighted about the wedding. It's far too quick — seven months isn't long enough to know you're ready to spend the rest of your life with someone. Mum said she knew (she absolutely, positively *knew*) she wanted to marry him the day she asked him to buy tampons. He didn't even blink, just asked if her flow was light, regular or heavy. Seems a pretty low bar to me, thinking someone's worth marrying because they're not embarrassed to talk about periods, but Mum's easily impressed.

'How's Tim doing?' I ask. 'Is he upset about Lewis?'

Mum follows my gaze, and it's as if Tim senses her looking, as if their vows have forged some super-sensory connection between them. He smiles and Mum beams back at him.

'He's . . . disappointed. I'd be devastated if you

and Billy weren't here. This is supposed to be about our families coming together. Yeah, yeah, I know you think it's sentimental old bollocks, but if I can't be sentimental on my wedding day, when can I be?'

'Are you sure *you're* not the one who's had too much to drink?' I say with a sly smile. Her smile falters, if only for a second. Mum never has more than a couple of drinks these days. She's always a bit touchy about me drinking, even though she's resigned herself to the fact that she can't stop me.

'Everyone keeps asking about Lewis. Maybe it would have been better if we'd just told people the truth?'

Gastroenteritus is the official explanation for my new stepbrother's absence; his flat-out refusal to leave his room is the actual truth. *I'd* never have got away with it, but he's nineteen years old and apparently those two extra years mean he gets to do whatever the hell he likes.

I shake my head. 'People wouldn't understand. Now stop worrying about Lewis and focus on enjoying yourself. This is *your* day.'

She leans in close. 'You do like him, don't you? Tim, I mean.'

'*Yes*! How many times do I have to tell you? He makes you happy, and that makes *me* happy.' Plus there's the fact that he isn't a total drunken mess. That's a definite bonus.

There are tears in Mum's eyes. She squeezes my arm and whispers, 'You're my best girl.'

I roll my eyes. 'You'll ruin your make-up if you're not careful. Now go, mingle. Your public awaits.' I gesture to a couple of Mum's colleagues hovering nearby.

She fixes her bridal smile back in place and straightens her shoulders. 'Promise me you're on soft drinks for the rest of the night?'

'I promise.'

'And you and Billy have to come up and dance for at least one song . . .'

I gently push my mother in the direction of her friends, who immediately envelop her in hugs and kisses and don't-you-look-beautifuls.

I don't exactly *break* my promise; I stretch it and mould it to my purposes. I do have a soft drink – several, in fact. It's just that Marcus adds a couple of generous splashes of vodka to my glass each time. He keeps looking at me and smiling. I wasn't sure how to feel about that, at first. But I decide that I like it.

'You're thirsty tonight, aren't you?' he says with a grin.

It sounds sexual, the way he says it. I'm fully aware of that, but I don't mind one little bit.

A little later – three drinks later to be precise – Marcus sidles over to where I'm sitting with my brother.

'I'm on my break now.'

I blink twice; my vision isn't exactly blurry, but it's not crystal clear either. 'And you're telling me this *why?*'

He likes that – his eyes flash with delight. He shrugs. 'I thought you might want to join me.' There's no doubt in my mind about his intentions.

I'm about to say no when my drunken gaze lands on Tim with his arms around my mother. It will never not be weird, seeing her with a man who isn't my father. I turn to Billy. 'You OK on your own for a bit, Bill?' My brother doesn't look up from his phone, mumbling something about trying to beat his best score.

Marcus holds out his hand and pulls me to my feet. He doesn't let go, even when I stumble. The stumble is a warning sign, which I ignore: I'm too drunk to cope with walking, so why exactly am I letting this boy lead me out of the marquee?

Next thing I know I'm sitting on a pile of fruit boxes with my dress hitched up round my waist while Marcus Bloom kisses my neck and fumbles with my underwear.

He smells of sweat and cigarettes. His stubble scratches my face when he kisses me; I turn my head away and notice the caterer's van parked a few metres away. It's not even dark yet. Anyone could see us.

Someone unbuckles Marcus's belt. Surely that someone can't be me.

But it is.

This is me. Evan Page. Little Miss Know Your Limits. Little Miss Responsible. Having frantic, uncomfortable sex with Marcus Bloom.

I'm vaguely aware of the extenuating circumstances, even while we're doing it. It's been a tough day – in so many ways – but I've had to keep smiling the whole time. I've kept it together even when I wanted to fall apart. And it's not just today; for years I've been playing the dutiful daughter role and maybe I'm finally sick of it. Add into the mix that I also happen to be drunker than I've ever been in my life.

Circumstances, reasons, excuses.

But what is exactly is my excuse for having frantic, uncomfortable, *unprotected* sex with Marcus Bloom?

TWO

Later, Billy and I stand on the edge of the dance floor, watching Mum and Tim's first dance. There's precisely zero chance of it going viral on YouTube.

'Who was that boy?' Billy whispers, scuffing his feet on the shiny floor.

'Just a friend from school.'

'I think he looks like a wolf.' My baby brother can be surprisingly perceptive. 'I prefer Sid.' I think Billy was more heartbroken than I was when Sid and I broke up at Easter.

I turn to see Marcus clearing glasses from the tables, taking time to stop and flirt with Mum's cousin, Norah. I know I'm far from sober, but everything suddenly feels painfully clear. It hurts to think.

'It's always the quiet ones.' That's what he said as he zipped himself up, shaking his head and smiling. Then he asked for my number. I told him to fuck off, which surprised him (and me), but didn't particularly bother him (or me). 'Feisty . . . I like it.'

I left him behind and hurried across the courtyard to the toilets – smiling at people along the way and trying to ignore the fact that my legs felt too weak to support me. Trying to ignore the wetness in my underwear.

STD names are running through my head as Tim twirls Mum round the dance floor. If Marcus didn't use a condom with me, what are the chances he uses them at all? My only hope is that the other girls he has sex with aren't as reckless as me. It's not as if I didn't think about it. Was it deliberate? Taking that risk, knowing it'll mean a trip to the chemist first thing tomorrow morning? I don't even know.

Billy reaches for my hand and looks up at me with those big blue eyes. 'Things are going to be better now, aren't they?'

'Yes.' There's really no other answer when a ten-year-old is looking at you like that.

'Aw, why are you crying? People always cry at weddings on TV, don't they? It's weird if you ask me.'

I laugh and squeeze his hand. 'It's happy crying.' I wish that was true.

'Come on, you two!' Mum and Tim have danced

11

their way towards us, laughing and smiling. Mum grabs Billy's hand and Tim takes mine. I don't seem to have a choice in the matter. The four of us dance together while the photographer snaps away. Everyone's so distracted by Billy's ridiculous moves that no one seems to care when I escape from the dance floor at the earliest opportunity.

Mum and Tim are still dancing two hours later. Tim's Tango-coloured hair is damp with sweat and his face is red. He's got rid of his jacket and rolled up his sleeves, and she kicked off her heels as soon as 'Dancing Queen' came on.

I find an empty table and get my phone out to message Daze. I don't want to have to tell her about Marcus Bloom face to face. Of course I'd never have had sex with him if she'd been here, but Daze doesn't *do* weddings. She's going to give me hell for it, but I'd still rather stay at her place tonight than go to Harry's with Billy. The thought of staying at my father's flat is unappealing at the best of times, but tonight it's unimaginable.

I type out several versions of the message and delete each one. I'm starting to wonder if maybe it would be best not to say anything at all when Gary Strout shimmies over. Middle-aged men should be banned from shimmying – and from wearing novelty ties. 'Mind if I join you?' He doesn't wait for an answer before sitting down and loosening his tie.

Gary is Tim's best man, and the producer on his show. Apparently he's a nice bloke, but I think he's a dick – especially after that innuendo-laden speech of his. Tim must have mentioned that I'm into music, which seems to be Gary's cue to bore me to tears on the subject. He isn't remotely interested in what I have to say, as long as I keep nodding in the right places. This guy could get a degree in mansplaining.

'Did Tim tell you about the time I met Bowie? What a legend. *Total* legend.'

That's definitely worth a nod. I even manage to muster the enthusiasm to ask what Bowie was like.

'Oh, *amazing*, totally amazing. Inspiring, really.'

'So what did you guys talk about?'

Gary's finger traces a red wine stain on the tablecloth. 'It was all a bit manic . . . you know how things are backstage. All sorts going on . . . *wild*.' His eyes widen and he wiggles his eyebrows.

Gary never met David Bowie. That much is obvious. A stifled giggle emerges from under the table and I realise that Billy's holed up under there. If it were socially acceptable for a seventeen-year-old to do the same I'd have cheerfully joined him. Instead, I grab my brother's arm and pull him up to sit beside me, forming a Billy-shaped barrier between Gary and me. Gary ruffles Billy's hair and starts asking him the sort of questions adults ask children when they have no idea what to say. *What's your favourite subject at school? Are you glad the summer holidays have started? Do you like football?* Billy's answers are suitably monosyllabic: art; yeah; no. Thankfully Gary gets the hint and shimmies off to get another drink. I spy Marcus behind the bar. As far as I'm aware he hasn't looked my way in hours. Not that I want him to, but still.

'You tired, kiddo?' I ask, smoothing down his hair. Billy yawns, but shakes his head – an automatic reflex when you're ten years old and staying up long past your bedtime is the ultimate victory. I check the time – 11.27 p.m. Mum and Tim are due to be chauffeured away at midnight in a clapped-out orange VW Beetle. Mum cried when Norah parked it in front of the house first thing this morning; her first-ever car was an orange VW. I like that Tim isn't flashy – that he didn't go for a fancy limo just to impress people. I like that he asked Billy to write 'JUST MARRIED' on the rear window using white shoe polish.

I call for a taxi, then message Harry to say Billy will be on his way at twelve. Mum's given strict instructions to make sure he'll be watching out of the window when Billy's taxi pulls up.

'Why do you never want to stay at Dad's?' Billy

14

asks, before popping an ice cube into his mouth and crunching on it.

'You know why,' I say, a little more sharply than intended. 'Besides, there isn't room.' I check my phone; Harry hasn't seen the message. If he doesn't reply soon, I'll have to call him and I really don't want to speak to him.

Mum and Tim are about to leave the dance floor when the opening chords of Mum's favourite song kick in. She claps her hands and turns to Tim, but he's frowning at his phone. I watch as he puts the phone to his ear, moving away from the speakers.

Tim stands with his back to the room, huddled next to a fake olive tree twinkling with fairy lights. It's only when he turns to look at Mum that I realise something is wrong. His face is blank, his lips compressed into a thin line. He jams the phone into his pocket and hurries back to Mum. A few whispered words and her face crumples. I'm out of my seat in an instant, running to her. Other people are making their way over, but I get there first and Billy's only a few steps behind.

'What's wrong? What's happened?' My eyes flit from Tim to Mum.

'We need to get to the hospital.' Tim looks around helplessly.

'I'll sort it. You sort *them*,' I say, taking Mum's hand.

I grab her shoes and lead her outside while Tim fends off worried wedding guests.

'What's going on?' Billy asks, his bottom lip beginning to tremble. 'Tell me what's happening!'

'Billy, I need you to find Norah, OK? Tell her to bring the car round right now.' For a second I'm sure he's going to argue, but he nods and hurries off.

Mum starts shivering when we get outside, even though the night air is warm and thick as soup. Inside, the music is still blasting and Meat Loaf is still wailing that he would do anything for love (but he won't do that).

'Who's in the hospital, Mum?' I ask as gently as possible.

'It's . . . it's Lewis.' Her voice is shaky.

I feel anger, brittle as ice and twice as cold. I will kill him for ruining Mum's wedding day.

THREE

A rust-red line runs along the middle of the floor, stopping abruptly at the double doors. Or perhaps the line continues beyond the doors. I won't know unless someone opens them. I could go and see for myself but I don't want to wake Billy.

No one's told us anything. All we know is that Lewis has been involved in some sort of accident. The harried nurse at the desk said someone would come and talk to us soon, before her attention was diverted by a bearded guy in a Thor costume. Blood was dripping from Thor's nose, while his mates Batman and Spider-Man tried to figure out how to work the drinks machine. Claybourne-on-Sea is a magnet for stag and hen parties, especially in summer. The *Claybourne Courier* ran a series of articles last year, warning about the 'plague of pleasure-seekers threatening to destroy our seaside idyll'. Then Harry wrote an article saying that our town would most likely wither and die without the influx of cash from those so-called pleasure-seekers. The letters page went nuts.

Mum alternates between watching Tim pace up and down and staring at the TV mounted on the wall. Depressing news from around the globe scrolls along the ticker at the bottom of the screen. Norah's outside, making pointless calls to tell people there's no news yet.

Tim sits down heavily in the chair next to Mum and loosens his tie. 'This is getting ridiculous. What's taking so long?' Mum takes Tim's hand in hers and murmurs something in his ear. He nods and says, 'Fine, I'll give it ten more minutes.' He takes out a handkerchief and starts cleaning his glasses, holding them up to the light to look for smudges.

Mum goes back to staring at the TV, now showing the weather. I'm impressed she's holding it together. Most people would lose their shit if their wedding day ended up like this. People keep glancing over at her, scanning for signs of injury. She may not be wearing the big white meringue dress, but she looks unmistakably bridal: cream knee-length dress with matching heels. All that's missing is the bouquet – caught by Norah, mostly because she was the only one who actually tried to catch it.

I'm glad to have Billy nestled against me, even if he's periodically drooling on my shoulder. Four years ago he was the one lying in the hospital bed while Harry paced up and down the corridor. Mum was away on a management-training weekend in the Lake District. I vividly remember sitting on a chair down the hall, waiting for a phone call from Mum and studiously ignoring Harry.

The smell of the place hasn't changed in four years – thickly antiseptic, with underlying notes of something that doesn't bear thinking about. It's hard to tell whether the anxious, sick feeling in the pit of my stomach is worry about Lewis or an echo of the worry about Billy all those years ago.

We were all relieved that Billy didn't remember how he got his scar on his forehead. The version Mum and Harry decided on was close enough to the truth to satisfy him. As far as Billy's concerned, he was sleepwalking and tripped on the bottom stair, cutting his head open on the corner of the radiator. Billy doesn't know how often Mum's cried about it over the years, blaming herself for not being here that weekend. Billy doesn't know who's really to blame.

I shouldn't have insisted on coming here. There's nothing I can do to help; I can't fix this. We don't even know what *this* is yet. Tim and Mum were too dazed to put up much of a fight when I bundled them and Billy into the back of the VW Beetle. Norah hastily removed the chauffeur's hat she'd bought for the occasion. She drove at the speed limit and didn't ask questions. I kept calling Harry, but there was no answer.

'Can you try your dad again?' Mum says to me, when Tim goes off to queue up at the desk. I shake my head when the call goes to voicemail, and Mum and I exchange a look. We're both thinking – dreading – the same thing.

We can't see Tim, but we can hear him, begging for information about his son. The nurse's responses are inaudible, but you get the gist from what Tim's saying: she can't tell him anything. I half-expect Tim to start kicking up a fuss but instead he goes quiet. I crane my neck to see what's happening, but he's already on his way back over.

'Any news, love?' asks Mum.

Tim's shaking his head when the double doors at the end of the corridor open and a woman comes striding towards us. She's wearing pristine blue surgical scrubs and Billy's favourite brand of trainers. 'Lewis Rossi?'

Tim springs to his feet. 'Can I see my son now?'

'I'll be able to take you to Lewis soon. But first I need to speak to you . . .' she pauses and looks down at Billy who's slowly waking up, '. . . in private.'

'Yes, yes, of course. This is my . . . my wife. Diane.'

The woman shakes Mum's hand. 'I'm Angela Mabaso. If you could just come this way.'

'We won't be long,' says Mum, flashing a reassuring smile at Billy and me. Then Mum and Tim follow the woman – surgeon, surely? – back through the double doors. And Billy begins a barrage of questions. None of my answers satisfy him, but that doesn't stop the onslaught. *Where have they gone? What's happening? Where's Lewis? Can I get a drink, please?*

I give him some money for the machine, and he spends a long time staring through the glass, considering his options. I check my phone to see that Daze messaged a while ago, asking where the hell I was and saying that she was going to bed. I fire off a quick reply: *At the hospital. Something's happened to Lewis.*

Daze replies straight away: *Sprained wrist from all that wanking?*

Another message pops up before I have a chance to reply: *Sorry, not funny. Hope he's OK. Call me. x*

I keep thinking about Angela Mabaso's scrubs. It has to be a good sign, that they're so pristine. Doesn't it? And she didn't look particularly worried or anxious. Businesslike would be the best description. So Lewis must be OK.

'Evan! The police are here!' Billy's back, with a can of Coke for himself and a bottle of water for me.

I look over to see a couple of police officers talking

21

to the nurse on reception. It's only when they start walking towards us, shiny black shoes squeaking on the lino, high-vis jackets too bright under the strip lighting that it hits me: maybe Lewis isn't OK after all.

FOUR

I couldn't compute it, when Mum told me what had happened. She'd ushered us through the double doors and down a short corridor to the relatives' room. Tim stayed to talk to the police. There was a box of tissues on the coffee table in front of us; I've never understood the concept of man-size tissues. Mum took one and blew her nose before she told me what had happened.

A car crash. That was the first thing that didn't make any sense. What was Lewis doing in a car in the first place? He should have been at home, in his room, doing whatever he does in there. The boy is practically a hermit.

Mum only told me more when Billy went to the loo. The words spilled out in a torrent. The car had crashed into the primary school on Fairfax Road. No other vehicles were involved. Luckily a guy had been passing and heard the crash, otherwise . . .

'What, Mum? What is it? Was Lewis driving? Whose

car was it?' I don't even know if he has a licence. Add that to the list of things I don't know about him.

Mum shook her head. 'There were three people in the car with him.' She sighed heavily. 'The car didn't have airbags, and Lewis was the only one wearing a seatbelt.' *Three people?* Lewis doesn't have any friends – unless you count ones on the internet.

'Who are the others? Are they here too?'

She shook her head again. She took my hand and squeezed it. The sight of her wedding ring shocked me. My mother was married now. 'They're . . .' She swallowed hard. 'They're dead, sweetheart.'

When Billy came back, Mum glossed over how bad it was. She said he'd be able to visit Lewis soon, and that there was nothing to worry about. I don't know if he believed her or not, but he was abnormally quiet, which made me wonder. He didn't even kick up a fuss when Norah said she'd take him back to her place. Mum said I should go too, but I told her I wanted to stay. She squeezed my hand again and I think she was glad even though she wouldn't admit it.

I hugged Billy close to me before he left. He was painfully sincere when he said, 'Tell Lewis not to worry about Indy. She can sleep on my bed tomorrow night.' Our cocker spaniel's love for Lewis defies all explanation. She latched on as soon as Lewis moved in, the little traitor. Indy's supposed to be staying with a dogsitter for the next few days, because Mum and Tim were meant to be on their way to Paris in the morning. No point wasting money on the dogsitter now they're going nowhere.

I was grateful that Tim didn't try to shield the truth from me when he finally sat down on the other side of my mother. He explained Lewis's condition and somehow I managed to nod as calmly as if he were reeling off a shopping list.

'They asked me if Lewis uses drugs. What kind of question is that? He wasn't even driving the car.' He went on to tell us that they suspected drugs or alcohol might be involved, owing to the 'particular circumstances' of the crash site.

'What did you tell them?' Mum asked. She was holding Tim's hand now; he needed the comfort more than me. He hadn't been able to see Lewis yet. He looked pale and haggard, a million miles away from the bridegroom who'd beamed with pride as he proposed a toast to the 'blushing, beautiful bride'.

Tim looked over his shoulder, even though the room was empty. 'I said no. What else was I supposed to say?'

Mum shifted in her chair. She'd been less than impressed when she saw the poster Lewis hung above his bed – a doctored photo of Barack Obama smoking a massive spliff (*'Yes we cannabis'*). She kept quiet, though, because Lewis is an adult and adults are allowed

25

to have crappy posters on their walls. She was even *less* impressed when the unmistakable smell came wafting through the house that very first night, straight after our first official 'family' dinner.

'They asked if I had any idea who was in the car with him. And I had to say no. They looked at me as if I was mad!' Tim shook his head. 'This is my fault.'

'It is *not*.' Mum's voice was as firm as I'd ever heard it. 'How can you say that?'

'He should have been at the wedding. He should have been with us.'

'You couldn't *force* him to come, Tim. You tried your best – we all did. And that's all we can ever do. We don't even know what happened yet. Let's focus on Lewis for now. One step at a time, OK?'

Tim shook his head but didn't say anything more. We settled into exhausted silence that was broken a few minutes later when Dr Mabaso came back in. She smiled warmly, but she looked as weary as we felt. 'You can see your son now.'

Mum went with Tim. Lewis is her son too now. In a way.

I picked a leaflet – *Coping with Bereavement* – off the rack on the wall and read it from cover to cover, wondering about the families of the other people in the car. Where would they be when they found out? At home? Would it be a knock at the door from a

26

police officer? Perhaps one of the officers who'd spoken to Tim. Of course the police would have had to identify the bodies first. It wasn't as if they could ask Lewis.

Were the bodies in this building somewhere, lying side by side on stainless steel tables? I'd seen enough hospital dramas to know the morgue is always in the basement. It shocked me that I didn't feel sad when I thought about the people who'd died. But they weren't real to me, because I had no idea who they were. They were shadows of ghosts.

Lewis Rossi has been my stepbrother for less than twelve hours. For two of those hours he's been in a coma. This whole day feels like some sort of hallucination. Seeing my mother descend the stairs in her wedding dress. Trying so hard to smile during the ceremony. Making that monumental error with Marcus Bloom. None of it seems real.

Until Mum and Tim come back into the room, looking diminished. Faces slack from shock.

Until I insist – why? – on being allowed to see Lewis, even only for a couple of minutes.

The broken boy in front of me is all too real.

Under the bandage around his forehead, his face is a mixture of vicious reds and pinks. His eyelids are shiny and swollen, his mouth slack around the breathing tube. A tangle of wires and tubes surrounds him, linking him up to machines which rhythmically beep and hiss.

I keep my eyes on his face – his battered, almost unrecognisable face – because I can't bring myself to look a little further down the bed. At the space where his arm should be.

FIVE

The next morning I pour three litres of perfectly good milk down the sink before telling Mum we've run out and that I'll pop to the shops to get some more. She was already on the phone, answering questions from anxious relatives.

I'm at the chemist five minutes before it opens. I stand, leaning against the wall, music blaring in my headphones to try to drown out the thoughts. The drumbeat is too fast, though, and instead of soothing me it makes me feel anxious.

I'm ready for the pharmacist's questions, and make a point of looking him in the eye when I answer each one. I tell him I had to come off the pill because it was driving me loopy. To be fair to the guy, he doesn't try to make me feel ashamed or embarrassed, even when he advises me to get tested for various STDs. After the consultation, I hand over the money at the till. Twenty-five bloody quid – half a day's wages I might as well have flushed down the toilet.

I sit on a bench outside the newsagent and open the paper bag. The box is purple and white, and inside there's a single pill in a foil packet. I pop it out and swallow it dry. I picture the pill making its way through my body, forming a force field around my womb, protecting it from Marcus Bloom's sperm. Or however it actually works.

I decide there and then not to tell Daze about Marcus. She wouldn't bat an eyelid at me having sex with someone I barely know, but not using a condom? She'd kill me dead, and I wouldn't even blame her. I need to get Marcus – and Daze, for that matter – out of my head and focus on being there for Mum. And for Tim, I guess.

Images of Lewis in that ICU bed punctuate every step of my walk home. The empty space where his right arm has been amputated above the elbow. I wasn't even sure if Lewis was right- or left-handed, which shows just how well I know my stepbrother.

Bizarrely, the fact that he's in a coma is less of a worry than the arm. The doctors induced it, and won't let him regain consciousness until the swelling in his brain has reduced. They're optimistic that he won't have any permanent brain damage. 'Optimistic' doesn't sound sure enough for my liking; I'd want them to be absolutely fucking certain.

Mum and I left the hospital just before four this morning. I gave Tim a quick hug, said I was sorry and that I was sure Lewis would be OK. It's strange, the things you say in a situation like that. The words don't have to make any sense, or be true, they just have to be spoken. Mum and Tim embraced for a long time; I had to look away.

My key is in the front door when I remember: the milk. As I turn to head back to the shops, I glance in through the bay window and see the back of a man's head.

I ram my key back in the lock and storm inside.

'Get out.'

Harry flinches. He doesn't get up from his chair but he does have the decency to look ashamed. He looks like shit and smells even worse. His face is pale and doughy, and his eyes are bloodshot. He probably slept in his clothes but it's hard to tell; rumpled seems to be his go-to look these days. Looking at him, it's almost impossible to believe that my father used to be handsome.

Mum comes through from the kitchen in her dressing gown and slippers, carrying two steaming mugs of black coffee.

'What the fuck, Mum? What is he doing here?'

Mum shakes her head and hands Harry one of the

31

mugs. He takes a gulp and winces. He never waits for his coffee to cool when he's got a hangover.

'Where the hell were you last night? Did Mum tell you what happened? While you were getting wasted, Lewis was—'

'He *knows*, love.'

Harry runs his hand through his hair. It's so greasy that it slicks back and stays there. 'I came as soon as I heard. Jane called me this morning.' Jane is Harry's boss at the *Courier*. I've never met her, but she sounds terrifying.

'Oh, so you'd sobered up enough to answer *her* call?'

'*Evan*.' Mum casts a warning glance in my direction. Why does she always defend him? Even now?

'It's OK, Di. I fucked up yesterday.' He looks at Mum and his face softens. 'It . . . it was a hard day.'

'Yeah, well, tell that to Billy. You know he was actually excited about staying at your place?'

Harry winces. 'He can come today. I'd be happy to . . .' His words peter off as Mum shakes her head.

'I think it's best if Billy just comes home. Evan can pick him up on the way back from the dogsitter.' Mum's gaze lands on the pile of unopened wedding cards on the coffee table. The card Billy made is on top. He spent ages decorating the envelope with multi-coloured hearts.

'So that's settled, then. You can leave.' I cross my arms and glare down at this man who calls himself a father yet refuses to act like one.

Harry meets my gaze. 'Jane talked to the police. She has the names.'

'What names?'

'Of the people in the car with Lewis,' Mum supplies, and I finally understand why she let Harry into the house.

I perch on the sofa next to Mum. 'Tell me.'

Harry takes a scrap of paper from the pocket of his jeans. 'James Gayle, Phoebe Mackintosh and . . .' He looks at Mum, then back at me.

I've never heard of James Gayle, but Phoebe Mackintosh is in my year at school. I only know Phoebe's name because the head teacher gave her some award in assembly last term. Something to do with an essay or a poem, I think. I can't even picture her face — not clearly, anyway. Brown shoulder-length hair in a ponytail. Medium height. Medium everything. And now she's dead. But what the hell was she doing in a car with Lewis?

Mum takes my hand. 'Evan,' she says gently, and I feel my heart go into freefall and I want to stop her from talking because I know it's going to be bad. 'I'm afraid Karolina was in the car too.'

I close my eyes and take a deep breath.

'I'm so sorry, love,' says Mum.

I say nothing, because the truth is that I used to be friends with Karolina Zabek, but that was a long time ago. The news that she's dead has no discernible effect on me, but I can't let Mum and Harry see that. You're supposed to feel something when someone you know dies, aren't you?

SIX

Harry has one last bombshell to drop before he leaves. Well, two, really. Phoebe was the one driving the car even though she doesn't have her licence yet. But the car belonged to Lewis.

Mum calls Tim the moment the front door closes behind Harry, but it turns out the police already told him. Mum paces the living room, pausing to shake her head every so often. 'But I don't understand . . . we'd know if Lewis had a *car*. Where was he keeping it? Are they *sure*?'

While she's fixated on the car, I'm fixated on something else: what was Lewis doing with Phoebe Mackintosh, Karolina Zabek and James Gayle in the first place? They can't have been his friends. Lewis doesn't *have* friends. I head up to my room and fire up my laptop.

A quick Google brings up results for James Gayle. There are photos of him smiling, holding oversized trophies. Football, sprinting and swimming. It must be exhausting being so good at so many things. He is – *was* – a sixth former at Belmont Hall – the boys' school on the north side of Claybourne. Lewis went to Belmont Hall too, but left two years ago before finishing his A-Levels – a fact I only know because I once overheard Billy asking Mum why Lewis didn't go to school or have a job.

James Gayle has the same smile in each triumphant photo – wide, brimming with perfect teeth. Flawless brown skin, with exactly the kind of body you'd expect from someone whose life revolves around sport.

I bet he was popular too. People like that usually are. James Gayle appears to have been everything that Lewis Rossi isn't. The *anti*-Lewis. And he didn't exactly look like the kind of boy Phoebe Mackintosh would be hanging around with either. Karolina, though? James looks exactly like someone she would want to get to know.

Eleven missed calls from Sid, five from Daze, and a few messages from some mates from school. It seems like the whole world knows what happened, which makes sense when Daze messages to say the crash was the first story on the local news and that rumours are flying online.

I tell Daze what I know, and she asks if I'm OK,

if I'm still on for band practice at Sid's tomorrow. With everything that's going on, my first instinct is to say no, but I end up saying yes – partly because I want to see Daze.

I message Sid and apologise for ignoring his calls. My finger hovers over the 'x' on my phone for a few seconds. Why is it more complicated with him than it is with Daze? It's more recent, I guess. The thing with me and Daze ('thing' is the only word we ever used to describe it) is ancient history. Mostly. As soon as we had the idea for the band, we decided it'd be better to just be friends. Well, *I* decided, and Daze seemed to agree. Then things got complicated when I started going out with Sid and *he* wanted to be in the band. Of course, then he had to go and dump me, which meant that I found myself in a band with two of my exes. The biggest surprise about that is that it's only *occasionally* awkward and confusing.

Indy is delighted when I arrive at the dogsitter's house to pick her up. The dogsitter – a ruddy-faced woman called Margaret – is less thrilled. She wants to know if she's still getting paid for the full week. She doesn't even relent when I explain about the accident. I make a mental note to tell Mum we need to find a new dogsitter.

As soon as we get home, Indy scampers up to

Lewis's room. When I get there she's sniffing around. I swear she knows something's wrong, but how is that even possible? I try to coax her out but she's having none of it. She jumps on his bed, turns around three times and settles down. She doesn't even come downstairs when Mum gets back with Billy.

I can tell by the look on my brother's face that Mum's told him the truth about Lewis, and my suspicion is confirmed when he barrels into me for a hug. He often does that – coming to me for comfort when you'd expect him to make a beeline for his mother. 'I want him to be OK, Evan. Do you think he's going to be OK?' His voice is muffled by my T-shirt.

I look at Mum over the top of Billy's head. She looks helpless. 'I hope so, Bill. I really hope so.'

When Tim gets back from the hospital, Mum suggests we call for pizza but Tim insists we all sit down together for a proper dinner. He raids the fridge and starts chopping vegetables like it's a perfectly normal evening.

'I can do that, Tim,' says Mum, hovering behind him. 'You should get some rest.'

'Yeah, why don't you sit down?' I chip in. 'You must be knackered.'

'I'm *fine*,' he says sharply, but then turns around with an apologetic smile on his face. 'I'd rather do it myself, if that's OK. It's nice to focus on something mundane for a little while . . . and it doesn't get more mundane than chopping onions.'

Half an hour later the four of us sit down to eat. Billy pulls a face when he looks at his plate. He *hates* risotto, but he doesn't say a word. He picks up his fork and starts to eat. When Tim asks if it's OK, he even says yes. I'm proud of my little brother.

The silence at the table is unbearable, but I can't think of anything to say. Luckily, Billy never has that problem.

'I want to make a Get Well Soon card for Lewis. I'm going to draw Indy on the front. You know that face she does when she's waiting for you to throw a tennis ball? Where she sort of tilts her head to one side and looks like she's smiling? I want to draw her *exactly* like that. Then we can put the card next to Lewis's bed so she'll be the first thing Lewis sees when he wakes up and—'

Mum cuts in. 'That's a lovely idea, isn't it, Tim?'

Tim nods, but I can tell he's not really paying attention. He's too busy staring at the empty chair across the table as he mechanically shovels food into his mouth.

Billy keeps up the chatter for the rest of the meal, probably to distract himself from the risotto. Mum and Tim don't seem to notice that he's only eaten a few mouthfuls. He's careful to cover the rest of the risotto with napkin, because Tim doesn't like us to waste food.

I clear the plates from the table and put the kettle on for tea. When I pass behind Tim's chair, I put a hand on his shoulder. It's nothing, really. A small, inadequate gesture because I can't find the right words to say.

I spend the rest of the evening in my room. Usually I'd be messing around on my guitar, but tonight I get stuck in an endless social media cycle – flicking from one site to the next on my phone.

The memorial pages are already up and running on Facebook. There's one for Karolina, and another for James Gayle, but I can't find one for Phoebe. I can't find her at all, actually, on any of the social networks.

I check Karolina's Facebook profile; I'm friends with her on there, even though I muted her posts years ago. Her last post was a selfie three days ago – two days before she died. Her face is made up to the max, glossy brown hair cascading over her shoulders. There's a glint in her eye, almost a challenge, defying the viewer not to find her attractive. It's hard to disagree with the first comment on the photo: *sexy af*. The most recent comments are mostly RIPs and sad face emojis. And then Davey Coates posted a comment half an hour ago: *fukin tragic. Why is it never the munters???*

Several people have replied to Davey, calling him

disgusting and disrespectful, but four people have liked the comment, including his best friend, who just so happens to be Marcus Bloom. It doesn't surprise me that Davey and Marcus are Facebook friends with Karolina, despite her not going to the same school as us. She became a bit of a local celebrity when she was chosen to be the Mermaid Queen at last year's summer solstice parade. I reckon the clamshell bikini top had a lot to do with it.

A few people I know have posted about the accident on Twitter and Facebook. Most of them talk about how shocked and upset they are, but I get the feeling some of them are secretly enjoying the drama of it all.

I turn my music down so I can hear what's happening downstairs, but there's nothing to hear. Earlier, the phone wouldn't stop ringing with friends and family calling to ask about Lewis. A couple of journalists too. Tim dealt with those calls, politely but firmly, with several 'no comments'.

Another message from Daze pops up on my phone: *Heads up: bullshit article on Courier Online. x*

I only ever go on the *Claybourne Courier* site to read Harry's articles. He's a surprisingly good writer, for a completely hopeless human being. Of course, I'd never tell *him* that. Sometimes he'll ask if I've read something of his, and I usually say no, unless I'm feeling particularly charitable. I know it hurts him when I do that. He's always so interested in the band and my songs and pretty much everything I do, and I act like I couldn't give a toss about him and the things he cares about. He never complains, though; he knows he doesn't have a leg to stand on.

Daze was right. The article is *bullshit*, but it's even worse than that. Tim's going to hit the fucking roof.

SEVEN

Walking down Morley Hill to Sid's house, guitar case in hand, I feel like myself for the first time in days. The weather is postcard perfect — a few cotton wool clouds meandering across the azure sky. The sun glints off the sea, and the pier looks like somewhere actually worth visiting. A lone seagull pecking at a splatter of vomit on the pavement only serves to add a certain grittiness to the holiday vibe.

I feel guilty that I'm able to enjoy the warm air on my skin, given everything that's happened. It's not like I can even use the excuse that Lewis would *want* me to enjoy it. I've no idea what Lewis would want me to do.

I unlatch the garden gate and head for the garage.

'Evan! Come here, sweetheart.' I hadn't noticed Sid's mum, Tanya, lying on a sun lounger on the patio. Tanya loves me. She even sent me a letter when Sid and I broke up, saying she thought Sid was 'daft as a broken loo brush' for breaking up with me, and that she wanted to know that she's always there for me if I need her. It was a bit weird – nice, but weird.

Tanya hugs me, and it's definitely strange to hug your ex-boyfriend's mum when she's practically naked. Her suntan lotion smells delicious, though. Her pale blue eyes are moist when she pulls her sunglasses up on to her head. 'Awful, just awful news. I'm so sorry about Lewis. How is he? Is there anything I can do to help?' Pause for breath. 'When I think that it could have been you or Sid . . . or Daze . . .' Tanya shudders, and I make a mental note to tell Daze that she was definitely an afterthought. Like a lot of people, Tanya doesn't 'get' Daze.

Tanya leans close and whispers. 'So *was* it drugs-related?' She suddenly holds up her hands as if I've accused her of something. 'No. Sorry. I can't abide gossip like that. Ignore me. I'll let you get on. I know Sid's ever so keen to see you.'

Tanya is a tiring woman to be around – better in small doses, Sid reckons. I thank her and head down the garden towards the garage. It's looking a lot more welcoming since we painted it. I don't know why there aren't more pastel-pink garages, really.

We share the space with Sid's dad, Gil, who calls it his studio. He spends most Sunday afternoons in here, creating his 'art' (inverted commas non-negotiable) and drinking craft beer. The garage is always hot in summer, but this summer is proving particularly brutal. The fridge Gil installed is a lifesaver. We're not officially meant to nick his beers, but he's such a nice guy that he never complains.

I peek in through the window to see Daze with Sid's bass slung round her neck, playing the riff Sid's been struggling with. Sid's standing there with his arms crossed, brow furrowed in concentration. He's looking a little tired, but summer suits him: white vest, baggy grey shorts and Havaianas. He's still wearing the leather bracelet I got him when we were going out. I stopped wearing anything he bought me. It seems silly now. Childish to deny myself something I love just because things changed.

Daze is wearing a cherry-patterned fifties-style dress and white Chelsea boots. Not the most practical clothing for the weather, or for drumming, but I've seen what happens to people who dare to suggest that. Besides, she looks good. Her trademark red lipstick is in place, but it's unwise for me to start thinking about her lips.

Daze looks up and catches me spying. 'Get in here!'

Sid rushes over to hug me. He holds me gently, as if he's worried I might shatter into a thousand pieces. Then it's Daze's turn and I have to swallow down the lump in my throat.

I step back and put my guitar case on the workbench. 'Can we just play some music? Right now?'

We play for an hour, song after song after song. Sid finally manages to nail that riff, and Daze is on fire, and my voice is strong. It sounds different, to my ears, at least. There's something raw there I've never noticed before. Something real.

I knew I wouldn't be able to avoid the talking for ever. Sid's the one who instigates it, claiming he'll pass out if we don't take a break. He grabs three beers from the fridge and we sit on a blanket on the floor. Sid and I had sex on this blanket once. I thought he was gazing at me adoringly afterwards, but it turned out I had a spider in my hair.

I watch as Daze tilts her head back to drink from her beer. The curve of her neck makes me think unthinkable thoughts. 'Take a picture – it'll last longer,' she says as she winks at me, and I blush. 'So tell me – did Breakfast Tim see the *Courier* article?'

Daze refuses to call him anything other than Breakfast Tim. She thinks his radio persona is hilarious and one of her favourite things to do is imitate his spiel . . . *Wakey, wakey, rise and shine! You're listening to Breakfast Tim at Breakfast Time – the best possible way to start your day. We've got the choicest tunes ready to spin for your delectation and delight* . . . Breakfast Tim is a massive nerd.

I tell them what happened last night. I was too late to warn Mum and Tim about the *Courier*. When I came down from my room, they were sitting on the sofa with Mum's iPad on Tim's lap, staring at the screen with stony faces. Harry had just called to apologise – said he'd spoken to his editor, but the editor wouldn't listen. The journalist who wrote the article is new – a graduate out to make a name for themselves.

TEEN CRASH HORROR was the headline, which was fine, I guess; I mean, at least it was *true*. It was the rest of the article, and the photos that went with it, that were the issue. The photos of Phoebe Mackintosh, Karolina Zabek and James Gayle were side by side at the top. Each one was a classic school photo – neat hair, pristine uniforms against a bland background. Karolina's photo is ancient – she looks sweet and innocent, the epitome of butter wouldn't melt. I haven't seen her look sweet *or* innocent for at least three years. James looks like the kind of kid a school would plaster all over its website – smiling and confident, shoulders straight. Eyes looking towards a bright future.

Phoebe's not smiling. You have to respect her for that, considering the pressure those photographers always put on you. She's staring right down the camera – chin slightly raised and jutting forward. It almost makes me wish I'd known her.

The article was hazy on the details of the crash: *The police are still trying to piece together the chain of events that led to this terrible tragedy*. Didn't stop the journalist speculating, though.

I've no idea where the photo of Lewis came from. They could have used the one in our living room, nestled behind the pictures of Billy and me. Tim likes to joke that it's the last photo of Lewis looking respectable: a studious-looking fifteen-year-old engrossed in a battered copy of *The Lord of the Rings*.

The photo the *Courier* used may be the kind of picture friends of mine post online all the time, but it's not the kind of picture you'd want in the local paper. It's slightly out of focus, but Lewis is easily identifiable despite the locks of lank hair that hang over one of his eyes. The eye that's visible is glassy and red. Smoke wisps and curls from a joint, dominating the foreground of the photo. The caption underneath says, *Known drug user Lewis Rossi, son of local DJ Tim Rossi*.

The article says the car belonged to Lewis, but neglects to mention that he wasn't the one driving it. It cites 'a reliable anonymous source' who claims Lewis supplied drugs to his friends. (*What friends?*) The article doesn't even bother to mention that he's in a coma, for fuck's sake. Perhaps that would have made readers sympathise with him too much? It's clear as anything that the guy who wrote the article has done his utmost to make sure *that* doesn't happen.

Tim was on the phone to the *Courier* right away last night, but he couldn't get through to the editor. He tried again this morning – telling them to take the article down if they don't want to hear from his lawyer. They said they stood behind the article, but they'd be more than happy to hear his side of the story. They even offered to send someone round to interview him. He slammed the phone down, as angry as I've ever seen him.

He kept saying, 'My son is *not* a drug dealer,' and Mum kept saying, 'Of course he's not.' But they couldn't make sense of the car – when did Lewis get it and where did he get the money from? It was an old car – a Saab 900 – but it would still have cost a fair bit. And then how did he manage to keep it a secret?

Of course they turned to me, as if I would automatically know about drugs just because I'm not a thousand years old. I said I had no idea what he was into, which is the truth. When they started to search Lewis's room, I felt sick as I watched from the doorway. If they were so convinced he wasn't dealing, why were they doing it? They found some roaches and Rizlas and a minuscule amount of marijuana in an old pencil tin in his desk drawer, but we always knew he smoked dope.

When I've finished telling them everything, Sid shakes his head. 'If someone went through my stuff like that I would fucking kill them.'

'Lewis isn't exactly in a position to complain, is he?' says Daze. 'You never answered my message, Ev. Did you know Phoebe?'

I shake my head. 'Not really. I used to live next door to Karolina, though.'

Daze does a double-take. 'You never said!'

'It might come as a shock to you, but you don't know *everything* about me.' Back when we were seeing each other, talking wasn't exactly the priority.

'OK, Little Miss-terious,' she says with her eyes narrowed. Then she switches her attention to Sid. 'Karolina used to be in my English class. You knew her too, didn't you, Sidders?'

Sid frowns and shakes his head. 'Nope.' He gets up and heads to the fridge, bending over to give me a perfect view of his arse.

'I thought you met her at George Fearnley's party?' she says. I missed George Fearnley's party; I was looking after Billy while Mum and Tim were away for the weekend. It was the weekend he proposed.

'Nope,' says Sid again as he cracks open another beer.

We fall silent, and I wonder if it's hitting us at the same time. That this is a real thing that's happened.

The last remotely dramatic thing that happened in Claybourne was two years ago when a guy on a stag weekend thought it was a stellar idea to dive off the end of the pier in the middle of the night. He ended up paralysed from the neck down.

A few minutes later, Sid asks if I think Lewis was dealing, and Daze answers before I get the chance. 'If he was, it was small-time. I asked Jaime and she's never even heard of him.' Jaime is Daze's older sister; she knows everyone who's anyone in Claybourne, particularly if they're dodgy. 'Jaime was at a party in the old tyre warehouse on Saturday – do you reckon they could have been headed for that?'

I consider it before shaking my head. 'Lewis isn't really the partying type, is he? What I can't get my head around is what were the four of them doing *together*? How did they even know each other? Lewis and James were the only ones who went to the same school – but there's no way those two would have been mates, even if they'd been in the same year. I mean, come on . . . have you ever seen anyone so clean-cut and wholesome in your life? Someone like James Gayle wouldn't be seen dead hanging out with someone like Lewis.' All three of us wince at my poor choice of words. 'Then you've got Karolina, boy-magnet, and . . .'

Daze leans forward. 'And Phoebe?'

'I don't know about Phoebe . . . she was kind of a nerd, I suppose?'

'Great job on the stereotyping there, Ev.'

She has a point, but I think I do too. It just doesn't add up – the four of them – and I can't stop thinking about it. Perhaps there's a perfectly reasonable explanation. I can't help wondering if maybe I would know what that is if I'd ever given Lewis the time of day.

EIGHT

A few days later, Mum and I sit at the kitchen table with our mugs of tea. She's dressed for work, I'm in pyjamas. I turn on the radio at 6.59 a.m.

Mum tried to convince Tim not to go back to work so soon, but he was adamant he didn't want to hide away. I think he needs the distraction – something else to focus on between hospital visits.

Tim skips his usual intro spiel today. This version of Breakfast Tim is sombre, at least to start off with. He reads out a brief statement that we helped him write last night – his thoughts are with the families and friends of the crash victims, asking for privacy at this difficult time. He ad-libs a bit, asking for thoughts and prayers for his son – it's an effective way of telling people that Lewis is in a bad way, because the papers seem oddly reluctant to mention it.

Mum breathes a sigh of relief when I turn off the radio after twenty minutes. 'That wasn't so bad, was it?'

'He did well.'

Mum smiles gratefully. Her jaw cracks with a massive yawn. She hasn't been sleeping properly; none of us have – not even Indy. Every night she starts pacing the hallway at three a.m. and it seems to have fallen to me to be the one to let her out into the garden. I lead her back to my room afterwards, even though she tries to stop outside Lewis's room every time. She's been my dog for *three* years. Mum got her for me (and Billy, but mostly me) when we moved in here after the divorce. (*Sorry your dad's a drunken douchebag, but look! A puppy!*) You'd think those three years would mean more to Indy; Lewis must have bribed her with treats when I wasn't looking.

'Maybe you two can think about rebooking your Paris trip for the autumn, when Lewis is better?' For some reason I can't bear to say the word 'honeymoon'.

I half-expect her to say that we don't know for sure that Lewis will get better, that it's too soon to be thinking about holidays, but she surprises me by putting her arms around me. Her hug is fierce. 'What did I do to deserve a daughter like you?'

I hate it when she talks like this. You're supposed to want your mother's approval. But every time she says something like this, all I feel is pressure. It feels like a warning – *you can't fuck up, I'm counting on you.* It makes me want to take drugs and get drunk and have sex with all the wrong people. It makes me want to reply to the message Marcus Bloom sent last night. But I won't.

There's no sign of the heatwave breaking, and people have moved on from basking in the sun to moaning about it. My boss, Eddie, is a prime example. The first thing he says to me when I arrive at The Pit is, 'Hot enough to melt the baws off a brass monkey out there, eh?' He's from Glasgow; the sun is not his friend.

Eddie doesn't mention the accident – not even once. The only difference in his behaviour is a none-too-gentle pat on the back and an offer to make me a coffee. The shop is quiet so Eddie lets me spend a good chunk of the day playing the guitar of my dreams – a Martin D-18. I'm determined to buy it one day. So far I've saved up seven hundred pounds. Only another eleven hundred and fifty to go.

No matter how I feel about Harry, it's him I have to thank for bringing me to The Pit and buying me my first guitar when I was seven years old. Even if it was a bribe to stop me kicking up a fuss about all the attention my newborn baby brother was getting.

The shop is probably my favourite place in Claybourne; it's where I met Daze. I'll never forget the day she wandered in, took a seat at the drum kit and blew us all away. That was the day I learned not to judge a book by its cover. The day I realised that maybe, just maybe, I wasn't a hundred per cent straight. Sometimes I think about how different my life would be if Daze had decided to pay a visit to Claybourne's *other* music shop that day instead of coming into The Pit, but she assures me we would still have met. She says it was fate.

Tim picks me up at the end of my shift. I could have walked, but it's a trek in this heat. He's surprisingly upbeat, tapping his fingers on the steering wheel in time to the music.

It's the first day there haven't been journalists or photographers lurking outside the hospital. There's an old man in a wheelchair, though. His hospital gown is hitched up above his knees, revealing his veined, milk-pale legs. He lights his cigarette directly underneath the 'No Smoking' sign, coughing up some phlegm after the first drag. 'Cheer up, love,' he says as I walk past, and miraculously I manage not to tell him to go fuck himself.

Tim and I are too early for visiting hours, so we have to wait in the relatives' room. This time it's not empty; a couple in their twenties sit huddled in the corner. They don't even look up when we walk in. Every couple of minutes the woman sniffs, even though the box of tissues is right there on the table. The air con is on full blast and I've got goosebumps within minutes. Tim offers to lend me his jumper, but I say I'm fine, because I think it would be weird to wear his jumper.

Tim picks up the folded copy of the *Courier* from the seat next to him and I read over his shoulder. The headline is: DAD'S GRIEF FOR FOOTBALL STAR SON. The photo shows a man with red-rimmed eyes and a worn-out face, sitting in what looks to be a teenage boy's bedroom, surrounded by trophies. In Donovan Gayle's hands there's a framed photo of James wearing a pristine football strip and grinning at the camera.

'Lewis used to play football,' says Tim, his eyes still on the photo. 'He scored a hat-trick in the under-elevens match against St Joseph's. We took him out for ice cream after the match and he ordered the biggest sundae on the menu.'

'Why did he stop playing?'

Tim puts the newspaper down and sighs. 'He never sticks at anything. He's not driven like you, Evan.'

It's an uncomfortable moment; I don't know what to say, so I pick up the paper and leaf through the pages. Harry's latest article is on page eight – a short piece about the impending closure of a youth drop-in centre. I've never even heard of the place. It's a typical Harry story – railing against funding cuts and the shortsightedness of the council. They never make a difference.

'Did you listen to the show this morning?' Tim asks as I'm reading an article about the heatwave.

I nod.

'What did you think?'

'I don't know how you did it, to be honest.'

He tilts his head. 'What do you mean?'

'Managed to act normal with all this going on.'

Tim takes off his glasses and rubs his eyes. 'It . . . it wasn't easy. But it's my job. You learn how to switch it on when you need to.' He gives a half-shrug, almost embarrassed. Then he smiles. 'So, anyway . . . when are you guys going to come on the show?' He's been trying to get the band to make an appearance; he often features local bands doing acoustic sessions.

'We're not that desperate,' I say with a smile, and he laughs. It's turning into a bit of a running joke between Tim and me. He keeps asking, and I keep saying no. He says it would be great exposure for the band, and he's not wrong about that. But we're not ready. *Sid's* not ready, anyway.

I look at the clock and nudge him. Visiting hours started five minutes ago.

I hesitate as we approach Lewis's room. 'I'll wait out here.'

Tim turns to me, his expression puzzled. 'Why?'

'You should have some time alone with him. I'm happy to wait, honestly.'

'Don't be daft,' he says, and puts his arm around my shoulders. 'We're family now.'

So in we go. Tim sits on one side of the bed, and I sit on the other. If anything, Lewis looks worse than he did on Saturday night. His face is terribly swollen. There's some kind of tube snaking out from the bandages on the stump of his arm.

For ten minutes, neither of us says a word. I can't resist glancing up at Tim's face every now and then. Each time I find his gaze fixed on Lewis's face. His jaw is tight, as if he's clenching his teeth.

Eventually I can't bear the silence any more – even though it's not really silence, with all the machines hooked up to Lewis. 'Maybe you should talk to him?' I whisper.

'I don't know what to say,' Tim says helplessly, just as the doctor walks in. It's not the same doctor as before, but Tim obviously knows him. He's called Dr Harroch; he's French, and taller than anyone I've seen in real life. When he leans across to shake my hand, the edge of a tattoo peeks out from under his cuff. He grabs Lewis's chart from the end of the bed and gives it a quick scan. Then he asks Tim if he would like to step outside to discuss Lewis's progress. It doesn't look like Lewis is making any progress to me, but what the hell do I know?

Now that I'm alone, I'm free to really look at Lewis. I think I see his eyeballs moving under his eyelids, but when I lean in closer I see it's a trick of the light – one of the strip lights over the bed is flickering. A lock of hair lies on top of the bandage on his forehead, a few strands skimming his left nostril. It would tickle, if he were awake. Maybe it's annoying the fuck out of him. I hesitate, looking over my shoulder to check I'm still alone, and then I gently brush the hair back. His hair is clean. Someone must have washed it. How would they even do that? The colour is lighter than I realised – mid-brown, with a reddish tinge. The red must come from Tim.

I touch Lewis's hair again, almost furtively, because if Tim saw I would die of embarrassment. 'Is this what it takes to get you to have a wash?' I whisper. Another furtive look over the shoulder before I lean in closer. Just in case he can actually hear me. 'Indy's really missing you, by the way. I swear I've never seen a dog look so sad in my life – not even on those adverts for Dogs Trust. Billy's doing his best with her – we all are – but it's you she wants. Last night she came downstairs with your Che Guevara T-shirt in her mouth, set it down in front of the fireplace and lay on top of it. Then she *sighed*, as if she was saying, "What even is the point of life without my favourite person in the whole wide world?"' I stop talking and wait for a response I know full well isn't going to come.

Lewis's remaining hand is next to me. There's an IV thing taped on to the back of it, and something plastic clipped on to his middle finger. I don't know what any of this stuff does, exactly. Perhaps I should make an effort to find out.

His nails are bitten to the quick. I can't remember seeing him bite them, but did I ever really pay him that much attention? Not that I've had much of a chance. I only met him three times before he and Tim moved into our house, and after that he spent ninety per cent of his time alone in his room. The one time I actually made an effort — asked him if he wanted to come to the cinema with me and Daze — he looked like I'd just asked him to strip naked and run down the promenade on a Saturday night. He said no before I'd even told him what film we were going to see.

I hook my fingers round his pinkie finger. 'I'm sorry,' I whisper. And I'm not even sure what I'm sorry for, exactly. That it's taken him being comatose for me to notice even the most basic things about him?

I open my mouth to say something else — equally inane and pointless, no doubt — when the door opens.

'Any news?'

Tim shakes his head and sighs. 'There's no change

to the brain swelling, but Dr Harroch says that's normal. It's still early days. He said they're keeping a close eye on Lewis's lungs because of the increased risk of infection.' Tim's gaze alights on my hand, clasping Lewis's little finger. I let my hand fall back to my lap, almost guiltily. Visiting time is over. I don't say goodbye to Lewis, and neither does Tim. I think we both feel weird about talking to someone who isn't even conscious.

At dinner that night, I watch as Tim reaches across and takes Mum's hand. She has to finish the rest of her meal one-handed, but she doesn't seem to mind. That's when it occurs to me that Tim didn't touch Lewis. He didn't kiss him on the forehead or stroke his cheek or do any of the things you might expect from a parent whose only child is in a coma. He's really not been himself since the accident.

NINE

Sid and I step out of the church and into blazing, blinding sunshine. We both reach for our sunglasses. It seems almost obscene to have a funeral on a day like this. Inside the church, several people in the back rows used their orders of service to fan themselves.

It's far too hot to be wearing black, but pretty much everyone is. Sid's gone for skinny black jeans, black Converse and a plain grey T-shirt paired with a faded black cardigan, which is him in maximum smart mode. You can't get away with that shit when you're a girl, particularly if you're a girl with blue hair. I've gone for the black trousers Mum bought me when I did work experience with her at the supermarket and a burgundy top I found in her wardrobe. I nicked a pair of her shoes too. They're one size too small.

It was Karolina's funeral yesterday. Family only,

according to Mum, so I couldn't have gone even if I'd wanted to. And I definitely didn't want to.

Mum's sure that people blame Lewis for the crash, just because of that stupid newspaper story; she reckons we should be lying low for a while. So I neglected to mention to her that I was coming today. I knew exactly what she would say (*'Do you think that's* wise, *Evan?'*), so I decided to bypass the situation entirely. What she doesn't know, etc.

A lot of people cried during the service – the woman next to me sort of whimpered when the vicar said, 'Phoebe will be deeply missed by her siblings, Conrad and Ruth.' Towards the end, a little girl sitting in the front row – Ruth, I guess? – turned around to gaze at the pews behind her. She looked about eight or nine years old; her chin was trembling but her eyes were dry. She was holding it together, as if she didn't want to let anyone down. I know the feeling.

'That was horrible,' says Sid as we watch the rest of the mourners spill out into the sunshine. He's right, but I'm glad we came.

A voice close to my ear says, 'Hey, Blue,' and I turn around, coming face to face with Marcus Bloom. What the fuck is *he* doing here? As if he would ever have given Phoebe the time of day when she was alive. We're all hypocrites – every last one of us.

'My name's not Blue,' I say, keeping my expression neutral.

Marcus isn't sure how to take that, so he half-smiles and half-frowns. 'It's just a nickname.'

'I don't have a nickname.' It's one of my pet hates – people not respecting you enough to use your actual name.

'Okaaaay.' He puts his hands in his pockets and turns to survey the crowd. I almost feel sorry for him but at the same time it's nice to watch him squirm. Sid tries to catch my eye, but I look away.

'Seems like she was a nice girl. Phoebe, I mean.' It's an inane thing for Marcus to say, but at least it's not offensive. 'How's your brother doing? I heard he's in a coma.'

'He's her *step*brother,' says Sid, stepping closer, and I could swear Marcus didn't even notice him before now.

Marcus shrugs. 'Same difference. It's still family, right?'

'What's it to you?' Sid crosses his arms in front of his chest, and I almost burst out laughing at the absurdity of the situation.

'Look,' Marcus says with a grin, 'I was just registering my concern that Blue's brother – sorry, *step*brother – is in a coma.'

'And why should you care?' Alpha Male really isn't a good look on Sid – or on anyone wearing a cardigan, for that matter. 'You don't even know Evan.'

Marcus turns to me, a slow smile creeping across his face. *Don't say it. Don't you dare say it.* 'Oh, I know her very well. We go way back, don't we, Blue?' He turns and saunters away before I can reply.

So he didn't say it. But he put just enough suggestiveness in his voice to ensure that Sid will have a ton of questions for me. Thankfully, a bunch of people from school come to the rescue before Sid can start the interrogation. They're Sid's friends, rather than mine. He's always found it easy to make friends; people seem to be drawn to him. I know I was.

None of this lot seems to know the connection between me and Lewis yet. Or if they *do* know, they're being spectacularly insensitive, whispering the latest theories about the accident. One girl, Lenore, says she heard there was another car involved. Some kind of drag race, she reckons. 'That Lewis guy looks well shady, don't you think?'

Sid steers me away from the conversation rather than intervening on Lewis's behalf. We head towards the older part of the graveyard, where it's quieter. Phoebe's little sister, Ruth, is darting about amongst the small clusters of people, her eyes scanning the crowd. When she reaches us I ask her if she's looking for someone.

The girl comes to an abrupt halt in front of us. 'Yeah, I am.'

'Who? Maybe we can help you.'

She fiddles with her necklace, a silver pendant in the shape of a question mark. 'I'm looking for the nice boy.'

Sid smiles. 'OK . . . any nice boy in particular? I'm a nice boy . . . kind of.'

'Not *you*.' The utter disdain on Ruth's face is a delight. 'Although I do like your cardigan. I'm looking for Phoebe's friend.'

At the mention of her sister I feel like I should say something – offer some typical funeral platitude. But I don't want to upset her; she seems all right at the moment. So what if it's just an act? I have no right to take that away from her.

'What does he look like? The nice boy?'

She starts describing him, haltingly. White boy, brownish hair, a bit skinny. I'm shaking my head until she says, 'Oh, yes, and he has a muddy green T-shirt with a man's face on the front.'

Sid shrugs. 'Doesn't ring a bell, sorry.'

He doesn't know that she's talking about a Che Guevara T-shirt. He doesn't know who she's talking about. And Ruth obviously doesn't know what actually happened that night.

'Lewis *must* be here somewhere . . .' Ruth stops and takes a steadying breath. 'Phoebe would want him to be here.'

Sid manages to mask his surprise at hearing Lewis's name. 'If you knew his name in the first place, why didn't you just say so?'

Ruth sticks her chin out, pouting a little. 'Because . . . *reasons*.'

Sid narrows his eyes. 'You're an interesting kid, you know that?'

'I *do* know that.'

'I'm really sorry about your sister,' Sid says gently.

Ruth nods, and the corners of her mouth turn down. 'I miss her.' She shakes herself and tries a brave little smile. 'Do you like my necklace? She gave me it, even though it was her favourite. Said I could look after it for her.'

'It's a cool necklace.' Sid nods appreciatively.

I clear my throat. 'Lewis is my stepbrother. He . . . couldn't come. I'm sorry. How did . . . um . . . was he a friend—'

A hand clamps on to Ruth's shoulder and her eyes widen in surprise. 'I've been looking everywhere for you. Come on . . . the cars are leaving in a minute.'

There's a family resemblance, definitely, but Phoebe's older brother has this whole pristine preppy look going on. He looks young, too, even though I know he must be about nineteen – around the same age as Lewis. For a second I can't think how I know that. Then I remember he was quoted in one of the articles I read. He said that Lewis hadn't been popular at Belmont Hall. As if being popular at school has got anything to do with anything.

He looks terrible. Dark circles beneath bloodshot eyes. He sniffs and pulls a red hanky out of his pocket.

'Conrad!' Ruth pulls on the sleeve of his jacket. 'This is Lewis's sister!'

Stepsister, I think, but I don't correct her. I'm sure Phoebe's brother doesn't care about the distinction. I steel myself for his reaction. I feel Sid's hand on the small of my back.

Conrad blinks a few times. It's hard to breathe as I wait to see what he's going to do. He stares and I stare back. There's something indecisive about his face – the look in his eyes doesn't match the hard set of his mouth.

'Conrad!' Ruth tugs his arm again. 'Did you hear what I said?'

He looks down at his little sister and puts his hand on her head. 'I heard you, Newt.' And when he looks back to me, his face is different somehow –

everything matches. 'Thank you for coming,' he says stiffly.

Then he takes his sister by the hand and walks away. Ruth manages to turn and wave, but I can't quite bring myself to wave back.

TEN

The shop is deathly quiet today. Eddie was panicking that he hadn't got his daughter a birthday present yet, so I sent him out with specific instructions about what *not* to get.

I tip a box of plectrums on to the floor and sit cross-legged to sort through them, putting them back in their individual compartments. It's my little ritual when the shop's empty.

The plectrums were always my favourite – all the different colours and logos, different types and gauges. I was allowed to choose a plectrum each time Harry brought me in here when I was little. This was back before I even had a guitar. I still have them all in a hexagonal tin on my bedside table.

My brain is too busy for the plectrum sorting to work its usual magic today. Daze's message from last night is still front and centre of my mind: *Something you're not telling me about you and some guy called Marcus Bloom?*

Sid must have told her about Marcus and his weirdness at the funeral. I thought he and Daze only talked about band stuff, but now it seems they talk about me too. It should be a good thing – that they're proper friends now. So why doesn't it feel like that?

I try to pretend it's perfectly normal to be best friends with your exes. And that works, most of the time. But Sid telling Daze about Marcus Bloom feels a lot like betrayal, even if it technically isn't. He was on my case before we'd even left the church grounds. *'What did he mean? That you two go way back?'*

I said I had no idea what Marcus was on about. I didn't mean to lie; I don't even know why I did. I'm not worried about what Sid would think of me if he knew the truth. I'm not remotely interested in his opinion on the matter. But I know he wouldn't just accept that I had sex with Marcus. He would ask questions. He would ask *why*.

I could tell Daze the truth, and ask her not to say anything to Sid. Daze is good at keeping secrets. Plus, it's not unusual for her to hook up with randoms, so I know she wouldn't judge me for it. But that's not the point; I don't want her to know. I just don't. I messaged her back to say that Sid was just being a jealous fool. She didn't reply.

I couldn't stop thinking about Conrad last night, and that weird expression on his face when he realised who I was. Could it be that he was feeling guilty that his sister was the one responsible for Lewis being in a coma?

When I got home I looked up Conrad Mackintosh on every conceivable social network. I found him quickly, unlike Phoebe, but every account was locked. The same preppy profile picture smiled back at me, but all the good stuff – the interesting stuff – was protected by a padlock.

I'm hanging a Lake Placid blue Fender Stratocaster when the bell goes to indicate someone's come into the shop – except it's not a bell. Eddie has it wired to play 'the greatest guitar riff in history'. Eddie is so obsessed with Jimi Hendrix that he has Hendrix's face tattooed on his chest. On a hot day like today, when Eddie leaves the top buttons of his shirt undone you can just see the top of an Afro peeking out.

'I'll be with you in a second!' I call out from the top of the stepladder. Then I turn round to look. Fuck. 'Eddie's out,' I say, without a hint of warmth.

'I'm not here to see Eddie.' Harry's voice is mild, but I can feel the sharp edges of his words.

I take my time putting the ladder away. When I finally look at him properly, I'm relieved to see he looks better than the last time I saw him. His eyes are clear, and his hair is clean. He hasn't shaved, but that would be expecting too much.

'What are you doing here?'

'I'm taking you to lunch.'

I cross my arms. 'I can't leave the shop.'

Harry crosses *his* arms, waiting. He knows full well that Eddie closes the shop for an hour every lunchtime. Eddie reckons there's no point running your own business unless you do it in a civilised way. He doesn't seem to care that it loses him money.

'There's a street food truck parked up in front of the pier. It's their first day. Half-price tacos . . . and they make their own tortillas from scratch.'

Harry has many, many faults, but the man knows his food, and he knows me. I could happily eat Mexican food every day for the rest of my life. Unfortunately, the only Mexican place in town is a) always full of hen and stag parties and b) fucking terrible. The guacamole tastes like creamy vomit.

I reckon that if I have lunch with him now, I won't have to spend time with him for at least a couple of weeks.

Plus there are tacos to consider.

It was a good decision — food-wise, at least. We get six tacos each, and guacamole and tortilla chips to share. The pier is packed with people, but we manage to snag a bench from an elderly couple packing up their thermos and sandwich crusts.

We don't talk as we eat. The tacos are *epic*. I have nothing to say, and Harry never talks when he's trying new food. He likes to think about the flavours. Apparently you can't just think something's delicious; you have to analyse *why*.

There's hardly a bare patch of sand to be seen on the beach below. It's always busy during the summer holidays, but this is another level. Costa del Claybourne.

Harry wipes his mouth with a napkin and sighs happily.

I stare at the sign telling people not to jump from the pier. They only put the sign up *after* that guy got paralysed. 'When was your last drink?' I ask.

'*Thanks for the delicious lunch, Dad. You take me to all the best places. Oh, and sorry I've been ignoring your calls and messages.*'

'Thanks for the delicious lunch, Harry. When was your last drink?'

'I haven't had a drink since the night your mum got married. I've been to my meetings every day.'

'And I'm just supposed to believe that, am I?'

His sigh isn't so happy this time. 'You can believe it or not believe it, but that doesn't change the fact that it's the truth.' His tone is matter-of-fact.

'You can drink yourself to death for all I care, but it's not fair on Billy. He doesn't understand.'

Harry nods, which isn't the reaction I'm expecting

75

after essentially saying I don't give a fuck if he dies. 'I'm trying, Evan. I want you to know that. I should have gone to a meeting on the day of the wedding. I know that now.' He's been going to AA on and off for years. More off than on, unfortunately. You might think that getting so blind drunk it seems like a good idea to run down the stairs with your sleeping six-year-old son in your arms would be enough to make you change your ways, but you'd be wrong.

'Why didn't you go, then?'

'Because I wanted to get so wasted I'd be able to forget that your mother was marrying some knob off the radio.'

I laugh. I can't help myself. 'Tim's not a knob.'

Harry shrugs. 'He could be the best bloke on the planet and I'd still think he was a knob. It's the sworn duty of the ex-husband to think the new fella's a knob.'

Fair enough.

'So anyway . . . there's something I wanted to talk to you about.'

'And you thought you'd buy me tacos to butter me up first?'

'Odd choice of idiom. Guacamole you up would surely be more appropriate.'

'Hilarious, Harry. Truly.'

'You always used to laugh at my jokes.' He hesitates. 'I don't want you getting the wrong idea.'

I raise an eyebrow and wait.

'It's about the accident.'

I wait some more.

'What they're saying about Lewis . . .'

'What *your* newspaper is saying about him, you mean? All the drug-dealing bollocks.'

He ignores the gibe. 'It *is* bollocks, isn't it? I wasn't sure at first but I'm pretty sure now.'

'What makes you say that?'

Harry shrugs. 'Been doing a bit of digging. Asked a few people.'

'What sort of people?' I ask, and I'm not surprised when he shakes his head. Let's just say Harry has more than a passing acquaintance with some of Claybourne's shadier characters.

'If you know the stuff about Lewis isn't true, why aren't you writing a story about it instead of telling me?'

'Jane won't let me anywhere near the crash story – she reckons it's a conflict of interest. Anyway, I couldn't write the story even if she did give me the go-ahead. It's much harder to prove something *isn't* true than imply that it is.'

I think about that for a second and realise he's right. 'So what do you want me to do?'

He grins, and it's so cheeky and boyish that I can see a glimpse of who he used to be. The scruffy long-haired guy from Mum's old photos, guitar slung extra low, bottle of beer in one hand.

'Search his room.' His eyes narrow as he lays down the challenge.

'Mum and Tim have already done that. What makes you think there's anything there they haven't found?'

'There might be nothing, but I want to be sure. Plus it wouldn't do any harm to have a sniff around, get a better idea of the kind of kid he is.' He stares down at his left hand. He still hasn't taken off his wedding ring. Billy noticed a while back, but had the sense not to ask Harry about it. When Harry looks up, his eyes are sad. 'Will you do it? Not for me . . . for Lewis.'

'I don't know.'

'He's in for a hell of a shock when he wakes up. Can you even imagine being the only survivor?' Harry shakes his head. 'That's going to be hard enough without these accusations flying around.'

'Why do you care so much? Is this just about getting one over on the guys at the *Courier*?' I'm curious, in spite of myself. There's something else going on here, I'm sure of it.

Harry doesn't answer straight away. When he finally speaks, he sounds weary. 'Jane told me that the police found drug paraphernalia in the car, and there was a significant amount of ketamine in Phoebe's bloodstream.' He pauses, then says, reluctantly, 'Lewis tested positive for the drug too.'

I'm not that shocked about Lewis, but Phoebe didn't seem like the type. Even as I think this, I realise how ridiculous it is. How can you expect to know *anything* about a person when you never even spoke to them?

'So what happens now? Are the police trying to say that Lewis was the one that got hold of the drugs?'

Harry shakes his head. 'There wasn't enough ketamine in the car to warrant investigating any further. As far as they're concerned, they've got their explanation. Phoebe was high and lost control of the car. The other two were probably high as well – otherwise there's no way they'd have let her get behind the wheel.'

'So that's it? Case closed?'

He shrugs. 'I guess so. But the problem is that Phoebe's family wants to keep this quiet – understandable, really – and that means that the rumours and speculation about Lewis aren't going to go anywhere any time soon. So I just want to rule him out as the dealer – for my own peace of mind as much as anything – then maybe think about trying to find out where Phoebe *did* get the drugs from. Because no matter what the family wants, something like this isn't going to stay quiet for long. It'll be all too easy for people to point the finger at Lewis. And once a reputation like that is set in stone – even if no one can prove anything – it's almost impossible to shift.' He looks away, rubbing at the stubble on his chin. 'When something like that happens, there's a temptation to become exactly the kind of person they already think you are. And I don't want that to happen to Lewis. Not if I can help it, anyway.' He lets out a huff of air and looks at me almost sheepishly. 'So that's why I'm asking you to take a look in Lewis's room.'

'I'm sorry.' I can count on one hand the number of times I've apologised to Harry since he and Mum split up. And I've never actually meant it before. He doesn't ask what I'm apologising *for*, because we both know I always assume the worst of him. 'I'll do it. Of course I will.'

Ten minutes later, I leave Harry sitting there, staring out to sea. The questions only occur to me when I replay the conversation in my head later. Is that what happened to him? Did he turn into the kind of person people already thought he was?

ELEVEN

Indy tilts her head to one side, her doleful gaze following my every move. 'It would really help if you'd stop looking at me like that. I'm trying to help Lewis, you know. You're just going to have to trust me. Remember when you used to trust me?'

Trust. There doesn't seem to be enough of that to go round at the moment. Mum and Tim were told about the ketamine, but obviously didn't think they could trust me with that information. Harry practically had to beg me not to confront them about it. So now I have to pretend I'm none the wiser, and do Harry's dubious detective work for him.

It's not just for him, though. I know that. I want to know what happened that night. So what if Phoebe Mackintosh was tripping on ketamine and lost control of the car? It still doesn't explain why the four of them were together in the first place. Karolina would never have been friends with someone like her – even if she did have a secret wild side. And Karolina certainly wouldn't have wanted to be seen with someone like Lewis. It doesn't add up, and no one else seems to care. Apart from Harry.

So here I am, in Lewis's room, trying to work out where I would hide my stash if I were a drug dealer, and trying to convince my dog that I'm *not* up to no good. To be fair to Mum and Tim, they didn't leave it in as bad a state as they found it when they conducted their search. Mum obviously couldn't resist picking up the dirty washing from the floor and the collection of mouldy mugs next to the bed.

I flick through the book on the bedside table, and then immediately feel stupid for doing so. If Lewis really is a dealer, I highly doubt he will have carved out a secret compartment in a book, like I tried – and failed miserably – to do when I was little. His choice of reading matter isn't quite my cup of tea – the book is as thick as a dictionary. It has a sword-wielding man wearing a hooded cloak on the front. The only books I like are ones that have stuff that could actually happen in real life.

Indy seems to have decided to trust me after all. She yawns and stretches before lying down on the striped rug next to Lewis's bed. I lie next to her and scratch behind her ears. Her eyes half-close in doggy ecstasy. 'I'm not snooping, Indy. I'm . . . investigating.

There's a difference.' Her reply is a little snuffling sort of sigh.

I can't get over how different the room looks now. Six months ago it was our spare room – floral curtains, floral bedspread and more cushions on the bed than anyone could ever possibly need. The first thing to go was the curtains. I was annoyed about that, because I've been stuck with the same ones since we moved in. I didn't say anything, though. I never do.

I search quickly and methodically but come up blank, even though I try all the places Harry suggested. I know Mum and Tim already looked in the bedside drawers, but I can't resist a quick peek. They're jammed full of stuff – magazines and old notebooks and a crusty old sock (too gross to contemplate).

I go to close the bottom drawer and realise that it doesn't close properly no matter how hard I push it. I remove the drawer and place it next to Indy on the rug, and crouch down to see what was jamming it. 'Bingo,' I whisper when I spy the cardboard box nestled in the empty space. I pull it out from its hiding place, already mentally composing the message to Harry saying we were wrong after all. It's an L.K. Bennett shoebox. Ladies' size five. My heart pounds as I lift up the lid.

My heart returns to its regular beat when I see what's inside. Nothing but keepsakes and mementoes.

A swimming certificate (ten metres) and assorted badges. An empty limited edition Coke bottle. A Lego Severus Snape. Right at the bottom of the box there's a torn-out page from the *Claybourne Courier*, dated two years ago. There's an article about scuba divers exploring the detritus left over from the construction of the pier back in 1886. It seems like an odd thing to keep, but then I notice the article about Tim in the bottom right-hand corner of the page. There's a picture of him holding a giant cheque; he raised £3,462.94 for a children's charity by broadcasting his show while sitting in a bath of baked beans on the beach.

The guilt I feel at invading Lewis's privacy isn't quite strong enough to stop me rummaging through the rest of the box. I pull out the last few things. A cream-coloured pamphlet – the order of service from the funeral of Imogen Rossi, 1967–2014. Lewis's mother. Born the same year as my mum, which makes me feel something like vertigo.

It takes seeing a photo of Tim's first wife on the front of the order of service for her to seem real to me – and for me to really think about what it must have been like for Lewis to lose his mum when he was only fifteen. The photo is lovely. Imogen Rossi sits in an armchair, mug of tea in hand, newspaper folded on her lap. Her eyes crinkle as she smiles at whoever's taking the photo. The smile is tinged with fond exasperation. I'm willing to bet Imogen hated having her photo taken.

There are some more photos of his mum. My favourite is a blurry one of her on the top the Ferris wheel that used to be at the end of the pier. She's gripping the safety bar with gloved hands, looking half-delighted, half-terrified.

The last photo in the stack is an old one of Lewis and Tim. It looks at least ten years old. Lewis and Tim are both wearing shorts and garish T-shirts, standing in front of a log flume and soaked to the skin. Father and son have matching awkward smiles.

My phone buzzes, making me jump, but it's only Harry checking up on me. I tell him the room seems to be a drugs-free zone and he replies with a thumbs-up emoji.

From downstairs, there's the sound of the front door opening, and the jangle of keys landing in the bowl on the sideboard. I hurry to put things back exactly as I found them. Everything's where it should be and I'm sprawled next to Indy on the rug by the time Mum reaches the top of the stairs.

'I'm in Lewis's room!' She pokes her head round the door and smiles when she sees us. She kicks off her shoes and sits down on Lewis's bed with sigh.

'What are you doing in here?'

I shake my head, smiling. 'The lengths I have to go

to these days to hang out with Indy. I think the only thing that could lure her back to my room is a whole roast chicken.'

I ask Mum about her day. She's the manager of the complaints department at the big supermarket outside town. The shit she has to deal with on a daily basis is unbelievable. 'I've got one to add to the list of all-time greats,' she says, shaking her head. 'Poor Darren was the one who took the call.' Darren's a uni student working his second summer at the call centre.

Mum proceeds to tell me about a man who called to complain about a pizza. He was outraged that it didn't have any of the advertised toppings on it – no cheese, no tomato sauce, no ham, no pineapple. Mum clears her throat, then launches into an impression. 'You know what I call that? *Bread*, that's what. And if I'd wanted bread I could have just opened the bread bin instead of trekking *all the way across town* to your sorry excuse for a supermarket.'

I narrow my eyes, trying to work out the puzzle. 'He'd bought flatbread instead of pizza? Or those ready-made bases?'

Mum shakes her head, her eyes sparkling with glee. 'Wrong! Ten points from Gryffindor! Five minutes into the phone call, the guy goes quiet. "Oh," he says. "I seem to have opened the box upside down."'

We laugh for two minutes straight, and it feels so

good. It feels normal. And then I'm left with a strange yearning for frozen pizza. We used to have it at least twice a week before Tim came along.

'I must have listened to the call ten times in my office this afternoon,' says Mum, when we've finally got a grip.

We head downstairs, and – to our surprise – Indy comes too. Then we realise it's her dinnertime. I get Indy's food ready while Mum raids the veg drawer of the fridge.

'Mum?' And it sounds like the word has two syllables because that's just how you say it when you're about to ask a difficult question.

'Ye-es?' she says, mimicking my tone.

'Does Tim ever talk about Lewis's mum?'

She shakes her head and closes the fridge door. 'Where did *that* come from?'

'I dunno. I was thinking it must have been hard for Tim, coping on his own, looking after Lewis. And that got me thinking it's sad that Lewis's mum isn't here to visit him in hospital.'

'That's a lot of thinking,' she says carefully.

'What can I say? I'm a thoughtful person.' I put down Indy's bowl and she finishes her food in ten seconds flat. Cocker spaniels have to be the greediest dogs in the entire world. She grabs the bowl in her mouth and takes it out into the hall where she will proceed to lick every last minuscule morsel. Tim will trip over the bowl on his way in, and will shake his head fondly and say, 'That dang dog will be the death of me!' which is the closest he ever gets to swearing.

I sit down at the kitchen table and begin chopping the veg under Mum's strict supervision. She sits down opposite me and starts peeling a gnarled piece of ginger. Finally, she starts to speak. 'He doesn't talk about her much. It's . . . complicated.'

I wait, and focus on cutting perfect batons of carrot. Harry taught me this trick years ago – to let the other person fill the silence; it was one of the first things he learned about conducting interviews.

'In some ways he's still grieving.'

I nod. It hadn't occurred to me that Tim was grieving; before the accident, Tim seemed like the most cheerful person I'd ever met. But I guess being happy on the outside has nothing to do with how you're feeling inside – particularly when 'cheerful' is part of your job description.

'It was a stroke, wasn't it?' I almost whisper.

'An aneurysm in her brain. It was very sudden.' Mums stops peeling the ginger and looks at me. 'She was forty-seven. It's no age at all.'

It's no age at all. I've heard my grandmother use this phrase before. It must get passed down through the generations, like a family recipe. The words don't quite fit my mother's mouth; she's too young for them.

'It must have been awful. For Tim and Lewis.'

The clatter of the front door interrupts my thoughts; Tim and Billy are back. Mum flinches. 'Don't say anything to Tim, OK?' she says quickly, and I nod. We listen to the thump-thump-thump of Billy charging up the stairs, followed by a door closing with a not-quite-slam. Mum shakes her head. 'He doesn't like talking about her.'

We set our faces into expectant smiles just before Tim enters the kitchen. His face lights up when he sees us. 'How are my best girls?' He leans down and kisses the top of Mum's head, before taking the seat next to hers.

'Fine, love.' Her smile matches his in brightness. 'How's Lewis?'

Tim takes off his glasses and pinches the bridge of his nose. 'No news. But the doctor did say that his arm is healing nicely. He said there are some amazing prosthetics available these days.'

Mum nods encouragingly. 'We should research the options, so we've got all the information ready for him.' She's good at saying the right thing sometimes, my mum.

Music starts blaring from upstairs and we all raise our eyes as if we can see through the ceiling into Billy's room.

'What's up with him?' I ask. It's got to be something,

because that boy always heads straight to the kitchen as soon as he gets home. His first priority is always his stomach. Lately he's had an obsession with strange sandwiches – yesterday it was peanut butter and pickle.

Tim pops a piece of carrot into his mouth and crunches away. 'Bad day at the office, I think. Some picture not quite turning out how he wanted it to.' Billy's goes to an art club at the community centre every summer. 'I said, "That's life, mate. What matters is how you deal with adversity. That's what makes you a man."' He nods emphatically, raising his eyebrows at the same time.

Mum snorts. 'You didn't actually say that, did you?'

Tim frowns and puts his glasses back on. 'Yes, I *actually* did, Diane.' His words are clipped, precise.

Mum and I look at each other and burst out laughing. Eventually Tim joins in.

TWELVE

'I think that boy might be doing a poo,' says Billy.

I take off my sunglasses and squint; it's hard to tell, but the kid is squatting in the shallows, and I can't see if he's wearing shorts or not. Billy and I decide to get out of the water, just to be on the safe side.

The paddling was his idea. He said he never gets to come to the beach *properly* – like a real day out – and that walking Indy doesn't count. He's too young to remember that Mum and Harry used to bring us down every Sunday – wind breakers, buckets, spades, the whole shebang.

I thought this might cheer him up. I even added in a couple of bribes to sweeten the deal: I promised we'd visit Sid at work *and* I gave Billy a tenner to spend in the arcade. Billy said I was the best sister he'd ever had. I choose to take it as a compliment.

I tried to get to the bottom of what was the matter the other day after he'd stormed upstairs.

When I asked what was wrong, he said, 'Drawing is stupid,' and the words hurt my heart. Billy loves drawing more than anything. He said he didn't want to go back to art club and no one could make him, so there. I suggested he try something else, if he wasn't enjoying drawing so much at the moment – collage or print-making or sculpture. It didn't take much to talk him round; he went back to art club the next day.

Still, something's not quite right. Normally you can't shut Billy up when we're all sitting round the dinner table, but he's been quieter the past couple of days. Mum and Tim don't seem to have noticed, and I don't want to bother them about it. Billy's probably just feeling a bit neglected. It's not that anyone's ignoring him, but he's not even close to being the centre of attention right now. Tim's worried about Lewis, and Mum's worried about Tim and Lewis, and I'm worried about Mum and Tim and Lewis.

My guess is that Billy's mature enough to understand that things have to be this way at the moment, so he's just keeping his head down and getting on with it. He's a good kid. It's not easy, that moment when you realise the world doesn't revolve around you. Billy's too young for it, even though he's putting on a brave face. I was even younger.

We're sitting on the sand, waiting for our feet to

dry, when Billy says, 'Rory Slater says that everyone wants Lewis to die.'

'Is this why you didn't want to go back to art club?'

'No. I mean, yes, but then I decided I don't care what he . . . what Rory says. He's a total dingleberry.'

I may have to start stealing insults from my ten-year-old brother. 'Well, then. Just ignore Rory Slater.'

Billy starts drawing in the sand with his finger. 'I wish they'd let me see him. Lewis, I mean. Not Rory Slater.'

'I know, Bill. I'm sorry. It's just for a bit. It'll be different when he wakes up, you'll see.' I did actually try to persuade Mum and Tim they should let Billy visit Lewis, but they think it would traumatise him. Sure, it wouldn't be easy for Billy to see Lewis like that, but maybe it's even worse *not* seeing him. Not knowing. Imagining the worst. I thought Mum was coming round to my way of thinking, but she said it's Tim's decision in the end. He said that the ICU is no place for a little boy, and there was something in his tone of voice that stopped me from pushing the matter.

I've been going to see Lewis every couple of days; I've started reading to him. I took along the book that was next to his bed – there was a scrap of paper marking his place. He was just a third of the way through when he stopped reading. For all I know he stopped there because it's a bad book, but perhaps he put it down the night before the accident because his eyes were drooping closed even though he was desperate to find out what happened next.

The book really isn't my sort of thing – magic and elves and a seemingly endless quest to find something Very Important. I'd rather watch the film version – two and a half hours and you're done. Plus you can have popcorn. I like reading to Lewis, though. I felt self-conscious at first, same as when I started talking to him the first couple of times. But now that I'm used to it, it's almost fun. My reading voice is posher than my actual voice. Sometimes I give the characters unlikely accents. I don't think Lewis would approve of my cockney elf, but he doesn't get a say in the matter.

I haven't told Mum or Tim what I'm doing, and I stop as soon as one of them comes in and pretend I'm just reading myself. When Mum first saw me she came over and put the back of her hand to my forehead. 'A book! In the summer holidays! Are you sure you're feeling all right?'

Last night, when I couldn't sleep because of the heat, I started reading the book from the beginning. Mostly to fuel my outrage about the lack of female characters. When Lewis wakes up I'm going to have to have a word about his terrible taste in reading matter.

'SCREAM IF YOU WANNA GO FASTER!' Sid is in full showman mode on the waltzer, and Billy's transfixed. We watch as Sid hops effortlessly from car to car, spinning them, singing along to the music, winking at all the girls and one or two boys.

The fairground is a bit rough around the edges – faded signs, blown lightbulbs and usually more than one ride out of action at any one time – but to Billy it might as well be Disney World.

Sid sees us watching, grins at me, and gives Billy a solemn salute. Billy salutes back. It's their 'thing', apparently.

It's only when Sid's on his break and we're sitting at a grubby table next to the burger stand that I get a proper look at him. He has dark circles under his eyes and his face is pale under his summer tan. I wait until Billy's had his fill of Sid banter and headed off to the arcade, tenner in hand, before saying, 'You look like shit.'

He raises one eyebrow. 'The girls on the waltzer beg to disagree.'

'Seriously, though, what's up? You look like you haven't slept in a week.'

He takes several gulps from his bottle of water then licks his lips. 'It's too hot to sleep.'

'You should get a fan for your room. Mum's got one — says it really helps.' Sid stares at the empty ketchup and mustard sachets on the table. 'Is everything OK? Other than the not sleeping?'

The smile he switches on is extra bright, eyes wide, as if that will convince me. 'Yeah, why wouldn't it be?'

'You'd tell me, wouldn't you? If anything was wrong?'

He rolls his eyes. 'I'm *fine*. Honestly. What's going on with you, anyway?' He gives me a sly look. 'Seen Marcus recently?'

'Why would I have seen him?'

'*You* tell me.'

Luckily, Billy comes tearing towards us, screeching to a halt next to Sid's chair. He asks Sid for some tips on how to get to the next level on one of the video games and Sid checks his watch and says he's got time to show him. The two of them head off without so much as a backwards glance. Saved by the Bill.

Billy manages to convince me that we should have ice cream for lunch, and there's only one place in town worth bothering with. Gio's Gelato is worth the queue, which seems to get longer every year. It used to be only locals, but now the tourists have discovered it. The prices have stayed the same, though, and the general opinion is it's still the best ice cream you can get this side of Naples.

Billy and I are busy debating whether it's weird to have a scoop of melon sorbet with a scoop of chocolate ice cream (I vote yes, he votes no) when I notice Daze and her sister Jaime on the other side of the street. I watch them for a few seconds. I like the way Daze walks; there's something gloriously languid about it. She's never in a rush, even when she's late for something.

Maybe Daze feels the strength of my gaze, because she looks over and waves. She takes Jaime's arm and drags her across the street. Daze looks immaculate; Perfect make-up, ruby red lips. Jaime looks wasted.

Jaime takes off her sunglasses and looks Billy up and down. 'You,' she says finally, 'are a very short person.'

Billy considers that for a moment. 'I'm ten.'

'I don't think I was that short when I was ten. I think I would remember.'

Daze slings her arm over my brother's shoulder. 'Just ignore her, Bill. She's . . . tired. Come on, you, let's get you home to bed.'

'Noooooooo, I want ice cream first. Buy me an ice cream and I'll love you for ever, little sis.'

Daze rolls her eyes, and soon the four of us are sitting in the park with our ice creams. Daze and I try our best to have a semi-normal conversation, while

Billy tries his best to answer the random questions Jaime keeps posing to him. (*'Do you think slugs are jealous of snails?'*)

As soon as he's done with his ice cream, Billy starts messing around on his phone. After a while, Jaime lies back on the grass and closes her eyes.

'Sorry about her,' says Daze, scraping the last remnants of mint choc chip from her cup.

'I heard that,' Jaime mumbles.

'You were meant to.'

'So where was the party last night and why wasn't I invited?' I take Daze's cup and slip it inside mine.

'Some guy's house. I didn't catch his name. And you weren't invited because, if I remember correctly, you hate house parties even more than you hate every other type of party.'

I nod. 'You make a good point.'

'It was pretty civilised, actually. Unless you count my dear sister here, who suggested skinny-dipping in the pool. She was stripped down to her underwear before someone broke the news that there *wasn't* a pool.'

Jaime giggles softly. 'Good times, man. Good times.'

I don't know how Daze puts up with Jaime. She's always looking out for her, even though she's two years younger. It helps that she only ever drinks in moderation, and would never do drugs, not even if they were offered to her on a silver platter.

'I met someone, actually . . .' says Daze quietly. She's looking at her nails, short and blunt but perfectly manicured. 'This girl. I mean, I'd already *met* her – she's in my year at school. We got talking and . . .'

'And . . . ?' I'm suddenly aware of every part of my body.

She glances over at Billy, but he's engrossed in his game. 'I kissed her.'

'Right. Does this mystery girl have a name?' I sound breezy as anything. I'm almost impressed with myself.

'Alice. Weird thing, actually. She's . . . she *was* . . . friends with Karolina. She was in quite a bad way – really cut up about it.'

'And you comforted her in her time of need?'

Daze looks up sharply. Jealousy is not a thing with us; we don't *do* jealousy.

'She said the family are really struggling,' Daze goes on after a pause. 'They're thinking of moving back to Poland.'

I remember Mr Zabek and how he was always nice to me when I used to play round at Karolina's house. I remember him saying he'd wanted to live in England ever since he was a little kid – mostly to be closer to his favourite football team. I remember him saying that this was their forever home. 'And you're telling me this why?'

Daze hesitates. 'I wondered if you'd thought about

going to see them.' She chances a quick look at me. 'You know, pay your respects or whatever.'

Of course I've thought about it, but that's very different from actually doing it. 'They wouldn't want to see me, would they? Not with everything the papers are saying about Lewis.'

'People don't believe that crap,' she says, though we both know that a lot of people do. 'And even if it was true, and the whole thing was somehow – inexplicably – Lewis's fault, it's got nothing to do with *you*. What's the worst that can happen? They slam the door in your face? So what? At least you'll have tried.'

I want to tell Daze that Karolina's family aren't my responsibility; that I hadn't even talked to her in years. These things are true. And yet. I should go. I just don't think I can. Not only because I can't face her family – because it means going back *there*. I haven't even walked down that street in the last three years. The memories are too much. Shouting and crying, doors slamming. My little brother lying crumpled at the bottom of the stairs, blood pouring from his head.

I was sure she'd fallen asleep but Jaime must have been listening, because she rolls over to face us. 'That Zabek girl was crazy. With a capital K, if you get my drift.'

'What drift might that be?' asks Daze.

Jaime smiles sloppily and blinks a few times. 'You

think I'm bad, sis? That girl . . . she was fucking legendary. A couple of years ago I heard she climbed out of the sunroof of a car going down the motorway at eighty miles an hour. Said she wanted to know what it felt like to fly. Silly cow nearly got herself killed.' Jaime grimaces. 'She didn't deserve to die. No one does. Except for old people. I mean, they don't deserve it, but they kind of have to, don't they? Otherwise there'd be no room for the rest of us.'

I tune Jaime out, lying back on the grass next to Daze. I try to relax, let my mind go blank. I try not to think about Karolina, or any of the others.

So of course I end up wondering about this Alice person, this stranger.

Kissing Daze.

I shake my head to clear the image, and decide that I *will* go and see Karolina's parents. It's the right thing to do; I'm just not sure I can do it alone.

THIRTEEN

Harry walks towards me, carrying a bunch of flowers. When he gets close I see they're not shit ones from the garage like the flowers he used to get Mum whenever he'd fucked up – *again*.

I've brought cake. A traybake. Nothing that could be construed as celebratory.

Harry doesn't try to hug me. I'm glad he's finally got the message about that. At least, I think I'm glad.

'You told them I'm coming too?' I ask, unable to keep the anxiety from my voice. He nods. 'And they're fine with it?'

'Of course they're fine with it,' Harry reassures me. 'These are our *friends*, Evan.'

'Oh, really? When's the last time you saw them?'

'Last week,' he says, and I look at him in surprise.

'For work?' I ask.

'To offer my support,' he says neutrally. 'Come on.'

We start walking. I have to say something to fill

the silence. 'So why did you agree to come with me today?'

'Because you asked.'

We turn down the street towards the Zabeks' house, right next door to the one we used to live in. My heart starts thudding extra fast.

Our old house looks different – new double-glazed windows with grey trim, yellow front door instead of red, front garden blanketed in AstroTurf instead of real grass. I thought I would feel something when I saw it, but I don't. It's just a building – nothing more, nothing less. The house was never the problem.

'Travesty. What good is plastic grass to the birds? Not going to find any worms in that, are they?' Harry mutters to himself.

The Zabeks' house looks exactly as I remember it, right down to the window box with pink flowers in it. The doorbell sounds the same too – Karolina and I used to mimic the off-key chimes. But as soon as the door is open, everything is different. The wallpaper may be the same, and the sofa and the cushions, and the ornaments on the mantelpiece, but the people in front of me are shadows of the ones I used to know.

Nik Zabek ushers us in and gestures to the sofa for us to sit. He sits in a chair next to the fireplace while Agata fusses around, making sure our tea is just the way we like it, putting out plates and napkins for the traybake even though it's clear that no one wants to eat.

'Thank you so much for coming. Both of you.' Agata pats her hair self-consciously. It always used to look perfect, as if she'd just stepped out of an advert. Today, it hangs lankly, two drooping curtains framing her face.

I nod mutely, and Harry says, 'It's nothing. The least we can do.'

Nik leans forward and says, 'How is the boy? Lewis?'

'Still in a coma,' says Harry. 'They might be able to bring him out of it soon, all being well.'

It's the first I've heard of it. I open my mouth to ask who told him, and promptly shut it again, because this isn't the time or the place.

Nik closes his eyes and nods once. 'That's good news. Finally, some good news.'

Agata almost manages a smile, but her mouth twists into something else at the last second and she stifles a sob. Nik grimaces and shakes his head. After an awkward moment or two, he comments on the heatwave we've been having, and Harry takes up the conversational baton with ease.

I stare at the picture on the mantelpiece, because it's easier to look at Karolina than her parents. It's easier to look at the little girl in that photo and remember when she taught me to dance like Beyoncé, and when we hung upside down from the monkey bars in her garden for a whole hour, and when I knocked her mum's favourite vase off the shelf at the top of the stairs and we tried to glue the pieces back together with a Pritt Stick. It's easier, until it isn't.

I ask if I can use the loo, not waiting for an answer before I hurry from the room. I make it halfway up the stairs before the tears start to fall. I sit on the side of the bath, sobbing.

I'm ashamed of myself – for crying now, for not crying sooner. I do not deserve to cry these tears in this house, when I felt nothing when Mum told me Karolina was dead. I don't even deserve to *be* in this house. Three toothbrushes sit in a mug on the shelf above the sink. Green, blue and pink. Pink was always her favourite colour when we were little. I splash water on my face before leaving the bathroom.

Her bedroom door is slightly ajar; I hesitate before pushing it. The walls are still pink, but everything else has changed. The furniture, the bedding, the posters on the wall. They all belong to a Karolina I never knew.

There's a small purple picture frame on the desk that looks familiar. It takes a moment for me to remember why. It was a present from me, for her eighth – or was it ninth? – birthday. Mum bought it, and I was upset because it wasn't pink and I thought Karolina wouldn't like it. But she loved it – or pretended to, at least. She put a photo of the two of us inside. I can't believe she still has it. I hesitate again before stepping over the threshold. I tiptoe my way across the thick carpet, well aware that this is crossing a line.

The photo inside the frame is different. Of course it is. This one must have been taken a year or two ago, by the looks of it. Karolina and a girl I don't recognise, heads tilted together, matching gazes brimming with confidence and disdain. They look ready to take on the world. They look like the sort of girls I cross the street to avoid, just in case that disdainful gaze falls on me. I always expect girls like that to look at me a certain way. Sometimes they do, and sometimes they don't. But I'm always ready for it. I'm ready for the whispers based purely on how I look and what I wear – *dyke, emo, goth, lesbian*. The truth is that it's a two-way street. While they're judging me, I'm judging them.

The last time I saw Karolina must have been last September or October; it was definitely after she'd been crowned Mermaid Queen. She was a few places ahead of me in the queue for the cinema, in the middle of a big group of friends. I was with Sid, having convinced him to see a horror film even though he hates horror films. I remember my relief when I realised Karolina and her friends were going to see something else. She smiled at me when they walked past, and there was nothing mean or false about it. There wasn't time for me to return the smile before she was gone.

That's a lie. There was time. I could have smiled, but I didn't.

I look at each and every photo on the wall and quickly scan the rest of the room, but there's nothing out of the ordinary. Nothing to tell me how she knew Lewis, anyway, which is the one thing I'm desperate to know.

Before leaving Karolina's room, I say a silent sorry. I'm not even sure what it is that I'm sorry about. I just know that I am.

When I get back downstairs, no one says anything about how long I've been gone, or the fact that I've clearly been crying. They carry on their conversation without missing a beat, and that conversation has moved from small talk to ketamine in my absence.

'Karolina . . . she's not an angel.' Nik looks at his wife before continuing. 'We have found . . . things . . . drugs in her room before.'

'It was just a phase!' says Agata, frowning at her husband. 'All teenagers experiment, don't they? We certainly did when we were that age.' I can't picture Agata getting high, no matter how hard I try.

Harry sits up straighter. 'Even if it *wasn't* a phase – even if all the kids were on something that night – there's so much that still doesn't add up. Have you ever seen Lewis with Karolina? Or did you see her with Phoebe or James?' I frown at him. I can sense the change; Harry's gone from sympathetic friend to inquisitive journalist and the Zabeks don't seem to have even noticed.

Instead of telling Harry to get the fuck out of her house, Agata leans forward to pour more tea into his cup. 'I don't think so, but it's hard to say. There were always different friends. So many friends! A popular girl, our little kotku. She loved . . . she loved *life*.' Agata and Nik share a look and it breaks my heart.

'Is it true?' I say eventually. 'That you're going back to Poland?'

Harry whips his head in my direction, but I ignore him and focus on Nik. He nods slowly. 'We think, maybe, yes. This place . . . it will not be the same now. And there is family . . . Especially with Agata's sister—'

'It is for the best,' Agata says firmly. 'For all of us.'

'You would be missed,' says Harry gently.

'We're not bad parents,' Agata almost whispers. 'We're not.'

'Nobody would ever think that,' says Harry at exactly the same time as I say, 'Of course you're not!'

Agata stares at the photo on the mantelpiece. 'She made the best chicken soup, you know. Better than mine. If one of her friends was ill, she would make a big batch and take it to them. This is my Karolina.'

Silent tears start to trickle down her face and I have to look away.

'She was a hard worker too,' says Nik. 'Never called in sick, never missed a shift. Always made sure her shirt was properly ironed. I think she was as surprised as we were at how much she enjoyed her job.'

'Where did she work?' I ask, and I can tell Harry was about to ask the same question.

'The Beach Hut, on the promenade.'

It's a tourist trap right next to the pier – the kind of place that charges four-fifty for a slice of cake.

I notice Agata looking at Harry while she dabs the tears from her eyes. It took her a while, but she's finally caught on. She clears her throat. 'You're not . . . this is not for the newspaper.'

It wasn't quite a question, but Harry answers it, anyway. 'Of course not. I'm here as a friend, Agata.' He sounds so sincere that even I couldn't say for sure if he's lying. He stands up and says we should be going, asks them if there's anything they need. But the only thing they need is for their daughter to still be alive.

Harry and Nik make their way out of the room, but Agata puts a hand on my arm to stop me. 'Thank you for the cake.' She smiles sadly. 'You remembered.'

'Remembered what?'

'Coconut. It was her favourite.'

The truth was I found a bag of desiccated coconut

at the back of the kitchen cupboard and thought it would be nice with the chocolate sponge. But now it comes back to me. Bounty was Karolina's favourite chocolate bar. She had coconut-scented shampoo. I could smell it when we used to hide in the cupboard under the stairs.

Now I remember.

Agata hugs me, clings on for a bit too long. 'She missed you. You were good for her, I think.' I think of the parallel universe in which I stayed friends with Karolina. In that universe, the Zabeks might have been invited to Mum's wedding, and Karolina and I would have spent the night laughing and dancing and taking the piss out of Gary Strout.

In a perfectly possible parallel universe, Karolina Zabek would still be alive.

FOURTEEN

Harry sets off walking down the street and I have to jog to catch up with him. 'You lied to them, didn't you? You're working on a story. That's why you wanted me to search Lewis's room.'

He hesitates, which is the only answer I need. 'I'm trying to find out what happened,' he says finally. 'And if there's a story that needs writing, I'll cross that bridge when I come to it.'

'You'd betray your friends, just for a story?'

'I'm not betraying anyone. I'm doing my job.' His pace quickens, but I keep pace with him.

'If you're so keen on doing your job, why don't you get the *Courier* to run the story about Phoebe and the ketamine?'

'I've told you . . . the families don't—'

'Since when has hurting people's feelings ever been an issue? What about Lewis's feelings – and his reputation? Phoebe was the one behind the wheel. End of story.'

Harry sighs. 'It's not that simple. The story isn't going to run because Donovan Gayle doesn't want it to run. He thinks it reflects badly on James — that people will just assume all the kids were high that night.'

This is all getting seriously confusing. 'Who asked his opinion?'

'My boss,' he says simply, before elaborating. 'Donovan Gayle provides the *Courier* with a quarter of its advertising revenue.'

Now it's starting to make sense. Almost. 'But the *Courier* has been implying Lewis is somehow to blame . . . Won't that make people think James was high too?'

'You'd think, wouldn't you? But people haven't connected the dots that way. Lewis is an easy target,' he says bitterly. 'He's alive. He's older than the others. Druggie college drop-out leading the others astray — it's not a hard sell. And the car is a problem, no matter which way you look at it. Especially since . . .'

'Since what?'

'OK, full disclosure, but this needs to be kept between you and me.'

I nod my assent.

'The Saab was seen parked outside Derek Lacey's house a few weeks ago.' Harry sees my blank expression.

'Derek Lacey's the closest thing Claybourne has to a bona fide gangster.'

'Friend of yours, is he?'

Harry laughs. 'I actually went to school with him, believe it or not.'

We reach the bus stop and sit on the bench.

'So what are you going to do now?' I ask.

'Keep digging, I suppose. And keep quiet about the connection with Lacey.' The bus pulls up and Harry suddenly looks worried. 'You need to do the same. Because even though you didn't find anything in Lewis's room, this Lacey thing doesn't exactly fill me with joy.'

I hop on the bus, glad that Harry didn't ask *me* what I'm going to do now. Because he's not the only one who wants to do some digging.

Band practice that afternoon starts off well, despite the garage being hotter than a sauna on the sun. Sid wrote some lyrics to go with the melody I came up with a couple of weeks ago. He pulls a piece of scrunched-up paper out of the pocket of his shorts and hands them over. The lyrics are dark and strange and surprising.

'Who knew you had such hidden depths?' Daze may be taking the piss but I can tell she's impressed. 'You nailed it, Sidders.'

Sid shrugs even though he's clearly delighted.

Then it all starts to go downhill. Daze asks me how it went with the Zabeks this morning, and Sid snaps at her, saying we should be practising, not chatting. So we get to work, playing some covers to warm up, and Sid is even worse than usual. Normally he can just about get the rhythm right but today he's all over the place. When he starts getting frustrated with himself, he makes even more mistakes.

'This is fucking useless. I'm fucking useless,' he says, slamming his guitar back on to the stand.

'You're not useless, you're . . .' Daze pats him on the shoulder. 'Sid. You're just Sid.'

He bats her hand away. 'Yeah, well maybe *just Sid* should stop kidding himself that he'll ever be a half-decent bass player.'

'Oh, man, stop being such a drama queen. You're having an off day. We all have off days. Why don't we give it a rest for now and order pizza?'

I pack my guitar away, because I don't trust myself to say the right thing. The truth is that it *is* annoying sometimes, and today is one of those times.

'*You* don't,' Sid says quietly.

'Huh?'

'You don't have off days. Neither of you do. You should find another bass player.'

Daze puts on this strange computer voice. 'I'm sorry. Your request has been denied. Please hang up and try again later.' Then, in her normal voice, 'Tell him, Evan.'

'Tell him what?'

'That it doesn't matter if he fucks up sometimes, because this is supposed to be fun. Remember *fun*, Sid? This thing we used to have before you went all Dark Willow?'

Sid doesn't get the Buffy reference, but at least it distracts him while Daze explains it. She takes a beer from the fridge and hands it to him. 'You haven't been yourself lately. What's up? You can tell us.' She manages to look serious for all of three seconds before launching into song. *'That's what friends are for . . .'*

When practice has officially been abandoned and we're sitting on the floor with our drinks, Daze switches to serious again. Sometimes I think she does it on purpose to keep us on our toes. 'Do you think you might be feeling down because of the accident?'

Sid frowns. 'The accident? No.' He glances at me. 'I mean, obviously I'm sorry about Lewis and everything but . . .' He shrugs.

'I had a nightmare about it. More than one, actually,' says Daze. Her voice is low and quiet. 'I keep thinking that they must have been so scared when they realised what was happening. Imagine knowing you're about to die and there's nothing you can do about it.'

The only sound is splashing and screaming and laughing as the kids who live next door play in the paddling pool. The smell of freshly cut grass wafts in through the window. The sounds and smells of summer surround me, but all I can think about is death.

'I have to go.' The words are out of my mouth before I know what I'm saying.

'But . . . but . . . *pizza*?' Daze implores me.

'I know, I'm sorry. I'm not feeling too well. Maybe it's the heat . . . it's just so . . .'

'Hot?'

Daze doesn't quiz me further as I pack up my stuff, but she mouths, 'Call me,' when Sid's not looking. He's too busy apologising for ruining the practice to notice. 'I'm sorry I was crap today. It'll be better next time, I promise.'

Daze makes a noise of pure exasperation. 'Could you two be any more British? *I'm sorry, no, I'm sorry, I'm sorry that you're sorry about me being sorry.* There's precisely nothing to be sorry about. We have an epic new song to work on, Sid and I will nail the bass line *after* we've stuffed ourselves stupid with pizza. Go home, Ev.'

She practically pushes me out of the garage, packing me off with a quick kiss on the cheek. The whole way home, my mind fizzes with memories.

Kissing Daze used to be my favourite thing in the whole world.

After dinner, Mum and Tim decide to watch a film. Tim asks if I want to join them, but I say no. The two of them deserve to spend some time alone together.

I keep Tim company while Mum makes popcorn, even though I'm desperate to get upstairs to work on the melody for Sid's lyrics. Tim asks how things are going with the band. He loves music but doesn't have a musical bone in his body. A bit like Sid, really. I tell him about the new song.

'That sounds amazing,' he says enthusiastically. 'I'd love to hear you guys play some time.'

'Oh, we're not ready. Not even close. But thanks . . . I'll let you know as soon as we *are* ready.'

'You creative types . . . always so set on perfection! I bet your songs are better than half the drivel on the station's playlist.'

'Well . . .' I say with a smile.

He laughs. 'I thought as much!'

'I was thinking . . .' I hesitate; I don't want to dampen Tim's good mood, but I have to ask. 'I was thinking about maybe bringing my guitar to the hospital. I thought I could play for Lewis. There's a lot online about the benefits of playing music to people in comas.' I now know *a lot* more about comas than I ever wanted to.

Tim nods slowly. 'I don't see why not.'

'What's Lewis's favourite song?'

He sits forward on the sofa, reaching back to plump up the cushion behind him. 'Do you know, I have no idea.' He shakes his head. 'You must think I'm terrible. What kind of a father can't even make a wild guess about something like that?'

'It's not terrible.' I rush to reassure him. 'Mum wouldn't have a clue about mine either.'

'Wouldn't have a clue about what?' Mum comes in with the popcorn and proceeds to make several way-off-the-mark guesses about my favourite song of all time.

Harry would know the answer, because it's his favourite song too.

When he finally stops laughing, Tim points his finger guns at me. Finger guns are his favourite. 'Tell you what, I'm covering Sian's lunchtime show tomorrow. Why don't you come down to the station, Evan? I can show you round the studio, explain how it all works. Bit of a backstage tour, if you like. Then I can drive you to the hospital after.'

Mum pats Tim's leg. 'Ooh, behind the scenes . . . Now, why have you never offered to take me?'

'We try to keep the stalkers *outside*, love.'

They laugh like it's the funniest thing ever, and I take it as my cue to leave. It's this big joke between them — that Mum was this stalker fan of Tim's. She used to call in for 'Guess the Year' every morning, so it's not an entirely baseless accusation. And I do remember her going on about his voice before they got together. '*Like caramel, don't you think?*' (No, I definitely did *not* think.) She couldn't believe her luck when he turned up on that dating site she'd signed up for.

I decide I might as well accept Tim's offer, since I have to take two buses to get to the hospital. Hot, sweaty buses with windows everyone seems weirdly reluctant to open, even when it's thirty degrees outside. Plus it *would* be interesting to get a behind-the-scenes look at a radio station. Maybe even useful one day . . .

I stomp down on my thoughts. These are the thoughts I hardly ever allow myself to think. The hopeful thoughts, the impossible dreams of a future of gigs and radio appearances and the cover of *NME*. They're embarrassing, these thoughts of mine. Childish and stupid. Which is why Daze thinks the band is just for fun, because that's what I told her. To admit anything else . . . No.

I sit on my bed with my guitar; it's the only thing guaranteed to stop me overthinking — to stop me thinking about anything at all. Billy's asleep next door, so I play softly. The same song again and again. I change the melody, though, and slow down the tempo.

I finally fall asleep around two in the morning, with Sid's lyrics playing on a loop inside my head.

We are old
Old enough to know better
We are young
Too young to be bitter

We are old
They say that we shouldn't cry
We are young
They say that we're too young to die

FIFTEEN

The next morning I wake up to two messages from Daze, sent at five a.m. The first is an image, white text on a black background.

JAMES GAYLE   KAROLINA ZABEK
PHOEBE MACKINTOSH

WE WILL NEVER FORGET

SATURDAY, WEST BEACH, 10 P.M.

The second message is Daze saying: *Seen this? We should go, yes?*

I message back: *Not sure . . . probably wouldn't be welcome??*

I get a reply straight away: *Bullshit. You have as much right to be there as anyone. Everyone's going.*

Me: *Don't you ever sleep???*

Daze: *Sleep is for losers.*

121

I put my phone under the pillow and go back to sleep.

I check the time on my phone. Forty minutes till I'm due at the radio station, which is only a couple of streets away. My guitar case sits propped on the chair opposite me, like I'm on a date with it. I was lucky to get a table, swooping in just as a couple of tourists left.

A waitress comes over and starts stacking up the plates and empty cups. As she's wiping the table, she asks what she can get for me, and I look up at her face for the first time.

It's the girl from Karolina's photo. The girl who replaced me in the frame. She looks less scary than she did in the photo. Softer, and prettier. Her features are delicate, and she's hardly wearing any make-up. Her blonde hair is pulled back into a bun, stray strands neatly pinned down. The biggest change, though, is her eyes. In the photo they were sparkling, challenging, fierce. Today, they're blank.

It felt stupid, coming here in the hope of finding answers. As if I was expecting to conveniently see a photo of Karolina and Lewis on the noticeboard, pinned next to the adverts for Bikram yoga lessons and Reiki healing. But now it looks like it wasn't such a stupid idea after all.

'Did you want anything?' The waitress is staring at me, waiting.

'Sorry, um, what kinds of tea do you have?'

She reels off a seemingly endless list.

'I think I'll go for English Breakfast, thanks.'

'Riiight,' she says, and there's a glimmer of life there. I'm glad to see it, even if she does think I'm a time-wasting arsehole.

She moves on to the next table to deal with a woman who has a lot of questions about the type of bread used for the avocado toast. She's patient with her, and clearly knows her stuff. You must get a lot of daft questions working in a place like this.

I'm steeling myself as I'm watching her. *Just ask her. Ask if she was friends with Karolina and take it from there.*

When she brings my tea, I'm ready to make my move. But even as I open my mouth the girl says, 'You used to be friends with Karolina, didn't you?'

I'm so taken aback that I say nothing for a second or two while she looks at me expectantly.

'How did you know that?'

The waitress shrugs. 'She pointed you out, last summer, I think it was. Said you used to live next door or something. Proper besties. How come you weren't at the funeral?'

'I thought it was family only . . .'

'Family and *friends*,' she says pointedly.

'I'm sorry . . . about Karolina. She used to work here?'

The girl looks over her shoulder, but the woman behind the counter – the boss, presumably – is too busy with takeaway coffee orders to be paying attention. 'Kaz got me the job. Said it would be fun, working together. Not sure this could ever be described as fun, but we had a laugh sometimes.' Her almost-smile fades into a scowl. 'I should just quit now. It's not like I need the money, and without her here . . . But I don't know. Sometimes it's good to keep busy.'

I'm surprised that she's this forthcoming with a complete stranger – but maybe that's precisely *why* she's so forthcoming. She doesn't care what I think of her.

'Can I ask you a question?' I don't wait for a response. 'Was she even friends with any of them? The others in the car?' I lower my voice. 'Like that Lewis guy?' I watch her face and it doesn't flicker; she doesn't know I'm connected to him.

'Not him. Or the Gayle kid. But the girl . . . Phoebe? She used to come in here. We would take the piss, because she was always on her own, and always at the same table, scribbling away in her notebook. This table, actually.'

A shiver passes through me. Not because I'm sitting

at the same table a dead girl once occupied, but because it's another link in the chain. First, Ruth at the funeral, saying that Phoebe knew Lewis, and now Phoebe hanging out where Karolina worked. It may not be much, but it's something.

'Did Karolina ever talk to her?' I try to sound casual, like I'm just making conversation for the sake of it.

'She took her order, but that was it.'

'So what do you think they were doing in that car together?'

'Fuck knows. Probably heading to the warehouse party, out on the City Road — she mentioned it earlier in the week. I just wouldn't have had Phoebe down as the partying type — same with that James guy.' My thoughts *exactly*.

'You didn't go to the party, then?' I ask.

'Not really my scene,' the girl says with a shrug. 'Kaz liked to party, though, big time.' Her smile is fond, sad. 'And who knows? Maybe that girl Phoebe wasn't such a Billy No-Mates after all. Maybe they ran into each other that night and decided to go together. Kaz was always on the look-out for people who could keep up with her.'

She looks over her shoulder again, and this time the woman at the counter is standing staring at us, arms crossed and a frown on her face. The waitress rolls her eyes. 'Better get back to work. You going to this memorial thing on Saturday night?'

'I don't know . . .'

'You should come. Remember them. As though anyone could forget Kaz.' She turns to walk away, then stops and looks back at me. 'Sorry, Karolina didn't mention your name . . . ?'

'Evan.'

She smiles. 'It was nice to meet you, Evan. I'm Alice.'

SIXTEEN

I manage to maintain my smile until she turns away. What I feel isn't jealousy, not exactly; I don't even know *what* it is. All I know is that my stomach suddenly churns and my face feels hot.

I finish my tea and leave a fiver on the table. Alice is busy with another customer when I start gathering my stuff to leave, and I'm glad, because I'm not sure I could conjure up another smile right now.

As I reach for the handle, the door opens so I step back to let the person in.

Harry. His surprise makes his eyebrows disappear under his hair. 'Evan!'

'What are you doing here?' I ask as he follows me outside. We move away from the Beach Hut to stand next to the railings overlooking the beach.

'Oh, you know, I just fancied a decaf soy latte . . .' He grins as I stare him out. 'Well, I'd imagine I'm here for the same reason as you. You're turning out to be a right ch—'

'If you say "chip off the old block", I may do you actual physical harm.'

Harry grins again and mimes zipping his lips.

'Don't bother going in – you might as well save yourself a few quid.' I tell him about Alice, and what she told me about Phoebe coming into the café. 'But she said she never saw Karolina speak to her,' I finish.

Harry looks thoughtful. 'I wonder what she was writing.'

'Bad poetry?'

'Harsh.' He leans on the railings, staring out to sea. 'OK, so we've got a connection between Karolina and Phoebe; that's something, at least.'

'Plus there's the fact that Lewis was friends with Phoebe.'

'*What?* Was he? You didn't think that was worth mentioning before?'

'You didn't ask.' I can't resist a smile at my childishness.

Harry shakes his head, managing to stop just short of an eye-roll. 'Anyway . . . as I was saying . . . maybe Karolina and Phoebe *did* become friendly, when Alice wasn't working. What do you reckon? There's the drugs angle, don't forget. Maybe Phoebe asked Karolina to get her some drugs . . .' He clicks his fingers and points at me. It makes me think of Tim's finger-gun obsession. 'We should talk to Phoebe's brother – what's his name again?'

I look at him, his eyes shining with excitement and I feel sick. This isn't a game, and even if it *was*, I don't want to be involved. 'Stop. Just stop, Harry. There is no "we" here, OK? You're doing your job and I'm . . .'

'You're what?' he says. 'What exactly *are* you doing, Evan?'

I sigh. 'I'm just . . . I'm just trying to make sense of this.'

'Seems to me that what you're doing and what I'm doing are one and the same.'

'Seems to me you're treating this like some kind of intriguing puzzle to solve, when it's actually a fucking tragedy.'

Harry takes that on the chin, because he knows it's true. He does enjoy this – chasing a story, following leads. He always has, and always will. But this isn't just any story. People are *dead*.

He looks helpless for a moment, before his gaze lands on my guitar. 'Where are you off to?'

I could pretend I'm headed straight to the hospital. There's no need for me to tell him about going to the studio to see Tim. But I tell him anyway.

Harry nods three or four times. 'That's nice of him. Offering to show you round like that.' A couple more nods, and then, 'You never wanted to come to see my office.'

'You never offered.'

He nods. 'Right.' His fists clench around the railing; his knuckles turn white. 'Well. I'll see you around, Evan.' He turns and walks away.

It's the first time he's ever walked away. I'm torn between satisfaction and guilt. It's the first time he's done exactly what I want. So why do I feel so crap about it?

'What do you think of my little kingdom, then, Evan?' Gary Strout leans right back in his chair, hands clasped behind his head. The sweat patches under his arms are impressive.

'It's . . . there are definitely a lot of knobs.'

He smiles and says, 'The thing about knobs is you just have to know what to do with them.' His smug, self-satisfied smirk turns my stomach.

I turn my attention back to Tim on the other side of the glass. He looks perfectly at ease through there, chatting away to a listener. I don't know how he does it — always finding something to say. He hardly ever hesitates or says 'um' or 'er'. It takes practice, I guess, just like anything else. I'm glad he's there, even on the other side of the glass. Gary makes my skin crawl.

I wonder if I should tell Tim about Gary. But what

would I say? Gary didn't technically say anything out of line; it would be my word against his. Daze would have sorted him right out, if she'd been here. But he wouldn't have implied whatever he was implying, if she'd been here. Men have a tendency not to mess with her. Certainly not more than once, anyway.

For the past hour I've been trying my best not to think about Daze and Alice. I'm sure it was just a one-time thing, and even if it wasn't, it's none of my business. Nothing to do with me. At all.

Next door, Tim's doing a phone interview with a man who swears he saw a great white shark while fishing from the pier. Tim's polite to the guy even though he's clearly a liar or a fantasist. As he's wrapping up the interview he turns and gives me a thumbs-up. 'Well, there you have it, folks. You heard it here first, on Claybourne FM. Coming up, we've got a nice little surprise – an exclusive, no less – for you lovely lunchtime listeners. Why don't you grab a sarnie – or a salad if that's more your thing – and meet me back here after this stone-cold classic from Coldplay.'

Tim takes off his headphones and gestures for me to come through. I shake my head, and mime something intended to mean, *I'm fine in here, thanks*. He smiles, rolls his eyes and beckons me again. I relent, because I don't want to seem rude or ungrateful. Plus I'd rather not spend another minute alone with Gary if I don't have to.

Tim points me to a chair opposite him, and takes a swig from a Breakfast Tim mug with a chip on the rim. 'I hope Gary's been looking after you?' Looking through the window it's obvious Gary can hear every word. Now is not the time to tell Tim that his best man is a perv.

'He's been very . . . welcoming.'

'What do you think of the show so far? I try to tone it down a bit if I'm covering the lunchtime show. No need to be so hyper when everyone's already awake.'

I tell him that I liked the interview with the shark guy, and he seems pleased. 'It's never dull, this job. Crazy, sometimes, but never dull.'

'So what's the exclusive you were talking about?'

Tim's momentarily distracted by something on the screen in front of him. 'Mmm?'

The last few bars of the Coldplay song remind me how much I dislike Coldplay. 'The big surprise you just mentioned. What is it?'

Tim smiles like a kid on Christmas morning. 'You are.'

SEVENTEEN

There's no time to say anything before Tim slips his headphones back on and leans into the microphone. 'That was Coldplay with "Paradise", and now, let me introduce you to a very special young lady who'll no doubt be rivalling Chris Martin in a few years . . .'

My stomach flip-flops like wet clothes in a washing machine. This can't be happening.

'Those of you who aren't regular listeners of the breakfast show may not know that I was lucky enough to marry a very special lady recently – hello, Diane, if you're listening – and with Diane, I was equally lucky to welcome a fabulous daughter and a wonderful son into the Rossi family.'

Tim winks at me. And despite my shock I can't help think of Lewis. What about him? Has he been airbrushed out of the picture?

'Anyway, let me tell you, my stepdaughter Evan is

a talent with a capital T. And guess what? She's right here in the studio with me . . . say hello, Evan.'

I can't believe I didn't even look at the microphone just next to me. Stupid. Unbelievably stupid. Instinctively, I push my chair back.

There are one, two, three beats of silence, and I know that dead air is Tim's worst nightmare. He's still smiling – just about – as he says, 'Aw, she's a little shy, folks. How about I play another song to give Evan a few moments to compose herself. I'm sure she'd love to play something for us, and share that talent of hers with all of Claybourne. In the meantime, here's the latest from Ariana Grande . . .'

Tim flicks a switch in front of him, and the headphones come off again.

I stand up, shaking my head. How many times do I have to shake my head before he gets the message? 'This isn't . . . I don't want to do this. I'm just going to go, OK? Say that . . . say I've lost my voice or something.'

'This is an incredible opportunity, Evan,' says Tim, his voice soft and sincere. 'Most people your age would kill for a chance like this – playing on live radio.'

'I don't play by myself. I'm in a band.'

'But they're not here, and you are. And this will be great exposure for the band.' He gets up from his chair and kneels down in front of me. 'Come on, it's just one song,' he coaxes me. 'You'll enjoy it. There's nothing to be scared of, I promise. Do you need to tune your guitar first?'

I turn to see my guitar case propped up next to the door. Gary must have put it there when he opened the door to usher me through. He's smiling at me through the glass.

'Tim, I'm grateful for this – honestly, I am – but I really don't want to do it. Maybe we can arrange it for another time? Get Sid and Daze on board, and we'd have time to practise and plan what to play.' I'll say anything to stop Tim looking at me like that, as if he's given me the greatest gift in the universe and I've just spat in his face.

He looks down to the floor, and shakes his head. 'I've told the listeners, Evan. They're waiting to hear you sing.'

'But you shouldn't have told them! You should have asked me first!'

His knees crack as he stands up. He takes my guitar out of the case and hands it to me. 'Tune up.'

'I said no.' The guitar feels alien in my hands.

'Well, then,' he says with a sigh. His hands are on his hips as he sizes me up. Mum's always telling him how stubborn I am. *'Once Evan's made up her mind about something, that's that.'*

Then he smiles and shakes his head, and I think

135

I've won. He looks contrite, and I'm glad he's realised that this is Not OK because the Ariana Grande song can't be much longer than three minutes, and it's definitely been at least two.

Tim leans down towards me and puts his hands on the arms of my chair. He leans in close so I can smell the coffee on his breath. 'I saw you,' he whispers.

'Saw me *what*?'

He pulls back a little so that I can see his face. He smiles as he says, 'I saw you fucking that waiter at my wedding.'

EIGHTEEN

Mum's so proud. That's what kills me. 'So professional! And that song – it gave me chills!'

I smile politely. 'It's Sid's song. He wrote it.'

'But you're the one who sung it on *live radio*, as if you'd been doing it your whole life!'

I had no choice, that's what I keep telling myself. It was the shock of what Tim said. The thought of him watching me and Marcus. The knowledge that he would tell Mum if I didn't go along with what he wanted. Not that he threatened me. He just left it hanging there, watching me panic.

I had no choice. If Mum finds out about Marcus and me, she'll never look at me the same way again. And Tim would have told her, I'm sure of it.

I can't even remember singing. I just remember staring at him numbly as he stood up and moved a mic so it would pick up the sound better. 'It'll be fun, you'll see,' he said brightly.

It made me feel that I'd imagined it. The weight of the threat. The swearing. Tim doesn't swear; he prides himself on it.

It was an act. All of it.

'Play something cheerful, OK?' Tim said, and winked. That's what made my decision. If I was going to do this, the song was going to be as far away from cheerful as it was possible to get. I told myself that Sid wouldn't mind. He'd understand, when I explained.

Ariana stopped singing.

'OK, we are good to go, people! Without further ado, let me introduce the one and only Evan Page!'

I knew he wanted me to say something first, maybe introduce the song or thank him for the opportunity. But instead I closed my eyes and started to play.

Afterwards, I opened my eyes and saw Tim staring at me. Then he quickly whooped and clapped. I didn't say a word, just started putting my guitar away.

'Wow. Just *wow*. I'm actually feeling quite emotional after that.' And his voice was different – almost choked up. 'I'm afraid Evan has to love us and leave us. She's a lady in demand, what can I say? But I'm sure she'd love to know your thoughts on her big radio debut, so hit us up on email, phone, Twitter, carrier pigeon. Right now we've got the five biggest hits from 1996, which officially count as "oldies", so I've been told. Let's get in the mood with the fifth biggest selling single of that year, "Children" by Robert Miles . . . Let me tell you, I busted some *serious* moves to this back in the day.'

I was almost at the studio door when he caught up with me. 'Hey, where are you running off to? I'm giving you a lift to the hospital, remember.'

I kept my hand on the door handle, an anchor in a storm. 'I'm going home.'

'Oh, don't be like that! You were brilliant – better than brilliant.' That was true, at least. Sometimes you just know, when the music flows out of you, that you've nailed it. I'm just shocked – almost appalled – that I was able to nail it in those circumstances. It makes me wonder what kind of person I really am.

'What? Why are you looking at me like that?' He smacked his hand against his forehead. 'That thing I said about the waiter? Oh, come on, Evan, that was just a bit of fun. You needed a little push, and I gave you one. And you can't tell me you didn't enjoy it – singing, I mean. I know you did.'

And fuck that guy, fuck him to the moon and back, because he was right. But he didn't just cross a line with me; he went so far past the line that I can't even remember what the line looks like. And now Sid and Daze are going to kill me.

'Oh, and don't worry,' he said, smiling. 'I won't tell your mum about what you did. I was young once, you know. Right little tearaway, I was. Anyway, your secret's safe with me.'

Now here we are, the four of us playing happy families, eating dinner together. Mum's positively beaming – I haven't seen her this happy since she said her vows. What would she do if I told her the truth – about what Tim said to me in that studio, and about what I did at the wedding? Would she be on my side or his?

Tim's eating his salmon with gusto, in between harping on about the great feedback the station's had about my performance. He's been showing Mum all the tweets, even though we usually have a strict rule about no phones at the table.

Billy's quiet, but it's hard to get a word in with these two. Mum played the clip from the radio website for him before dinner, and he listened with his eyes closed. He always does that when listening to music. He says it helps him to see. When the song was finished, he wrapped his arms around me. Mum thought it was the cutest thing ever. But when he pulled away, Billy wasn't smiling, and neither was I.

Mum asks about Lewis when we're stacking the dishwasher, and I have to admit that I didn't go to the hospital. If she's surprised, she doesn't show it.

'We decided it would be better if she went tomorrow, didn't we Ev?' I didn't realise Tim was right behind me. 'It was such a huge day – making your live radio debut is kind of a big deal, isn't that right?' He squeezes my shoulder, and my skin itches.

NINETEEN

I should know by now that burying your head in the sand never works. And yet somehow I can't bring myself to message Sid or Daze about the radio thing. If Sid sang a song of mine without crediting me, I'd be fucking furious. Worse than furious, though – I'd be *hurt*.

That night I receive two messages about the radio appearance. The first is Marcus Bloom who says that my voice is sexy and we should hook up again soon. I delete it without replying. Obviously.

The second message is from Harry: *Proud doesn't even come close. x.*

I don't know what to say to that, or how to feel about it. I find myself opening the message again and again, staring at the words. Because even though I don't want them to, they mean something to me.

Around midnight, I finally manage to summon up an iota of courage and send a message on the band WhatsApp group:

It was a dick move, singing that song. I'm sorry. Extenuating circumstances, though, big time. Will explain tomorrow. Still, total dick move. Sorry.

Two little ticks tell me that the message has been read, but I wait and I wait and there's no reply.

At work the next morning, Eddie manages to say exactly the wrong thing within five minutes of me walking through the door. 'Gone solo, have you?'

I tell him to fuck off, but he keeps taking the piss, listing lead singers who've dumped their bandmates. He only shuts up when a woman comes in looking for a ukulele. Eddie thinks ukuleles are the devil's work, but he has to keep them in stock because they're popular.

Later on, he makes me a cup of tea and offers his version of an apology. 'Your pa's proud as punch . . . non-alcoholic punch, of course. And I am too. You sounded . . .' he shakes his head and strokes his stubbled chin, 'you sounded *real.*'

I relent and tell him the truth – part of it, anyway. That I didn't want to do it, and I nicked Sid's song just to piss Tim off. Eddie's a good listener; it's one of my favourite things about him.

Eddie says that Sid will understand, and that he should be glad to have his song on the radio, whatever the circumstances. I'm not buying it, but I'd be lying if I said it didn't make me feel a little better. Until, that is, I finally get a message from Daze, about an hour before I'm due at Sid's house to practise. The message isn't on the band group, which makes me uneasy before I've even looked at it:

Band practice is off. He doesn't want to see you. That song was special to him, Ev.

She's writing another message even as I'm reading the first.

Maybe we should give the band a rest for a week or so. Give you guys a chance to sort things out.

My fingers feel numb as I type out a reply:

What?? No! I said I was sorry. I just need a chance to explain. I fucked up, OK?

Daze: *You did.*

Do you hate me? I hate myself, as I tap out the words.

Daze's reply is exactly what I deserve. She's always been an expert at deployment of the eye-roll emoji.

'If Sid needs space, he can have it. He's making a big thing of it, though, don't you reckon? I'm sure he'd understand if he'd just let me explain. But maybe a couple of weeks away from the band isn't such a bad idea, after all. There are more important things, right?'

Lewis doesn't answer, but that doesn't mean he isn't listening. He's probably waiting for me to get back to the book – the last chapter ended on a cliffhanger – but I'm tired of reading.

'It's all your dad's fault.' The words sound right, so I say them again, a little louder.

Who am I trying to kid? I could have told Tim to go fuck himself and walked straight out of there. Would it really be that terrible if he told Mum what he saw? Like Tim said of himself, she was young once too. Plus I could have played literally any other song and at least my favourite people wouldn't hate me right now. But it felt like my only option.

'You probably hate me too. Coming in here and offloading on you, as if you don't have enough problems of your own. Sorry about that. But maybe – God, this is going to sound stupid – maybe this could be the start of something. You and me, talking. You'll have to start talking back soon, though, OK? If only to tell me to shut the fuck up.' I take his hand in mine. His fingernails look better now that they've grown a little. 'Things will be different when you get out of here, I promise.'

I clear my throat, and force some happiness into my voice. I open the book, flicking through to find the right page. 'How about one more chapter?'

TWENTY

It's too hot to stand anywhere close to the bonfire, but that doesn't seem to put people off. The fire must be at least ten feet tall, flames leaping and dancing into the night sky.

Your average beach party typically consists of warm beer, tinny music from someone's phone, and a couple of those disposable barbecues you can get at Tesco for a fiver.

This is most definitely *not* your average beach party.

Whoever arranged this knows what they're doing – and has some serious cash. Decent music is pumping through speakers on stands set up at strategic intervals. There are kegs of beer next to a makeshift bar stacked with vodka, mixers and red paper cups. A couple of burly rugby types about my age are stationed next to the bar to make sure no one makes off with the vodka bottles.

'People really shouldn't have to die in order for

someone to throw a proper party,' says Nyisha Gill after downing her drink. She isn't known for her tact at the best of times, and right now she must be at least five drinks in.

'It's not a party, it's a *memorial*,' drawls Curtis Shepherd. His head is resting on Ellie Gattis's lap. She strokes his hair every so often.

Ellie called me over to join them when she spotted me. Half of me wanted to keep looking for Sid and Daze, but the other half was relieved I hadn't found them yet. It feels better – safer – to be part of a group, even if this particular group isn't my cup of tea.

I probably shouldn't have come, but I need to see Sid and Daze. Sid's still not answering my messages; Daze isn't exactly ignoring me, but not far from it. She didn't message to remind me about tonight – probably hoping I'd forgotten. I figured it would be better to see them in person – the two of them, together – to straighten things out. I miss them.

'If I die, promise me you'll throw an even bigger party – sorry, *memorial*.' I really wish Nyisha would stop talking about death and dying, but she keeps looping back to the topic.

Curtis pretends to scratch his chin, a thoughtful expression on his face. 'Hmm . . . I dunno . . . we could probably just about stretch to a few multipacks of Wotsits and a three-litre bottle of Frosty Jack's. Sitting on a park bench in the rain, probably.'

Nyisha hits him playfully in the stomach and Curtis laughs. 'OK, OK, we could maybe throw in a bag of Skittles, but you're pushing your luck!'

'I want to go quickly, like they did,' says Ellie, and the rest of them start debating the best ways to die. There's no consensus about the best way, but everyone agrees on the worst: fire. Ellie doesn't join in the conversation, even though she started it. When I try to catch her eye, she quickly looks away.

I get to my feet, muttering something about getting another drink. Loads more people have arrived on the beach since I sat down – there have got to be three or four hundred, at least. Sid and Daze *must* be here somewhere.

There are a lot of people I don't recognise; a lot of them must be from Karolina's school, St Joseph's, and Belmont Hall where James went. There's a bunch of older people too – I spy Jaime being given a piggyback by some guy with a mohawk. I'm about to go over and ask about Daze when someone barges into me. He stumbles to the water's edge and vomits. It takes a few seconds to realise it's him, because Conrad Mackintosh looks very different from when I last saw him. Bare feet, cut-off jeans, no top. I wait as he spits out the rest of the puke. He stays kneeling, as if he's praying to Poseidon.

'Are you OK?' My hand hovers uselessly above his back. I'm not going to touch him.

There's no sign of a reaction for a few seconds, then he finally tilts his head up to look at me. '*You.*'

'Can I get you some water or something? You have . . .' I make a vague gesture to my chin, even though my chin isn't the one with the trickle of vomit on it.

He wipes his chin with the back of his hand, then dips his hand in the water. The waves are lapping at his knees but he doesn't seem to mind. 'You shouldn't have come.'

I swallow. 'I have as much right to be here as anyone else.' My voice sounds feeble even to me.

'Whatever.' He shakes his head. 'Just leave me alone.'

'I'm not leaving you alone in this state. Where are your friends?'

Conrad snorts.

'Look, can you just come away from the water? I could do without a drowning on my conscience.'

I stand there with my arms crossed, and he stares up at me. Drunk people always look so gormless. He finally gets it – that I'm not going anywhere until he moves – and shuffles backwards. The tide's on its way out, anyway. Chances are he'll be fine.

'Just fuck off, will you?'

It suddenly dawns on me that although alcohol makes people belligerent and gormless, it also has a tendency to loosen their tongues. So I sit down next to him, and he glares at me. 'This is the very definition of *not* fucking off.' I suppress a gag at the stench of his breath.

'How's Ruth doing?' I ask, and the glare fades from his face.

'I'm not talking to you.'

'Why not?' I ask, even though I know the answer.

He stares at me as if he's memorising my features. I force myself not to look away. 'My sister would still be alive if it wasn't for Lewis.'

'He wasn't the one driving the car! Look, I'm not saying it was Phoebe's fault, but you can't blame Lewis.' I don't mention the ketamine, in case he doesn't already know; I have no right to tarnish the image he has of his little sister.

He picks up some sand and lets it run through his fingers. He does it again and again, still saying nothing. One last try. 'I didn't know Lewis was friends with your sister.' It's not quite a question, but then questions don't seem to be working out for me right now. I leave the statement hanging there, just like Harry taught me.

When I look at Conrad again, his face is wet with tears. He cries soundlessly, his facial expression unchanged.

The truth of it creeps up on me, sinks into my skin and seeps into my bones. His little sister is gone. Big brothers are supposed to be able to protect their little sisters, just like big sisters are supposed to look after their little brothers. Losing Billy is unimaginable. What Conrad is going through is unthinkable.

I want to say something to him. Find the words to lessen his pain. If only such words existed.

TWENTY-ONE

'Conrad? It's time.'

It's like waking from a trance. I turn my head to find a boy standing behind us, and I realise that the music has stopped. Everyone is gathered in a loose semi-circle facing the shore – with us smack bang in the middle. All eyes are on us.

The boy holds out his hand to help Conrad to his feet. I get up quickly and hurry off to one side, slipping into the crowd.

'All right, Blue?' An unwelcome whisper in my ear. An even more unwelcome hand rests on my waist, just for a second. Marcus Bloom. He moves away. I can tell he's still there, though, standing too close. I can practically feel the heat of his body.

The boy who spoke to Conrad is standing next to a cardboard box. Conrad stands just behind him, looking like he'd rather be anywhere else. A girl – Alice – emerges from the crowd and stands next to Conrad.

Her face is scrubbed clean of make-up, her hair tumbling loose across her shoulders.

The boy is clearly in charge. I'd put money on him being a Belmont boy. They just look different from regular people. They have better skin and whiter teeth, and they stand up straighter. They're usually taller too. You take one look at them and know they've never had an oven chip in their life, and that if they *have* had beans on toast for tea, it will have been slow-cooked borlotti beans served on griddled organic rye sourdough. Of course, there are exceptions – like Lewis – but there's no doubting that Belmont Hall is brimming with boys of a certain type.

The tall boy briefly confers with Conrad and Alice before facing the crowd. Crisp white shirt glowing in the moonlight, tailored grey shorts, black Birkenstocks. He's six foot one, or maybe even taller, broad shoulders. He could be a model.

He closes his eyes for a couple of seconds, then takes a deep breath and speaks.

'I'd like to thank you all for coming. I'm going to keep this brief. Public speaking has always been my greatest fear.' His slight accent isn't what I was expecting from a Belmont boy. Italian, maybe? Or French? 'For those of you who don't know me – and by the looks of things that's a lot of you – my name is Matthieu Fabre.' French, then.

I scan the faces in the crowd and catch a glimpse of Sid and Daze on the other side of the loose semi-circle of people. I'm not sure if they see me. The whole crowd is silent, waiting to hear what this guy has to say.

Matthieu shakes his head and smiles. 'That's a lie. It's true, I do hate public speaking. But my greatest fear was losing the person I loved most in the world.' He breathes hard. I can see his chest rise and fall from here. His next words are less composed, more real. 'And now this unimaginable, unbearable thing has happened, and the boy I love is dead.' He bows his head for a few moments, and I have to look away. It hurts to see someone in so much pain. 'James Donovan Gayle meant everything to me. Life without him is . . .' He shakes his head. 'But I made a promise to him, and tonight I'm here to keep that promise.' A ripple of interest runs through the crowd.

'I should explain . . . There was a film that we watched many times together, me and James. James loved it – me? Not so much. It is called *Lord of the Rings*.' A few people laugh, and someone shouts out, 'Fucking hobbits!' Someone else shouts, 'Now *that's* a film I'd watch.' Loads more people laugh, including me, and someone hushes us.

Matthieu is smiling, though. 'No, please, laughing is good. We have cried enough.' He turns to Conrad and Alice as though for confirmation; Alice nods, Conrad does not. After a tiny pause, Matthieu continues. 'So, in the first movie, a character dies – saving those fucking hobbits, as it happens. And his friends put his body in a boat, with his sword and shield, and push the boat out on to the river. James would always say they should have set fire to the boat – "proper Viking style". The last time we watched it together, maybe three or four months ago, James turned to me and said, "If I die, promise me a proper Viking burial."' Matthieu laughs again, but the laugh turns into a sob, and he shakes his head as if he's disappointed in himself. 'I laughed, of course, but James was serious. He asked me again to promise. And I did. I would have done anything he asked of me. But this was one promise I was unable to keep.' He starts crying properly now, and Alice puts her arm around him, whispering in his ear.

Other people are crying too. I'm just about managing to hold it together. 'So much for keeping it brief,' Matthieu eventually manages, and I have no idea where he's finding the strength for this. It's magnificent. He straightens his back and lifts his head. 'Anyway. I had this idea that I could honour my promise to James in some way, and at the same time pay my respects to Karolina Zabek and Phoebe Mackintosh. I didn't know them, but I take some comfort, knowing that he was not alone that night . . .'

That night. He must want answers too, surely.

'Tonight we honour the friends and family and loved ones we have lost. I like to think . . . I think this would make James smile.'

Matthieu reaches into the cardboard box and pulls out a boat made of white paper, just like the ones Harry taught me to make when I was little. There's a boat for Alice and one for Conrad too. Pinned to the sail of each boat there is a photograph. The three of them kneel down at the water's edge, and the crowd – instinctively it seems – shuffles to form a rough line behind them.

Matthieu uses a lighter to light a tea light in the prow of James's boat, then passes the lighter to Conrad and Alice who do the same. Conrad's hand shakes badly. It takes three attempts for him to light the wick.

All is silent as each boat is set adrift on the water. The tide is on the turn.

Silent sobs wracking shoulders.

White boats in black water, flickering flames.

TWENTY-TWO

I'm sitting close to a group of Belmont boys, watching Matthieu and waiting for my chance to speak to him, when Marcus sidles up to me and asks for a word in private. It's almost a relief. The truth is, I felt vulnerable by myself.

Marcus leads me away from the bonfire, towards the blocks – these huge cubes of concrete left embedded in the sand after the Second World War.

'So are you going to go out with me or what?'

'You're joking, right?' My arms are crossed.

'No!' He crosses his arms too, and I can't tell if the mirroring is subconscious or not. Marcus half-smiles. 'So it's a no, then, I guess?'

'Yes.'

'Yes, it's a no, or yes, it's a yes?' That charming smile again. 'It's a no,' I say firmly.

'Right.' He nods slowly.

'Right, as in, right, you'll leave me alone from now

on or, right, as in you're going to keep asking until I tell you to fuck off and die?'

Marcus winces, gesturing back towards the bonfire. 'Unfortunate choice of words, given the occasion.'

'Well, you seem to think it's a perfectly acceptable occasion to ask someone out.'

'Why do you hate me so much, Evan?' It's the first time he's used my real name.

'Why do you like me so much?'

'Fucked if I know.' He leans his head back against the concrete and looks up at the stars. I stare at his Adam's apple as he swallows. Finally, he looks at me again. 'I think we got off on the wrong foot.'

'You think? So plying someone with booze so that they'll shag you at their mother's wedding isn't your usual M.O.?'

'Look, I know you think I'm a dick, but I'm actually not that bad when you get to know me.' He could be telling the truth for all I know. His eyes widen all of a sudden. 'Oh my God, you're not *pregnant*, are you?'

The horror with which he says the word almost makes me laugh, but there's nothing funny about the thought of being pregnant with Marcus Bloom's baby. 'I took the morning-after pill.'

'Thank fuck for that.'

'Not that you seemed to care at the time. Plus I'm going to have to get tested for every STD in the book.'

158

He exhales loudly. 'I'm sorry. We should have – *I* should have – used something. I'm *sorry*. That's not . . . I haven't done that before. So you probably don't need to worry . . .' It's hard to tell in the darkness, but I think he might be blushing.

If he thinks I'm going to take his word for that he's even stupider than I thought. I need to end this conversation now. 'What happened at the wedding was a mistake. A never-to-be-repeated-under-any-circumstances mistake.'

'No one's ever called me a mistake before.'

'Probably because you've never bothered to ask.'

We lock eyes, and I'm ready for him to call me a bitch. But he doesn't call me anything.

Marcus Bloom says, 'I'm sorry,' and walks away.

I hate him even more than I did ten minutes ago, and I hated him a lot ten minutes ago. But at least then I didn't hate myself too.

'*Wow*.' The voice makes me jump. It comes from above and behind me.

'I never thought I would ever find myself feeling sorry for Marcus Bloom. And yet . . . here we are.'

I crane my neck to see Sid skip unsteadily from one block to the next until he's looming over me. His hair is even wilder than usual, as if he's been electrocuted. There's a half-empty bottle of vodka dangling from his fingers. He brings the bottle to his lips and takes a swig. He hardly ever drinks spirits.

'Get down from there before you fall and break your neck.'

He stands up straighter. 'Actually, I think I'll stay up here on the moral high ground, thank you very much.'

'You're wasted.'

Sid shrugs. 'You're a terrible person.'

He's drunk out of his mind, but the blow still lands – hard. I swallow down the pain and try to focus on what's important. 'Can we talk? Please? I've been looking for you all night.'

He snorts. 'You weren't looking very hard. Seems to me you had other things on your mind. I can't believe you – *you*! – had sex with Marcus Bloom.' He shakes his head, and keeps shaking it as he speaks. 'No, that's not it. I can't believe you had sex with him then *lied* about it. Why didn't you tell me? After we saw him at the funeral? I asked you what he was on about and you said you had no idea.'

'I'm not talking to you until you come down from there. Or I could come up there?'

'No. You don't get to do that. This is *my* place now.'

'What are you talking about?' But I remember as soon as the words are out of my mouth. Sid brought me here on a date once. Our fourth, I think. He'd even prepared a picnic; it became Our Place. 'OK, OK, it's your place. But the sooner you come down from there, the sooner I'll leave you in peace.'

He weighs that up for a few moments, before climbing down. He reaches up to retrieve his bottle and clutches it like he's worried I'm going to swipe it.

It's only now that I can see that his eyes are red and his face is puffy. He's been crying.

'Well?' He looks at me expectantly, combatively. 'I'm listening.'

I take a deep breath. 'Look. First of all, I'm sorry I lied about Marcus. I didn't mean to, but I was . . . I was embarrassed. It's not exactly something you talk to your ex about, is it? I have no idea who you've been hooking up with since we broke up – and I don't *want* to know.'

Sid considers that, as only a drunk person can, suspicious that his inebriation will allow him to be fooled by me. 'OK. Did you really not use anything, though? We were always so caref—' He slaps his own face and makes an anguished noise. 'Fuck. FUCK. I don't care. I *don't*.'

It's horrible, seeing him like this. I move towards him, but he backs away. There are tears in his eyes. 'What you did was unforgivable,' he spits.

'It was hardly unforgivable. Unbelievably stupid, maybe, but I didn't hurt anyone.' Apart from Marcus, it turns out.

'I'm not talking about Marcus! This isn't about him. This is about you and me. You had no right to play that song.' There's something about the look in his eyes that scares me. For the first time I think this might not be simple to fix. I'd been so sure that things would be OK as soon as we were face to face.

'You're right,' I say quietly. 'I shouldn't have played it.'

'So why did you, then?'

He would understand, I think, if I tell him the truth – that it was the first depressing song that popped into my head. But that's no excuse. I shouldn't have done it.

'I don't know,' I say dully.

'That's all you've got to say for yourself?'

'I'm sorry.'

His jaw clenches. 'That song means something to me, you know. *Meant* something. Being in the band meant something too.'

'The band still means something. The song too. It still exists, it's still yours. It's still beautiful. Nothing can change that.'

'*You* changed that. You changed everything.'

'Let me make it up to you. What can I do to prove how sorry I am? Don't let this affect how you feel about the band. You *love* being in the band.'

He laughs, but it's a harsh, guttural sound. 'Oh,

come on, Evan. I was kidding myself and we both know it. I'll never be good enough. You two will be better off without me.'

'We need you.' It's entirely true and I didn't even realise it until now. How could I have been so stupid? He's not the best bass player in the world, but that doesn't matter. What Sid brings to the band is much more important. He's the heart. 'There's no band without you.'

He shrugs. 'Then I guess there's no band.'

It's the biggest cliché ever, but it's true. You don't know what you've got till it's gone.

TWENTY-THREE

It was inevitable, I suppose, but that doesn't make it any less disappointing. The *Courier*'s headline is as stupid as ever: LOCAL TEENS' ILLEGAL BEACH RAVE.

The article is mostly bullshit. It focuses on drinking and drugs and debauchery, says it was a 'so-called memorial service that rapidly spiralled out of control'.

I'm reading the article for the third time when it dawns on me that they hate us. The media. It's the only explanation for the way they talk about us. They don't understand us, and they hate us for it.

They call us lazy, irresponsible, dangerous, ungrateful.

You hardly ever see positive stories about teenagers. There's the odd sporting or academic triumph, or a tragic battle with cancer. They only like us when we're excelling, or dying. No one's interested in the in-between.

I haven't touched my guitar since that day in the studio with Tim. It sits on its stand in the corner of my room, taunting me. Reminding me of what I did, and what I lost.

Any illusions I might have had about Daze having any sympathy for me were smashed to pieces with the message she sent the morning after the bonfire. It was short and not sweet: *Alice told me you turned up at her work, pretending you don't know Lewis. What the hell are you playing at?*

I typed out a message, explaining that I hadn't meant to lie to Alice; I just wanted some answers. I was about to hit send when the anger arrived in full force. *Daze should know better. She knows what kind of person I am. If she's so ready to think the worst of me, then fuck her.* I deleted my explanation, replacing it with a single word: *Whatever.*

Three days later and the anger's gone, leaving misery in its wake. I keep thinking about how smug we used to be – the three of us against the world, proving that being friends with your exes isn't the terrible idea people seem to think it is. The stereotypes didn't apply to us. Our break-ups had been amicable – inevitable, almost. There was no bitterness between us. We – mostly me, if I'm entirely honest – were so damn superior. We had no idea it would only be a matter of time before we unravelled.

The next day is Billy's eleventh birthday and I'm fully expecting an early morning wake-up call; it's the one day of the year he's allowed to wake me up by jumping on my bed. At eight o'clock he still hasn't emerged from his room and I start to worry. My first thought is that he's dead. Choked on his own vomit or stung by a bee that somehow lodged itself in his throat or struck down by some random, extremely rare undiagnosed illness.

As it turns out, Billy's sitting on his bed in his PJs, watching a video on Mum's old phone. I know which video it is straight away. It's Harry singing a song he wrote for Billy's seventh birthday. The song's called 'Billy is Somewhere Silly'. Each verse puts Billy in a ridiculous situation, culminating with a miniaturised version of Billy having a cup of tea while swinging from one of the Queen's earrings. When he first watched the video, Billy laughed so hard that he snotted everywhere. Today, he's crying.

It takes a while for me to get the truth out of him: that he's not looking forward to his birthday meal tonight because he wants to see Harry. I try to explain that Harry's going to take him out tomorrow, but that doesn't help one little bit.

'Why can't we be a normal family?' He flings the phone dramatically on the bed; it bounces off on to the carpet, undamaged.

There's no point explaining to Billy that there's no such thing as normal these days. Instead, I try the one tactic guaranteed to pique his interest. 'Pancakes?'

He pouts and does his best to maintain his frown, but the grumble from his stomach is a dead giveaway. He side-eyes me. 'With chocolate chips?'

'An entire bag,' I say, praying we actually have some in the cupboard.

'I guess pancakes would be sort of OK,' he says, and the smile grudgingly appears.

I pull my little brother into a hug and wish him a happy birthday.

Present-opening is delayed till lunchtime, when Mum hurries back on her lunch break. Tim was meant to be here too, but he messaged to say we should go ahead without him. It's nice, with just the three of us. Mum manages not to keep looking at her watch even though Billy is snail-slow at opening each gift. Indy amuses herself by batting a ball of wrapping paper with her paw. She's perked up a bit in the last couple of days. It's nice to see *someone* has, at least.

Mum starts clearing up the wrapping paper when Billy runs outside to try his new skateboard, but I tell her that I'm happy to do it later. She sighs her relief. 'Life-saver.'

'Bit of an exaggeration, but I'll take it. Got time for a quick cuppa before you head back?'

She checks the time and says, 'Go on, then. Another ten minutes should just about be OK.'

We're sitting at the kitchen table when Tim comes in. He looks fresh-faced, relaxed, and not for the first time I wonder whether I could have imagined what he said at the studio. It doesn't seem possible that those words came out of Tim's mouth. 'How's the birthday boy?' he asks, dropping his keys on the kitchen table. He has a Harry Potter key ring. How could someone who likes Harry Potter possibly say something so vile? I thought Harry Potter fans were meant to be the best people in the world?

Mum starts to speak but I talk over her. 'Actually, he seemed a bit down earlier. He's missing Harry. So I was wondering . . . could we maybe ask Harry along for the birthday dinner tonight?'

Mum starts shaking her head even before I've stopped talking. 'I don't think that's such a good idea.'

'But it would make Billy so happy!' *And I wouldn't mind either.*

Mum's face falls. 'I *know*, Evan. But he needs to understand that things have changed.' She reaches for Tim's hand, like she's reminding herself who she's married to. 'And Harry's taking him out tomorrow. This way he gets to celebrate twice!'

What is it with divorced parents thinking that two birthdays and two Christmases magically make everything OK?

'I don't mind, you know,' says Tim casually. 'Harry's

perfectly welcome to come along tonight as far as I'm concerned.'

Mum gapes at him. 'Tim, I really don't think it's . . . are you *sure*?'

He nods and slides his hand over hers. 'Harry's their father, Di, and that means he will always be a part of this family. We should have made this gesture a long time ago.'

I stare at Tim, gobsmacked. He's never mentioned including Harry before. But Mum flings her arms around his neck, and says, 'You never fail to surprise me, you gorgeous, *kind* man.'

Gorgeous? Absolutely not. Kind? I used to think so.

'Besides,' Tim says, his voice warm, 'it's a double celebration today.'

Mum pulls back to look at Tim, and he smiles. 'I spoke to the doctors. They're happy that Lewis's condition is stable . . .'

'And?' Mum says impatiently.

'They've started lowering the dose of anaesthetic. He should wake up in the next couple of days.'

Mum gasps and her eyes fill with tears. 'Oh, darling . . . that's wonderful news. Why didn't you say something before?'

'It's still early days,' Tim explains, just as Billy runs in. Billy's face falls when he sees Mum's tears and we all rush to reassure him and explain what's happening.

'Are you sure you don't need to be at the hospital tonight?' Mum asks. 'I'm sure Billy won't mind . . .'

'Not at all,' Tim reassures her, and I catch Billy's frown. 'It's not an exact science, but Dr Harroch's best guess is that Lewis will regain consciousness some time tomorrow.'

Billy still looks sad, so I sling my arm around his neck and tell him that Harry's invited too. Then he runs round the kitchen shouting, 'BEST DAY EVER!' and starts dancing with Indy, who's barking with joy as if she understands the news about Lewis. And Tim kisses Mum and Mum hugs me, and for a few minutes it looks like we're a proper family.

Looks can be deceiving.

TWENTY-FOUR

It's a round table, which is a good thing. Billy's sitting in between Mum and Harry, exactly where he wants to be, and I'm sitting between Harry and Tim – the only seat left by the time everyone else sat down.

Harry's wearing a tie even though the restaurant isn't exactly fancy. Tim's gone for a pink polo shirt and Mum's wearing a pink top, and the thought of them colour coordinating on purpose makes me faintly nauseous.

Tim went AWOL for a few hours this afternoon, tapping his nose and saying he had a top-secret mission, which suited Billy and me just fine. We watched *Despicable Me* and stuffed ourselves with popcorn.

Mum asked me to talk to Harry, but Billy insisted on doing it himself. It was adorable listening to him stumbling over his words in his excitement, telling Harry about Lewis, then shyly inviting him to the restaurant. If Harry was taken aback (and surely he must have been?), there was no delay in accepting, because straight away Billy pumped his fist and shouted, 'YES!'

Harry was already here when we arrived, sitting straight-backed at a table right in the middle of the restaurant. He stood to greet us, Billy first, then me, then Mum. Finally he took a step towards Tim and extended his hand. 'Wonderful news about your boy, Tim.'

Tim nodded, and shook Harry's hand more vigorously than was strictly necessary. 'Thank you. So glad you could join us tonight.' Just when I thought the handshake was never going to end, Tim took his hand back and clapped. 'Right! Let the Bilbo birthday celebrations commence!' When Tim turned away, Harry mouthed, 'Bilbo?' at Billy, who shook his head and rolled his eyes.

As soon as we sat down a waiter appeared with a bottle of champagne and four glasses. Mum said, 'I think that must be for another table,' but Tim smiled and said he'd called ahead.

The look of panic on Mum's face when the waiter started pouring a glass for Harry was almost comical, but he just shook his head and asked for a ginger ale. Billy asked for ginger ale too, even though he always – *always* – goes for Coke.

The conversation is less stilted than I thought it would be, mostly because Billy hardly shuts up. The only time he's quiet is when he's eating his lasagne; Billy takes lasagne very seriously.

Harry and Tim chat away about their favourite restaurants, and Mum barely says a word. I'm betting she's as surprised as I am at how well they're getting along. I notice that she hardly touches her food — probably because Tim badgered her to order the fish, even though she said she was in the mood for pasta.

When the mains are cleared away, Harry reaches under the table, producing a wrapped parcel he hands to Billy. 'Open it later, Bill.'

'Nonsense!' Tim cries and if I didn't know better I'd think he was drunk. 'Open it now!'

Billy stares at Tim for a couple of seconds, then at the gift in front of him. He puts his hand on it as if he'll be able to sense what's inside through his fingertips. Then he smiles at Harry. 'Thanks, Dad. I'll open it later.'

Harry rolls his eyes, smiling. 'Go on, then. Open it now before I change my mind and take it back.' He makes a grab for the parcel but Billy's too fast for him, turning his back and tearing into the wrapping with glee. Inside, there's a set of watercolour paints in a gorgeous lacquered wooden box.

I can tell straight away that Billy loves it. It's way better than anything he has at home. 'This is . . . this is *proper*,' he whispers.

'Is it OK?' Harry asks. 'The woman in the shop said a lot of professional artists use that brand. And I remembered you said you wanted to try watercolours instead of acrylic . . . that's right, isn't it? Oh, God, was it the other way round?'

'Dad!' Billy mimes zipping his lips. 'I *love* it. It's the best present ever.' He hugs Harry for a long moment. Tim has his arm resting on the back of Mum's chair and the two of them are smiling benevolently at Harry and Billy.

'What a lovely gift!' says Tim, drumming his fingers on the table. 'Right! My turn!'

'Sorry, mate, I didn't get you anything,' quips Harry.

Tim barks out a laugh, and points at him. 'Good one! But I'm talking about *my* gift for Bilbo.'

Mum's brows knit together in confusion. 'What gift? Billy's already opened our presents.'

'I know, I know, but not the extra-special bonus birthday bonanza gift!' He's using his radio voice. It's embarrassing. 'But first . . . Billy, I hope you don't mind . . . I got a little something for Evan.'

What the hell?

'But her birthday's ages away!' whines Billy.

Tim smiles, and turns to me. 'It's not a birthday present, it's a *thank-you* present. Things haven't been easy recently, and we've relied on you a lot, your

174

mother and me. I want you to know – from the bottom of my heart – that I appreciate it.'

'I really haven't done anything,' I mutter. Tim pushes his chair back, points two finger guns at me and says, 'Be right back!' His walk is jaunty as he makes his way to the back of the restaurant and disappears round a corner.

I ask Mum if she knows what's going on, but she shakes her head. Tim's walk is even jauntier when he reappears a few moments later. He's carrying a guitar case.

A nasty, sick feeling bubbles up in my stomach.

'I popped in this afternoon and asked Angelo to stash it in the back for me.' He hands me the case. 'Bet you can't guess what it is, eh?'

I can't speak. My fingers trace the letters embossed on the case. Martin & Co. He's gone and bought me a *Martin*.

'Go on, then. Open it.' Tim stands over me, arms crossed, eyes twinkling.

No. Way. It's a D-18. Sitka spruce top, mahogany back and sides. I've been saving for this exact guitar for over a year.

'How did you . . . ?'

Tim's smile is a mile wide. 'Eddie filled me in. Nice chap, isn't he, once you get past the tattoos?'

'Goodness.' Mum is frowning slightly. I don't think

she knows exactly how much a guitar like this costs, but she can tell it wasn't cheap. 'That's . . . very generous, Tim.'

I look at Harry, because he knows precisely how much a D-18 costs, knows how much I wanted it. His face is expressionless; his eyes are fixed on the guitar.

'Tim, this is . . . I don't know what to say.' I don't know how to feel either. But I manage a smile, because that's what everyone expects.

He chuckles. 'You don't need to say anything.'

'Thank you.' I know I should probably hug him. That would be the normal thing to do, but I can't. I just can't.

'You're very, very welcome. Now, don't think I've forgotten about you, Bilbo!' Billy's been sitting quietly, taking it all in, his eyes wide. The finger guns are aimed at him this time, and moments later Tim is back with a big box. 'Happy birthday, Billy,' he says as he hands it over.

All I can think is please, please, please let it not be a bigger, more expensive set of paints than the one Harry bought. And it's not. It's a games console – just released, already sold out in most shops.

Billy stares at the box for at least ten seconds, and it's as if his face is fighting itself. There's a smile and a frown and some expressions in between, but the smile emerges victorious. 'Thanks, Tim.' I wonder if I'm the only one to notice that the smile doesn't last.

'Those things are scarce as hen's teeth, you know?' Tim's looking at Harry.

'Is that so?' Harry's face is impassive.

'Yup. Had to pull a fair few strings to snag that one.' Tim sits back down next to Mum, and puts his arm around her shoulders. Mum's smile is tight.

'It's a very generous gift. The guitar too.'

Tim shrugs and says, 'Nothing but the best for family, right?'

Harry takes a sip of ginger ale before answering. 'Right.'

'Best birthday ever, Billy?' asks Tim.

Billy flicks a panicked glance at Harry. His answer, when it comes, sounds stilted. 'It's . . . it's been a good day.'

Tim's smile dims for a second before returning at full wattage. 'Well. Who's for pudding?' His phone rings, and at first I can't place the new ring tone, then I realise it's the song from their first dance at the wedding.

Tim winces and apologises before heading outside to take the call. I feel my shoulders relax as soon as he's gone. There's a strange silence between the four of us. Billy's the one to break it.

'My best birthday ever was when we were camping,'

he says, to no one in particular. Billy turned five when we camped in the Yorkshire Dales. It rained a lot. We spent most of Billy's birthday crammed together in one tent, playing cards. Billy was very good at Snap.

Mum smiles at the mention of the holiday. 'Do you remember when we got lost and that farmer chased us off his land?'

Harry grins, shaking his head. 'And then you went back and knocked on his door the next day and told him you didn't think much of the local hospitality.'

Mum nods. 'Damn right I did. He scared the kids half to death with all that shouting and swearing. Nobody treats my family like that and gets away with it.'

'Mama Bear,' says Harry softly, and Mum blushes.

This is who they used to be. Cute nicknames and holding hands and whispered jokes. I'd forgotten, somehow.

Just then Tim comes back. He doesn't sit down. He grips the back of his chair and speaks only to Mum. 'Lewis is awake.'

TWENTY-FIVE

Mum and Tim won't let me go with them to the hospital, so Harry takes us home on the bus. He spends the whole journey reassuring Billy it wasn't his fault that no one was there for Lewis when he woke up.

'But do you think Tim will blame me?' Billy asks, his fingers drumming nervously on the box of his new console. 'It must have taken ages to find one of these and he could have been at the hospital . . .'

Harry turns in his seat to look at Billy. 'Why would you think such a thing?' Billy shrugs, so Harry takes his hand. 'Coming out of a coma isn't like waking up from a night's sleep, Bill. It can take days before someone properly comes round. No one thought it was going to be today. And even if they *had* known, it would never be your fault. OK?'

'OK.' Billy rests his head on Harry's shoulder and Harry ruffles his hair. I remember doing the same, back when I was a little kid. It's been so long since I had a father to look to for reassurance. To find it there, and trust it. I should be happy that Billy still has that. I shouldn't be jealous.

When we get home, Billy hurries inside to let Indy out for a pee, leaving Harry and me standing on the front step. 'Do you want to . . . you could come in for a cup of tea? If you want.'

He doesn't manage to hide his look of surprise, or maybe he doesn't even try. 'I'd better be getting back. Thanks, though. Really.'

I'm hurt but I don't show it. 'Thanks for coming tonight. It made Billy's day, to have you there. And I know . . . I'm sure it can't have been easy. So . . . yeah.' Why does saying the right thing have to be so unfathomably awkward?

I hug him then, whispering a muffled thank you into his shoulder. The hug is over before Harry even seems to realise it's happening. I hurry inside and close the door behind me.

It's the first time I've hugged my father in more than three years.

'It was awful, Evan. Just awful.'

I put a mug of tea down in front of Mum and sit down next to her. It's two in the morning and Tim's still at the hospital; they didn't want to leave Lewis alone. I can't help feeling it's too little, too late.

'The doctor said it's to be expected – the confusion and agitation. But you should have seen him . . .' She shakes her head. 'I think he was having some kind of hallucination – thrashing around in a total panic. I spoke to the nurse who was there when he realised that his arm was gone, and she said Lewis just stared at the stump. He didn't say a thing.'

'He must be in shock. Did you . . . has anyone told him about the others yet?'

'Dr Harroch thought it best that we wait a few days. And of course the police will be wanting to talk to Lewis too, just to confirm what happened. It's a lot – it's too much . . . oh, it's all too much, Evan.' Mum starts crying, and I scoot my chair round and put my arm around her. 'He doesn't even remember the accident. How on earth are we going to tell him?'

'He doesn't remember anything? Does that mean . . . is there brain damage?'

'They don't think so. He remembers everything else – it's just that night. They say that's normal too . . .' She laughs hollowly. '*Normal?* How can *any* of this be normal?' She cries some more, and then snaps out of it with a suddenness that I've come to expect. When my mother loses it, it's never for long. She apologises and starts fussing around the kitchen, wiping down surfaces and tidying things away.

I cross my arms. 'Diane Louise Morgan. You're exhausted. Get to bed this instant, missy.'

'OK, *Mum*,' she says, pouting. It's a well-worn routine.

It's gone three by the time I get to bed, which means I'm dizzy with tiredness when I open up WhatsApp to tell Sid and Daze about Lewis. Even though things are weird between us, they'd want to know. Some things are more important than arguments.

I can't find the band's group chat. At first I think my mind's playing tricks on me. I scroll back – way back – but no matter how far I scroll, it's not there.

Someone's deleted it.

TWENTY-SIX

It's different, visiting Lewis, now that his eyes are open and he's out of ICU. But not *that* different, because he hasn't said a word since I got here. He's probably baffled that I'm here, given that as far as he knows I've shown zero interest in him before.

The bruises on his face have faded from purple to yellow, and the swelling has gone down. He looks more like the boy I remembered.

Lewis has been awake for two days, and they still haven't told him about the others. Tim maintains that it's the right thing to do, and Dr Harroch seems to agree. Tim reckons Lewis needs time to come to terms with his injuries first, and maybe it's for the best that he doesn't remember the accident yet. The police are keen to talk to him, but Dr Harroch's put a stop to it – for the moment, anyway.

The weird thing is, Lewis hasn't even asked about the accident – about how he got injured. I overheard

Tim telling Mum this morning. Tim sounded relieved, but I don't think it's a good thing. That would be the first thing you'd ask, wouldn't it? So why hasn't Lewis?

We made eye contact when I walked in, but since then his head's been tilted away from me. I felt cripplingly shy when I said hello, then awkward when he didn't reply. I know he's talked to Mum – he asked about Indy – so perhaps it's just me he doesn't want to talk to.

There's no point wittering on like I did when he was in the coma. I made a few attempts at conversation – said it was good to see him, that Indy's missing him loads – but there was no response. So now I sit and wait until I can leave. Another ten minutes should do it. I wish he'd just close his eyes so I could at least pretend he's asleep.

My gaze lands on the little table next to the bed. I reach over to pick up the book. 'I hope it's OK that I brought this.'

He has to turn his head to see what I'm talking about, but there isn't even a flicker of a reaction.

'I read to you. They . . . some people think you can hear things, when you're in a coma. I wasn't sure if it was a book you actually liked, though. Maybe it was just next to your bed because you used it to squash a massive spider.' Out of the corner of my eye I can see he's still looking at me. Progress, I guess.

'I could read to you now, if you like?'

The nod is so slight I could have easily missed it. But it's a nod. I clear my throat and start where I left off last time, with our heroes in mortal peril for the hundredth time. I stumble on my words a little at first, conscious of how different it feels. Because the truth is that I didn't really believe he could hear me, before. It was almost like I was acting, auditioning for the role of Compassionate Visitor.

After a few minutes I glance up to see that Lewis's eyes are closed. He's not asleep, though; I can tell. Still, it gives me the confidence to resume the stupid voices I'd made up to go with each character.

When the wizard turns up to save the day, I go full Australian. Another glance at Lewis to check for a reaction, and there *is* one. If a twitch of an eyebrow counts as a reaction.

I find myself falling into the story, in a way I haven't done since I was little. I don't even notice the minutes passing; I'm engrossed, and I think Lewis might be too.

'Story time, eh?' The voice from the doorway gives me such a start that I drop the book. It lands splayed out, spine broken. The scrap of paper that had marked Lewis's place floats under the bed.

Tim has a bunch of grapes in one hand, a bunch of flowers in the other. Seems like I'm not the only one adhering to clichés. Tim comes over, stopping abruptly at the end of the bed when he sees Lewis's eyes are closed. 'Oh! He's asleep,' Tim whispers.

'Looks that way.' The lie was instinctual. 'Let me help you with those.' I put the grapes on the table next to the bed and look around for somewhere to put the flowers.

Tim tells me not to worry. 'I'll track down one of the nurses and see about getting a vase.'

When the door closes behind him I lean over and pick up the book, then get down on my hands and knees to find the piece of paper. When I pick it up I realise there's a phone number and a date written on one side. I slip the paper back inside the book and I'm about to put the book back on the table, when something – I don't even know what – stops me. I check that Lewis's eyes are still closed, then I fold the scrap of paper and put it in my pocket. My heart's beating fast by the time I put the book down again.

'OK,' I say nervously, 'I'm going to head off now your dad's here. I'll come again soon, though. If you want me to. I can stay away if you'd prefer.'

Lewis's eyes remain closed, but they're all scrunched up. It makes me think of playing Hide and Seek with Billy, when he closes his eyes as hard as he possibly can to prove that he's not cheating.

'OK . . . I guess that's a no? Help me out here. Please?'

His eyes snap open, and his voice is almost inaudible when he whispers a single word.

'Phoebe?'

TWENTY-SEVEN

I'm sitting on the sofa with Mum when Tim comes in. He doesn't waste any time. 'What were you *thinking*? You knew full well I didn't want him told yet!'

Mum springs into action, standing up and putting herself between Tim and me. 'Calm down, Tim! What are you talking about?'

'Your *daughter* here thought it was a good idea to break the news to Lewis that he was the only survivor from the accident.' He looked over her shoulder at me. 'What on earth possessed you?'

'OK, that's enough.' Mum put her hand flat on his chest, right over his heart. 'Is it really such a bad thing, Tim? Maybe it's for the best. It could help him remember . . .'

He stares at her, chest heaving.

'Evan?' says Mum, without turning away from

Tim. 'Why don't you go up to your room for a bit?'

I don't need to be told twice.

Tim's not wrong. I had no right to tell Lewis that Phoebe and the others are dead, but that didn't stop me. Except it's not quite as simple as that. I froze when he said her name, and he *knew*. He took this deep, gasping breath and briefly closed his eyes again.

'I'm sorry,' I whispered. I took hold of his hand, but he shook it off with surprising strength. 'Tim – your dad – was going to tell you soon . . . I think he wanted you to build up a bit of strength first.' Now that the truth was out there was no point holding back the rest, so I told him that James and Karolina didn't make it either.

He didn't react this time.

That's when I realised what that meant. 'You remember, don't you? You remember that night.'

He just looked at me for a moment then turned away.

'Lewis? Talk to me.'

'Leave me alone.' He didn't sound angry, just tired.

Tim came in a few seconds later, brandishing a vase like it was the Wimbledon trophy. And I left.

I didn't know whether or not Lewis would tell Tim he knew the truth. But as soon as I saw Tim's face when he got home from the hospital it was obvious that I was busted.

The first thing I do when I get upstairs is take my new guitar out of its case. I haven't touched it since the other night. I hold it, just like I've held it a hundred times in the shop. It felt special back then, as if I were holding a dream. Today, knowing it's finally mine, knowing how I got it, it feels like something else. It feels rotten. I put it back in the case and put the case inside the wardrobe. I take out my battered old Epiphone instead. It feels better – much better – but oddly I can't bring myself to play. My fingers don't seem to want to; it's unnerving. I've never *not* wanted to play the guitar, almost as far back as I can remember. I've been able to escape into music whenever things are bad. Music is what I do. It's who I am.

The shouting downstairs has died down, and all I can feel is relief that Billy is over at a friend's house and doesn't have to listen to this. When Mum and Harry used to fight, I would sneak into Billy's room and tell him stories. There were a lot of stories; there were a lot of fights.

I force myself to play one song from start to finish, but it's just . . . *wrong*. I haven't played since that day at the radio station, unless you count Eddie making me demonstrate a couple of the guitars in the shop for a dithering customer.

Tim did this. He turned the thing I love most in the world into a weapon. Forcing me to play when I didn't want to. But then I had to go a step further; I turned that weapon against one of my favourite people in the world. No wonder playing my guitar doesn't feel right.

There's a tentative knock at the door and my fingers freeze on the frets. Must be Mum coming to see if I'm OK. I'm surprised when the door opens and it's Tim instead.

He stands by the door, leaning against the radiator. His face has lost some of its redness. 'Your mother thinks I overreacted.' He clears his throat. 'And she's right. I'm sorry, Evan. I know you were only doing what you thought was best. It must have been a very difficult moment for you and I appreciate it was hard to know the best thing to do.'

I nod slowly. All I can think is that I want this over with before Billy comes home. The words stick in my throat, but I manage to get them out with the required amount of sincerity. 'I'm sorry too, Tim.'

'Well, that's OK, then. Friends?' I nod again. His lightning smile is replaced by a frown when he sees the Epiphone in my hands. 'Where's your new guitar?'

'In the wardrobe,' I answer without thinking.

'OK . . .' Tim crosses his arms and waits.

I smile as if the explanation is obvious. 'So that Billy doesn't mess around with it.' As if my little brother would ever do something like that. He knows better than to mess with my stuff. Tim's expression is still sceptical. 'Tim, that guitar you got me . . . I want to look after it properly. It's not exactly an everyday sort of instrument. It's special. Really special.'

That does the trick; I knew it would. He tells me Mum's making some iced tea and wouldn't it be nice if we sat out in the garden for a bit. *As a family.*

So that's exactly what we do, and engage in the smallest small talk imaginable. Anyone who happened to be peeking through a hole in the fence would look at the three of us and see a happy family. That's what Mum is desperate for people to see. She implies as much when I go with her to pick up Billy later. 'Bit of a milestone, isn't it?' she says, looking straight ahead at the road and not at me. 'First family argument . . . it had to happen some time. At least we got it out of the way.'

She wants to believe it, and wants me to believe it. So I pretend to. 'Yeah, sorry about—'

'You don't need to apologise to me, Ev. Tim should never have shouted at you like that, and I told him as much. He knows he was in the wrong. And to be perfectly honest with you, I thought we should have told Lewis the truth straightaway.'

I love her for that. For not mindlessly taking Tim's side against me. It makes me wonder how she'd react if I told her about Tim threatening me at the radio station. But that would mean telling her what I did at the wedding. And I would rather rip out my own eyeballs and juggle with them than do that.

I'm emptying out the pockets of my jeans for the wash, when I come across the scrunched-up piece of paper I retrieved from the hospital floor. A mobile number and a date. 1989. I don't know what it refers to; I suppose it could be a PIN or combination for a lock or any number of things. The handwriting is messy and even worse than mine – I'm pretty sure it's Lewis's.

By the time I've brushed my teeth and finished getting ready for bed, I know what I'm going to do.

A quick Google tells me how to hide my own number from whoever picks up the phone. Then I punch in the numbers on the piece of paper and wait. The phone rings and rings, and I'm about to hang up when someone picks up.

'Hello?' A male voice, but the line is slightly muffled so it's hard to tell for sure.

'Hello?' I repeat stupidly. Perhaps I should have figured out a game plan *before* dialling the number.

'That's *my* line.' The voice on the other line is wryly amused. 'Who is this?'

'That was going to be *my* line.' I grimace.

'OK, this is fun and everything, but I've got stuff to do. What are you after?'

'You tell me.' I have no idea where that came from; probably from watching too many movies. There's silence on the other end of the line. Not quite silence, I realise, but music, ever so faint. Then: 'Did Carter give you this number?'

I stay silent.

'Fuck's sake. Tell him to give you the other number. Don't call this one again, you get me?'

Something niggles at the back of my mind. Something about his voice. 'But Carter told me . . .' I want to keep him talking but I have no clue what to say.

'Look, just fuck off, will you?' The line goes dead.

And just like that, I know who he is.

I message Daze: *Go back to ignoring me after this if you want, but this is important. Does the name Carter ring a bell with you?*

She's online. I picture her staring at her phone, weighing up her options. I send another message before she can go offline: *Please?*

I can practically hear her sigh from here. But she's typing a reply, which means that maybe she doesn't hate me after all.

The only Carter I know used to hang around outside the gates at St Joseph's selling bags of oregano and pretending it was weed.

Bingo. I thank Daze and ignore the five question marks she fires right back.

Then I do something I haven't done for a long time. I dial Harry's number.

TWENTY-EIGHT

'Do you want to be Woodward or Bernstein?' asks Harry, shaking his iced coffee to check if there's any left.

Woodward and Bernstein are the whole reason Harry wanted to get into journalism. He used to tell me about them instead of reading bedtime stories, so I grew up knowing more than the average person about the investigative journalists who brought down a corrupt presidency.

'God, this is so boring,' I say, ignoring him. It's our second night on 'stake-out', as Harry insists on calling it. Last night was uneventful – four hours and not even a hint of anything interesting, apart from an enormous ginger cat lounging on the top of a Porsche.

Harry didn't even bother to disguise his delight when I asked for his help. Mum seemed pleased too, when I told her I was going round to his place last night – and even more pleased when I said I was seeing him tonight too. I told her I wanted to spend some time with Harry – just the two of us – and she beamed. She's always on at me to see him more often, and banging on about alcoholism being a disease that Harry's doing his best to fight. She's a better person than me, I guess.

Harry's spread a map out on the steering wheel so that anyone walking past won't be suspicious, but there's hardly anyone around. It's a quiet neighbourhood, with detached houses partly hidden behind high hedges.

I show Harry the piece of paper from Lewis's book, but he doesn't have any bright ideas. 'Maybe it's something,' he says with a wry smile. 'Or maybe it's nothing, Evan. Either way, we're not going to solve it tonight. There's no point obsessing over it.'

I know he's probably right, but that doesn't stop me thinking about it. Wondering.

The cat is still lounging on the Porsche, and it's still hideously hot. Still boring. Until it isn't.

The crunch of gravel alerts us, and Harry and I both hunker down in our seats. A figure in a tracksuit hurries from the driveway, looking both ways before hopping on a mountain bike. Definitely shifty. He places a big pair of headphones over his head and sets off – fast.

'Headphones! Oh, this is going to be too easy,' says Harry, shaking his head.

'Go, go, go!' I whack Harry's arm.

'Patience, my child.' He waits a couple more seconds before turning the key in the ignition.

We follow the mountain bike through the quiet suburban streets of Claybourne.

'Eyes forward,' says Harry, driving slowly past a house on the Harewood estate. I've never been here before, but I've heard about it – everyone has.

I ignore Harry and gawk out of the window, even though there's nothing to see but the mountain bike leaning up against a sixties semi-detached house. The front door is already closed by the time we drive past. The curtains are closed in each of the four windows, but light leaks round the edges in every room.

Harry's eyes are shining with excitement. He doesn't stop, just drives smoothly past, and then pulls up round the corner. The truth dawns on me. 'You know whose house that is, don't you?'

'Yup,' says Harry, looking like the cat that got the cream *and* a bonus bowl of Whiskas. 'That, dearest daughter of mine, is none other than Derek Lacey's house.'

It takes a moment for the name to click. 'What the fuck?'

Harry raises his eyebrows. 'Seems to me that

Phoebe Mackintosh's brother has got more than a little bit of explaining to do.'

Conrad Mackintosh paying a late-night visit to Derek Lacey's house doesn't *necessarily* mean that he's dealing, but it's more than likely. According to Harry, no drugs come into Claybourne without Lacey knowing about it.

A thought burrows into my brain as Harry drives me home. 'Do you reckon he might have been the one who told the *Courier* that Lewis was dealing?'

Harry nods thoughtfully. 'If Conrad got the drugs for Phoebe he would have been shitting himself that the police would find out.'

'And Lewis is the perfect scapegoat. No one would suspect the preppy, loafer-wearing posh boy . . .' I sink into silence, my mind whirring. 'So the car – what was it? A Saab? – was seen outside Derek Lacey's house a couple of weeks before the accident, and now we know Conrad is connected to Lacey . . . that can't be coincidence, can it? I guess we need to find out if the car was spotted there before or after Lewis bought it . . .'

'Before,' says Harry. 'I haven't been able to track down the previous owner, though.'

I sigh. 'You know, this would be a whole lot easier if you told me what you know instead of keeping stuff from me.'

'Ditto,' he says, sounding amused.

By the time we pull up outside my house, it's just past midnight, and I have a plan. If you can call 'confronting Conrad' a plan.

'Absolutely not,' says Harry, pulling up the handbrake.

'I wasn't asking for your permission.'

'If anyone's going to talk to him it should be me. In case you'd forgotten, it's kind of my job.'

'In case *you'd* forgotten, you're not supposed to be working on the story.'

'This isn't a game, Evan.' Harry's voice is clipped.

'I never said it was. But I'll get more out of him and you know it. What should I do? Just knock on the front door and ask to speak to him?' The thought of talking to Phoebe's parents makes me want to throw up.

Harry's sigh is so long I worry his lungs are going to collapse in on themselves. 'Has anyone ever told you how stubborn you are?'

'Chip off the old block, I guess.'

'I thought we weren't allowed to say that?'

'Oh, *I'm* allowed to say it.' My smile is saccharine.

Harry scowls, but I know he's caving. 'Don't try to talk to him at home – you'll never get anything out of him. You might want to try the cemetery.' He clears his throat and looks shifty. 'I've . . . um . . . heard he visits his sister's grave almost every day. Around lunchtime.'

'You've *heard*? Fucking hell, Harry. Were you already following him?'

'It was a hunch. I get hunches sometimes,' he says sheepishly.

'You could have told me!'

The front door opens and Tim peers out. He waves when he spots the car.

Harry waves back, then starts the engine. 'I didn't want to get your hopes up,' he says quietly, keeping his eyes on Tim. 'I knew how badly you wanted Lewis not to be the one to blame.'

I get out of the car then lean back through the window. 'All I want is the truth.'

I don't say goodbye to Harry and I don't say hi to Tim either. I bypass all social niceties and head straight up to my room.

I do want people to stop blaming Lewis for the crash. But more than that – much more, I suddenly realise – I want to know what really happened that night. I *need* to know.

TWENTY-NINE

I can't remember the last time I woke up to find Indy curled up in the crook of my legs, but today she has graced me with her presence. I didn't realise how much I'd missed it – the solid weight of her head resting on my thigh, the sound of her breathing, her muffled dream woofs. When I turn over to hit snooze on the alarm, she yawns and stretches and creeps up the bed to lick my face.

'Lewis will be home soon,' I whisper, even though I'm not sure it's true. He started physio yesterday, but apparently it didn't go well. Mum was with him because Tim had a meeting at the radio station.

I overheard Mum on the phone to Tim, saying that Lewis refused to even talk to the physio, let alone try any of the exercises. It was straight after the police had come to talk to him for the second time – which went about as well as their first attempt. No matter what they asked, Lewis's answer was the same: he doesn't remember anything after the morning of the wedding. He doesn't remember meeting the others; he doesn't remember getting in the car or where they were going.

Mum lowered her voice for the next bit of the conversation, but I could still hear every word from the top of the stairs.

'He said he was ill with a stomach bug . . . and I didn't say anything. Should I have said something? I could tell they thought it was odd – they said as much. Wondering what he was doing in the car that night if he was too ill to attend the wedding. I wasn't sure whether I should . . .'

There was a long pause as she listened to Tim on the other end of the phone.

'Yes, but if it doesn't matter then what harm could it do to tell the truth?' Another pause, even longer. 'Yes, yes. I'm sure you're right. It's no one else's business.' She sighed. 'I can't help thinking that none of this would have happened if only we'd been able to convince him to come to the wedding. I didn't try hard enough with him.'

At this point in the conversation I had to scarper back to my room as Mum started making her way up the stairs. I could only hope that Tim was doing his best to convince her that none of this is even close to being her fault.

Tim hasn't said in so many words that he doesn't want me going to visit Lewis again — Mum would have something to say about that — but he *has* said that Lewis needs time to come to terms with that's happened, that we shouldn't crowd him.

Indy breaks my reverie with a paw to my face, and I bury my face in her fur. I can never get enough of her smell.

'Maybe what Lewis needs is a dad who's not a fucking creep who thinks it's perfectly acceptable to blackmail his own stepdaughter, eh?' I whisper. Indy blinks slowly, and I like to think she agrees with me. 'Maybe what Lewis *really* needs is someone to talk to.'

I roll out of bed. I have to be at work by nine-thirty, and somehow I've got to persuade Eddie to let me take a two-hour lunch if I'm going to be absolutely sure to catch Conrad at the cemetery.

It turns out that persuasion isn't necessary. When I ask about lunch, Eddie shrugs and says I can take the whole day off if I want. He's still feeling bad for selling the guitar to Tim after I gave him an earful about it. He said he should have known better. Eddie's fully aware I wanted to save up and buy it for myself, because he *knows* me — he's known me since I was seven years old. I tell him I'll take the rest of the day off, on the condition that he stops beating himself up about it. He looks at me appraisingly, before holding out his hand. 'You drive a hard bargain, Page.' The handshake seals the deal.

The phone rings just as I'm getting on the bus. The photo that comes up accompanying the number makes me stop in the aisle. She put it on there without me knowing a few months after we started dating. A blurry selfie, perfect lips puckered into a kiss. I never got around to changing the picture.

'Hi?' My voice is a whisper. I hate talking on the phone in public.

'Why didn't you tell me he's awake?' Daze's voice is so loud I have to move the phone away from ear.

'Here on Planet Earth it's customary to begin conversations with some version of "hello", usually – but not always – followed by "how are you?"' It's an old joke between us; I can't remember how it started.

'Why didn't you tell me?' She's not playing today.

There are several possible answers to this question – sensible, reasonable answers that wouldn't piss her off even more. They do not include, 'I figured you were too busy with your new girlfriend to care,' which, unfortunately, are the exact words that come out of my mouth.

'Jealousy doesn't suit you, Evan.'

'Yeah, well, being a sanctimonious bitch doesn't suit you.'

'That was a terrible comeback.' I hear her breathe in and out through her nostrils. 'You're not very good at this, are you?'

'Not particularly.' And I wonder if I will ever have the upper hand with this girl.

'You should have told me, Evan.' This time there's no recrimination. It's a simple fact, and she knows I know it.

'How did you find out?'

'Ah. Guessing you weren't listening, then? Sid messaged me that Tim just announced it on his show. Made a big thing of it, apparently. He even dedicated a song to Lewis. "Father and Son" – which, by the way, is one of the worst songs ever. Anyway, Sid said the whole thing was a bit weird.' I wish he'd messaged me instead of Daze, but perhaps the fact that he messaged at all is what matters. Because maybe it means he still cares. 'So, have you seen him?'

'Sid?'

'*Lewis.*'

'Oh. Yeah.'

'And? Is he OK? I mean, I know he's not OK, but how not OK is he? And what the fuck happened that night, anyway?'

Daze listens as I tell her about Lewis claiming not to remember anything about that night, and his refusal to work with the physio. I don't tell her that I'm sure he's faking the amnesia; it doesn't seem necessary. It feels so normal to be talking to her again, even though what we're talking about is anything but normal.

'Will you tell Sid? In case . . . just in case he wants to know.'

'You can tell him yourself.'

'He doesn't want to talk to me.'

'Evan, you did a crappy thing and it hurt him. And, no, I'm not talking about you shagging Marcus Bloom – can't blame you for keeping schtum about that, by the way. I'd have done the same . . . I mean, obviously I wouldn't have had sex with him, because of the whole him-having-a-penis thing . . . Anyway, what was I saying? Right. Sid is miserable. You hurt him, but that doesn't mean he never wants to talk to you ever again. He loves you. You know that.'

'And what about you?'

'What *about* me?'

I hesitate. *Do* you *love me?* 'You deleted the group chat on WhatsApp.'

Daze snorts. 'Oh, God, *that*! Well, it seemed like a good idea at the time. Sid didn't want to do the band any more and I was pissed off with you for stalking Alice.'

'I wasn't *stalking* her! I didn't even know she was the same girl you'd talked about. All I knew was that she was friends with Karolina. I was trying to . . .' It sounds stupid in my head, so I can guarantee it will sound even stupider when I say it out loud. 'I was trying to find out the truth about that night.'

'Jesus, I turn my back for two minutes and you go full Miss Marple on me. Wait, is that what that message about Carter was all about?'

Christ, I've missed her. I'm smiling so hard my cheeks hurt when I look out the window and realise the bus has sailed right past my stop. 'Shit! Daze, I'm going to have to go.' I say, scrambling to the front of the bus. The driver takes pity on me and pulls up to let me off. 'Thank you!'

'You are so welcome,' says Daze.

'I was talking to the driver, smartarse.'

'Why, thank you. My arse *is* smart. I've got a pretty great rack too.' Her voice is low and breathy. I know she's just taking the piss, but *God*.

We say our goodbyes and Daze says I should call her if I need anything. She means if I need any help; she doesn't mean *anything*.

I'm about to end the call when she says, 'She's not, you know.'

'What?' I'm distracted, focusing on getting out of the way of a kid careening towards me on a scooter.

'Alice. She's not girlfriend.'

Daze hangs up without another word.

THIRTY

Lewis recoils from the sunlight, but he doesn't say he wants to go back inside. I'll take that as a win.

I didn't even have to talk Dr Harroch round. He's fine with it – thinks it'll do Lewis good – as long as I get him back in time for his session with the physiotherapist.

Lewis was in his wheelchair when I arrived. He was staring out of the window, his left arm cradling the stump of his right.

He ignored me when I said hello. He ignored me when I said we were going outside. It was only when I'd managed to manoeuvre the chair into the corridor that he spoke – asking me to leave him alone. And then I ignored *him*.

I gave a cheery wave as we passed the nurses' station. I held my breath as we passed the smokers hanging around the entrance – a few of them leaning on their drip stands for support.

'Why are you doing this?' Lewis asks as we negotiate a narrow strip of pavement down the side of the pediatrics department.

I don't answer. Because it's obvious as soon as we turn the corner and see the parched rectangle of grass and wilting flower beds that serve as the hospital gardens. There's a rusting cast-iron bench with a boy sitting on it, his legs swinging back and forth. At the boy's feet, a dog sits patiently, tail sweeping across the dusty ground as if she's on a personal mission to make the place presentable for her favourite human.

'*Indy*!' Lewis's voice is halfway between a shout and a sob.

Indy's head whips round at the sound of his voice. Billy was under strict instructions to keep her under control, but nothing could have held Indy back; she bounds towards us as fast as her legs will carry her. Indy's modus operandi is to take a running leap straight on to the lap, but today she comes skidding to a halt in front of Lewis.

Indy starts making this high-pitched whine, a sound she usually reserves for begging for a slice of roast beef. 'Hey,' Lewis whispers, 'It's OK, girl. It's OK.' He holds out his right hand for her to sniff and she gives it a thorough going-over. 'Do I smell like hospital? Is that it?' Indy answers by getting up on her hind legs, with her front paws resting on Lewis's knees.

Lewis leans his head against hers, and they just stay like that for maybe thirty seconds. I'm worried she might be hurting him – she has a tendency to dig her claws in to get a better grip – but I don't want to say anything to break the spell. Eventually Lewis pulls away and just gazes at Indy's face as if he's trying to imprint it on his memory. Indy starts sniffing in the direction of his stump, so he moves it closer so she can investigate fully.

'Hi, Lewis.' Billy's voice is barely louder than a whisper. He's hopping from one foot to the other like he always does when he's anxious. 'Indy's missed you a lot.'

There are tears in Lewis's eyes when he finally manages to wrench his gaze away from the dog. 'Hi, Billy.'

I sit cross-legged on the grass and Billy crouches down next to me. He's doing well so far. Not staring or acting weird – no weirder than usual, anyway. I'm proud of him. Until he goes off-script and says, 'I'm sorry about your friends.' I told him not to mention the accident.

'Thank you,' Lewis says softly. And I realise that Billy was right to say something. Some things are too big to go unacknowledged. 'And thank you for the card you made. It was really nice of you to do that.'

Now it's Indy turn to go off-script. Without any

warning, she leaps on to Lewis's lap and starts licking his face.

'Indy, no! Get down from there!' I get up and grab her collar to try to haul her off, but Lewis's laughter stops me in my tracks. Indy starts licking his nose and his laugh is so joyful that I can't help but join in.

I sit back down again and watch as Indy turns in circles, a little unsteady on Lewis's skinny thighs. He was pretty scrawny before the accident, but now he looks painfully delicate. Indy settles down with a sigh. 'You're a good girl, aren't you?' Lewis whispers, scratching behind her ears, which makes her eyes close in ecstasy. 'You're my best girl.'

I check the time on my phone. We don't have long before we have to get Lewis back. 'Listen, don't tell anyone about us coming today, OK?' I say. 'Your dad doesn't know we're here, and something tells me he wouldn't be thrilled with the idea.'

'It's a covert mission,' says Billy proudly. '*Highly* classified. Mum doesn't know either.'

'Well, in that case, my lips are sealed.' Lewis's conspiratorial smile doesn't last long. 'She's been kind to me — your mum. It's . . . it's weird to think that she's married to my dad now.'

'Tell me about it,' I mutter before I can stop myself.

Lewis looks up sharply. 'Is it . . . are things OK?'

I hesitate, because I don't want to lie to Lewis, but I can't exactly tell the truth either. But just then Billy points at the stump of Lewis's arm. 'Does it hurt?'

'Billy!' I turn to Lewis. 'Just ignore him.'

Lewis shrugs and says that he doesn't mind. 'I reckon I'd be curious too.' I can't get over the change in him. Whether it's down to being outside for the first time in weeks, or Indy, or even Billy, he's like a different person. I can't help wondering if this is what Lewis was like all along. If this was the person I didn't bother to get to know, or if he's changed. And if Lewis has changed, then maybe I have too.

'It hurts sometimes, but they've got me on some serious pain medication. They're taking the staples out tomorrow – the doctor says that won't hurt at all.'

Billy nods, his eyes narrowed in thought. 'Are you going to get a new arm like the Terminator's?'

'Since when have *you* watched *Terminator*?' I ask.

Lewis looks sheepish. 'That may be slightly my fault.'

Billy looks proud. 'We watched it that night Indy was at the vet's just before Easter. I couldn't sleep.'

This is news to me. I can't decide how I feel about it, so I choose to feel nothing at all.

'Maybe not a Terminator arm, but they want me to get a prosthetic. It wouldn't be for another couple of months – when the incision's healed and the swelling's gone down.' He stares at the stump of his right arm, lightly resting on Indy's back. 'If I do my physio and all that.'

I nod. 'What's this about you missing physio? The sooner you start doing those exercises or stretches or whatever else they want you to do, the sooner they'll let you come home.' I have no idea if this is true, but it sounds like it could be.

'*Home*,' Lewis says, managing to make the word sound hollow. 'You have no idea.'

There is something desperate in his face. Before I can think whether or not this is a good idea, I get to my feet and crouch in front of him. I hesitate, before taking his hand in mine. 'Then tell me. Please.'

There's a moment when I think he might, when he looks at me as though he wants to speak. But then he moves his hand to dislodge mine. I've lost him. Somehow I've managed to lose whatever connection we had. Or perhaps I imagined the connection in the first place.

'I'd like you to come home, Lewis. It's better when you're there.' Trust my little brother to save the day when I least expect it. Billy leans towards Lewis and whispers loud enough for me to hear. 'Plus I really want to see *Terminator 2* and I don't think my boring old sister will let me.'

Lewis manages to muster a smile, and I do too. It's

hard to watch Lewis saying goodbye to Indy. He presses his lips to her forehead then gives her a gentle push so she jumps from his lap. Billy clips her lead back on, which is just as well because she's all set on following us into the hospital. She barks and whines and does her best to pull Billy off his feet as I push Lewis's wheelchair away from her.

When Lewis urges me to go faster, his voice is thick with tears.

THIRTY-ONE

I told Norah we were going to the beach, so of course she wants to hear all about it when I take Billy and Indy back to her place. Billy tells this elaborate story involving Indy joining in a game of beach volleyball and I don't know whether to be appalled or impressed.

I feel self-conscious passing through the cemetery gates, clutching my small bouquet of blue and white flowers. An elderly woman smiles at me and I feel the urge to confess that I'm here under false pretences.

I've never been to this cemetery before; it's peaceful. The only sounds are the rustling of leaves on the trees and birds twittering amongst the branches.

He's already there, sitting cross-legged next to a grave. The gravestone is a no-frills grey slab with several names on it. As I approach, I can see there's some space at the bottom, but Phoebe's name isn't there yet.

I deliberately scuff my shoes on the gravel to alert Conrad to my presence. When he doesn't look up, I try a tentative cough, which turns into an actual coughing fit. *Now* he looks up.

'What are you doing here?' Not quite hostile, but hardly friendly either.

I hold up the flowers and he makes a sweeping gesture with his hand. Permission, unspoken. There are two bunches of flowers already there; mine is smaller than both of them. A glass jar half-filled with shells sits on the grass. I prop my flowers up against the headstone, counting three generations of Mackintosh, each dying at ripe old ages. Ages when dying makes some kind of sense. Eighty-two. Seventy-nine. Ninety-three.

When I step back from the grave Conrad looks up at me, his hand shielding his eyes from the sun's glare. 'She liked blue.' When I say nothing, he keeps talking. 'Never pink. Never, ever pink. Not even when she was little.'

'I was the same.'

'You can sit, if you like.'

His politeness is disarming. Still, I sit. Not too close.

'Elizabeth Mackintosh, gone but not forgotten,' he reads aloud. It's the last name on the headstone. 'Our grandmother. They got that right. I don't think anyone could ever forget that old cow.'

A laugh escapes from my mouth and Conrad turns

to look at me. 'Seriously. She never had a kind word to say about anyone – apart from that stupid dog of hers. Vicious little bitch.'

'The dog or the grandmother?'

Now it's his turn to laugh, but he feels it – the wrongness of laughing in a place like this. His face closes itself off almost immediately.

'If you have something to say to me, you might as well come right out and say it.'

I swallow. 'I know you got the car for Lewis.' Harry's the one who came to that conclusion, reasoning that Lewis had been looking to buy a car and Conrad knew that Lacey – or a mate of his – had one they wanted to offload.

Conrad sighs. 'And?'

'And . . .' I realise I don't have anything else to say.

'There's nothing wrong with helping someone buy a car,' Conrad goes on. His voice is calm, like he's rehearsing his words. 'Lewis wanted one; I knew someone with cars to sell.'

That 'someone' just so happens to be the local gangster/drugs lord. I wait to see if he has more to say.

'I've gone over it again and again.' His voice is bitter. 'If only I'd said no when Lewis asked me . . . or if I'd got him a different car – a better car – but he wasn't interested in the Ford Focus that Lacey

needed to get rid of. He wanted something older –
a *classic,* he said. When I messaged him about the
Saab all he wanted to know was the licence plate
number. He didn't even want to see the fucking car
first. And I was glad, because it was less hassle for
me.' He shakes his head in disgust. 'I was fucking *glad.*
If I thought for one second that my sister would ever
get behind the wheel . . . It's *all* I think about. If only
I'd . . .' He sniffs hard, and wipes his nose on his
arm. He ignores the resulting slug trail of snot,
glistening in the sunshine.

'You can't think like that.' Paper-thin words of
comfort that he brushes off with a contemptuous shake
of the head.

It's the contempt that gives me the courage to
come out with it. My voice is gentle, even though my
words are not. 'That's not why you blame yourself,
though, is it?' I pause for a moment. 'Who gave Phoebe
the ketamine, Conrad?'

I watch closely for his reaction, but his face betrays
nothing. So he *definitely* knows about the ketamine. He
plucks at some grass next to his foot, lets it fall through
his fingers.

'You're a dealer, aren't you?'

The words hang in the air between us. Conrad
gathers his knees to his chest, folding up into the
smallest possible permutation of himself.

'You sold drugs to your little sister. Or maybe you gave them to her. Is that it? No wonder you feel guilty.' Deliberately goading him.

Conrad springs to his feet. 'I would *never!*' He stabs a pointed finger at me. 'How can you think that?'

I scramble to my feet too. 'How could I *possibly* think something like that? Maybe because you lied to the *Courier* about Lewis? That *was* you, wasn't it? Blaming a boy in a coma just to put the police off the scent is pretty fucking despicable if you ask me.' Three quick steps and he's in my face. Harry warned me to tread carefully, but I can't help myself. This boy doesn't scare me. 'What are you going to do? Hit me? Will that make you feel better?'

I force myself not to flinch under Conrad's glare; we're close enough to kiss. Close enough that I see the change in his eyes, when it comes. The anger evaporates in an instant, but it's harder to tell what's left in its place.

Conrad takes a step back, his eyes still on mine.

I try another approach; I'm almost certain Harry wouldn't approve. 'Look. I just want answers, for me. Not for the police, not for anyone else. I'm just trying to make sense of what happened that night.'

He looks away, his gaze pulled back to the headstone. 'What's there to make sense of?' he asks, his voice resigned. 'Cars crash, people die. It happens.' He looks

221

at his watch, but there's something unnatural about the movement – stilted somehow. He looks like a catalogue model, standing there in his crisp white shirt and chino shorts. 'I have to go,' he says. 'I'll . . . I suppose I'll see you around.' And just like that, he turns and walks away.

I hurry to keep up with him as he quickens his pace. 'Please. Just tell me. If you didn't give the drugs to Phoebe . . . was it Karolina?'

Conrad's head snaps round to me. 'I never even *met* Karolina – or James, for that matter. And I certainly didn't sell them the drugs.'

A couple comes towards us on the path. The man carries a helium balloon with the number seven on it. The woman carries a stuffed animal – a pink elephant. They're holding hands, but not talking. They both look straight ahead as we pass. I think of soldiers, marching off to war.

I wait until the couple is out of earshot. 'And what about Phoebe and Lewis? How did they know each other? Were they together?'

'I don't know.' His face is impassive. 'I'm the last person she'd have told if they were.'

'Over-protective big brother?'

For a second I think he's going to smile, but instead he sighs heavily. He doesn't answer until we reach the cemetery gates. Then he turns to me. 'If you must know, my sister barely said two words to me in the last year.' I can see how hard it is for him to admit this. 'I can't even remember the last conversation we had – no matter how hard I try.'

Conrad's mountain bike is chained to the fence. His hands are shaking as he takes a set of keys from his pocket and leans over the U-shaped lock. 'That day . . . the day it happened . . . I remember she told Dad she wanted roast potatoes instead of mash the next day, and she talked to Mum, suggesting ideas of what to get for Ruth's birthday. And Ruth had this big debate with her about who would win in a fight – Wonder Woman or Iron Man. But she didn't say a word to me. Fuck . . . why won't you just . . . give me a *fucking* break . . .' His hands are shaking too much to get the key in the lock.

'Here, let me.' I take the key from him and unlock the bike.

He mutters his thanks, fits the lock on its bracket and hops on the bike. 'So,' he says, embarrassed.

'So, what's the answer?'

'Answer to what?'

'Who'd come out on top in that fight?'

He gives a short, unsteady laugh. 'Wonder Woman. Obviously.' He cycles off before I can say anything.

I set off towards home, but less than a minute later, he's back. Cycling at snail speed to keep pace with me. 'I want you to know something.'

223

'OK.'

'I'm not dealing any more. Since the accident. It's
. . . done.'

'OK.'

'I don't expect you to believe me,' he says, 'but
it's the truth, so please don't say OK again.'

'OK.'

Conrad shakes his head, and something about the
way he does it makes me think of Harry. He stands on
the pedals and starts to pull ahead of me. He calls back
over his shoulder, just before he turns the corner. 'Lewis
is lucky to have someone like you looking out for him.'

On my phone there are two missed calls from
Harry, and a message consisting of seven question
marks. I type out a quick reply, reassuring him that
I'm safe and asking if he wants to meet up later. He
replies immediately, and I agree to go to his flat tonight.
Normally I'd do anything to avoid going there, but
things have changed. Nothing is normal any more.

THIRTY-TWO

I hang around in town until I'm sure Mum will be back from work, with Billy and Indy in tow. Home doesn't feel like home these days.

When I finally walk in, the smell wafting through from the kitchen tries to fool me that things are normal. A rich meat ragu and cheese going crisp at the edges. But it's Tim's lasagne bubbling away in the oven, while he sings along (badly) to his 'Summer Choons' playlist. It's little things like that – *choons*, for fuck's sake. They were endearing, in a way. Before. Now they're anything but.

Billy's in his room and Mum's on the sofa, mug of tea in one hand, book in the other, Indy curled up on her feet. God knows how she can concentrate on reading with that racket from the kitchen.

'Heard about your little trip to the beach today . . .' she says, eyes still glued to the page. When she's into a book, it's almost impossible to get her to focus on anything else.

'Eddie gave me the day off, thought I should make the most of it.'

'Indy went for her usual swim, then?' Indy always – without fail – goes in the sea. Swimming is her second favourite thing to do, after stealing tomatoes from Mum's plants in the back garden.

'Yeah, she did.' I wince as Tim sings the opening lines of 'Walking on Sunshine'. 'She had a blast.'

I'm turning to head upstairs when Mum says, 'Funny . . . she doesn't smell like the sea, and there's not a speck of sand on her.' She lets that hang in the air for a couple of seconds, eyes still on her book. 'I suppose you must have given her a bath – hosed her down when you got back to Norah's?' Now she looks up, a single eyebrow arched high, a small smile.

I nod.

'Well, I hope you enjoyed yourselves. The three of you. At the beach.'

She knows. Maybe someone spotted us at the hospital, or perhaps it was just too big a secret for Billy to keep.

'We had a great time, thanks.' I let my eyes meet hers. 'I'm really glad we went.'

Her smile is different now – fuller, warmer. 'I'm

glad too. It was a lovely thing for you to do. I wish I'd thought of it.' She leans forward and scruffles the fur on Indy's head. Indy pushes her nose under Mum's hand, which is her way of saying, 'Don't stop – ever.'

The door swings open and Tim comes in, oven gloves slung over his shoulder. 'Aha! There you are! Dinner will be ready in five . . . and I'm not one to brag, but I think this may just be the *ultimate* lasagne.'

'Great.' I can't bring myself to add the requisite exclamation mark. 'I'll just go dump my bag upstairs.'

'Oh, Evan,' says Mum. 'I meant to tell you—'

Tim interrupts smoothly. 'Good news about Lewis! Your mum popped in on the way home from work, and he's doing better. Much better. He had a good session with the physio – actually worked *with* him, from the sounds of it. You know, I think I really got through to him yesterday. I said that feeling sorry for himself wasn't going to get him anywhere in life. It's time to pick himself up, dust himself off and get on with things.'

'Man up, right?' I mutter.

Mum's head snaps round towards me – she knows when I'm being sarcastic – but Tim's oblivious. 'Exactly! Nail, head, right there. Anyway, I think it did the trick. Nothing like the right pep talk at the right time, eh?'

For a second I'm sure he's referencing the 'pep

talk' he gave me at the radio station, but his face gives nothing away. And of course I couldn't say anything even if he *was*. 'That's brilliant, Tim. Well done.' My words are flat, dry as a desert.

The oven beeps, snapping Tim out of his self-satisfied reverie.

'I wish you wouldn't do that,' Tim says as I squeeze a healthy dose of ketchup on to the side of my plate.

'I wish everyone in the world had clean water to drink and enough food to eat, but we don't always get what we want, do we?'

This earns me a kick under the table from Mum and a snort-laugh from Billy.

'Ha! Good one,' Tim says amiably, two seconds too late. 'Could you pass the salad, please, darling?'

Mum does as she's asked, and Tim uses the tongs to scoop some salad on to his plate. We never had salad tongs before Tim moved in. Tim spears a slice of cucumber and munches it before clearing his throat and turning to me. 'Now, Evan. I have some potentially very exciting news for you, but I don't want you to get your hopes up.'

A glance at Mum confirms she doesn't know what he's talking about. 'What kind of news?' I ask, interested in spite of myself.

'Well.' Tim wipes his mouth neatly with his napkin. 'Gary got in touch with a friend of his in London. Friend of a friend, really, but anyway . . . He's an A&R guy for a label. Not one of the biggies, but respectable. Gary sent him a recording of your song – what's it called? "I'm Too Young" or something? And guess what – this guy loved it!' Tim's eyes widen, like, *What do you think about that*?

And the answer to his unasked question is nothing. I think nothing about it. Tim talks into the silence. 'He wants to hear more from you – two or three songs, ideally. To get a better idea of your sound.' When I show no sign of reacting, Tim carries on talking. 'So . . . what do you think? Awesome, right? Now, I don't know how many other tracks you've got, but Gary's got a little studio set up in his garage, says you're more than welcome to use it.'

I've daydreamed about being scouted, of course I have. In the daydream, the band have just played a gig. The venue wouldn't be too big, or too small. We'd be coming off-stage, sweaty and buzzing with adrenaline, having nailed every song. And a woman – it's always a woman in my head, not some guy, some friend of a friend of Gary Strout's – comes up to us, hands me her business card and tells us to give her a call first thing on Monday. And the three of us, me, Sid and Daze, act all cool like this kind of thing happens all the time, but as soon as the woman's back is turned we're completely freaking out and . . .

That's as far as it goes, the daydream. There's never more.

'Well?' Tim's face is eager beaver.

I look at Billy, who's taking the opportunity to feed Indy some of his lasagne straight from his hand. I look at Mum, who's staring at Tim with a look I can't decipher.

Finally, I look back at Tim, a little less eager beaver, the expectant smile just about clinging to his face.

'The song's called "We Are Young". And it's not mine. It's Sid's.'

'Who cares? You're the one the A&R guy is interested in!'

'But Evan's in a *band*, Tim. And a band does things together.' And this is why I love my mum. She gets it, for the most part.

Tim ignores Mum. He doesn't even look at her. 'This could be your big break, Evan. Opportunities like this don't come along every day. You know as well as I do that the band isn't going anywhere. You've said it yourself – Sid's not up to the job. Don't get me wrong, he's a nice kid – a great kid – but he's not cut out for the music business.'

And now it's not Tim I hate, it's me. Because I'm sure I've let slip the odd negative thing about Sid in his presence. I feel sick with guilt. And that guilt rapidly hardens into anger.

'You can tell Gary to tell this friend of a friend of his that I'm not interested. It wasn't my song, I'm not a solo artist.'

There's a pause and Tim starts shaking his head. 'You can't be serious? You're just going to throw an opportunity like this away?'

'It's her decision, Tim,' Mum says gently. 'But I'm sure Evan's very grateful you've taken such an interest. Right, Ev?'

'Right. I'm very grateful.' The words are for Mum, not for him. And I think he knows it.

'Right,' he says, drawing the word out. He goes back to eating his lasagne. Three bites, far too much chewing. And then, suddenly, 'It would have been nice if you guys had played at the wedding.'

Early on in the planning, Mum had asked if we fancied it. I'd discussed it with Sid and Daze and we'd agreed that we weren't keen on playing covers. Plus we weren't ready to perform in public yet.

Mum's brow is furrowed in confusion. 'What's that got to do with anything? It wasn't an issue.'

Tim nods. 'Oh, I know,' he says airily. 'It was probably better that Evan was able to relax and enjoy herself at the reception – really let her hair down.' He smiles at me, showing far too many teeth.

Mum's staring at him with a confused look on her face. She probably just thinks Tim's being a bit random. She has no fucking idea, and I can't help judging her for it. How could she have married someone like him?

Mum's gaze lands on Billy, still absorbed in the task of feeding Indy under the table. She tries – and fails – to catch his eye. Tim notices.

'I thought lasagne was your favourite, Bilbo.'

Billy wipes his hands on his napkin, and when he looks up I swear he seems older somehow. 'My name is Billy.'

'Well, Billy, I went to a lot of effort to make this dinner and I would appreciate if you would do me the courtesy of eating it rather than feeding it to the dog.' Tim's tone and words are reasonable enough, but it's as if my ears are attuned to it now – the undercurrent. The *threat*.

'I'm not hungry.' Billy places his knife and fork on the plate at twelve o'clock, just like Mum taught him. He turns to her. 'Please can I be excused?'

Mum nods at the same moment that Tim says, 'No.' Mum puts a hand on Tim's arm. 'It's fine, Tim.'

'I won't be disrespected like this in my own house.'

A laugh bubbles up but I manage to swallow it down. Who does this guy think he is? 'It's not your house,' I say. I'm playing with fire, but fuck it.

The next thing Billy says is predictable, inevitable almost, but that doesn't make it any less satisfying to hear.

'And you're not our dad.'

THIRTY-THREE

When an expected argument doesn't materialise, it should be a relief. But that's not how it feels at all. Not tonight, anyway. It feels like an unexploded bomb.

Tim doesn't say a thing, doesn't even react. He picks up his plate and carries it through to the kitchen and we listen as he scrapes food into the bin.

In unison, Billy and I turn to Mum, fully expecting a bollocking. But that doesn't happen either. She carries on eating as if nothing's happened. So I do the same. I have to admit, it's a pretty decent lasagne.

An hour later, Billy's in the garden playing with Indy, and Mum and Tim are watching TV. Tim sits in his usual spot on the left side of the sofa. It's where I used to sit. He has his hand resting on Mum's knee, and the only sign that anything's amiss is the fact that he keeps his eyes glued to the screen and doesn't turn to Mum every couple of minutes to make some inane observation.

I grab my bag from upstairs and pop my head round the door to tell Mum I'm heading out for a bit. And all she says is, 'OK, have a good time.' Her voice is mechanical.

I hang there in the doorway for a second or two, waiting for her to ask where I'm going, but the question doesn't come. She *always* asks where I'm going. Mum's fine with me staying out late as long as she knows where I am. She trusts me.

So I tell her anyway, to make some point I don't completely understand. 'I'll be at Harry's if you need me.'

Mum's eyes widen in surprise, but she doesn't say anything. Tim puts his arm around her and pulls her closer. 'Give him our best, won't you?' he says.

I hate him.

The buzzer for Harry's flat is broken so I have to message him when I'm outside. The doorway smells like piss. Three bikes are propped against the wall in the hall and there's a pile of junk mail on the bottom step. I'm out of breath by the time I reach the top floor.

The door is open, but I hesitate before going inside. The last time I was here I sat staring out of the window while Harry and Billy played Scrabble.

'Hello?' A familiar smell stops me in my tracks. It

makes me think of Saturdays and cartoons and the green dressing gown I insisted on wearing even though it was far too small for me.

'I'm in the kitchen!'

I stand in the doorway because there's not enough room for two people in the tiny galley kitchen. Harry's crouched down so his eyes are level with the counter. On the counter, on a wire rack on top of a tea towel, there's a tray of muffins. Except they are kind-of muffins. Almost-muffins.

'They're not supposed to be flat. Why are they so flat? I followed the recipe to the letter. That Mary Berry has a lot to answer for. I've never trusted her, you know. Something sinister about her, an evil glint in the eyes.'

'You made muffins.'

He stares down at the tray. 'Your mother *makes* muffins. I *attempted* to make muffins.'

'Why?'

He starts fussing round the kitchen, wiping down the surface even though it looks clean to me. 'They were your favourite. When you were little.'

'OK.'

'I know, I know. I should have asked your mum for her recipe, but I . . . Anyway, do you want to try one? You don't have to. I can chuck them in the bin, nip down to Tesco Express and get something? What do you reckon? Evan? Ev . . . are you . . . why are you crying?'

Ten minutes later and I'm just about getting a grip. Harry ushered me through to the living room, sat me down on the sofa. Brown leather, worn and cracked. It's the only piece of furniture he got after the divorce. I don't know why. I remember Harry showing me how to make fart sounds if you sat down just the right way.

He let me cry and cry. I can't explain the tears – not entirely. Because there isn't one reason. It's the thought of Harry buying a muffin tray, because there was no way he already had one. Looking up a recipe online. Buying sugar and eggs and flour and chocolate chips. Measuring out the ingredients, mixing them together. Kneeling on the floor to peer into the oven. Using a tea towel to take out the tray.

Tim, standing in the living room – *our* living room – with oven gloves slung over his shoulder. Harry doesn't own oven gloves.

It's all of this, and none of it. It's Lewis and Conrad and nothing being straightforward. It's missing Daze so much I feel hollow inside. It's gnawing guilt about Sid. It's Billy, straight-backed at the dining table, looking older than he should. It's the thought of Nik and Agata sitting at their kitchen table, trying to work up the appetite to eat even a slice of the traybake I brought them. It's Phoebe's little sister, Ruth, so proud of the necklace her big sister gave her. It's Matthieu, trying to honour a joke promise he made to his boyfriend, never thinking for a moment he would have to keep it.

'I hate Tim,' is the only explanation I manage through the tears.

Harry doesn't look delighted like I might have expected when I haltingly explain what happened at dinner. He puts his hand to his face, scritch-scratching at his stubble.

'You don't think I'm stupid? For not wanting to follow up with the record company guy?'

'Not even a little bit. The guy might not even be legit, for all we know.'

I sigh. 'I don't understand how Mum could marry someone like Tim.'

'She married someone like me, didn't she?' he says with a rueful smile. 'You can't help who you fall in love with.'

'I *hate* him.'

'Yeah, you might have mentioned that a couple of times.'

'Are you taking the piss out of me?' I sniff, and he hands me a tissue.

'I would never do that. Unless you mock my muffins. All bets are off if you mock my muffins.'

'How am I supposed to know if they're worthy of mockery when I haven't even tasted one?'

'Do you want to? *Really?* You don't have to. I won't be offended, I promise. They're probably inedible, to be honest. I'm not sure . . . I think I might have—'

'Dad! Will you shut up for one second?'

His mouth snaps shut, and so does mine. Because it's been at least three years since I last called him that.

THIRTY-FOUR

Harry goes off to get muffins and tea. I look around the room and I can almost see why Billy likes it so much, despite the fact that there's no TV. One wall is all books, double- and triple-stacked. The other walls are painted a warm terracotta colour. Harry's old acoustic guitar has pride of place in front of the fireplace. There are only two photos on the mantelpiece – one of Billy, one of me. Billy's smiling, I am not.

The big bay window looks right out on to the sea. Tonight the windows are all wide open, and I can just about hear the rumbling thud-thud-thud of bass from the funfair.

Harry returns with two mugs of tea and a plate with four muffins on it. The edges of the muffins are raggedy – he must have had trouble getting them out of the tin.

They taste fine. Better than fine, actually. Harry doesn't believe me when I tell him, so I eat two just to prove it. The tea is exactly how I like it – strong, with plenty of milk.

'So,' Harry says when I'm dabbing at crumbs on the plate with my fingertip. 'Today?'

Somehow, with the crying and the muffins and the Tim-hating, I managed to forget why I'm here. It all comes flooding back, along with a wave of exhaustion. I tell Harry everything.

He listens well, only interrupting when something needs clarification. When I've finished, he closes his eyes for a few seconds, thinking.

'You believed Conrad, then? That he didn't get the drugs for them?'

I nod.

'What makes you so sure he's telling the truth?'

'It was his little sister, Harry.' Harry, not Dad. I can't tell if he notices or not.

'Yeah, but he could have got the drugs for Karolina or James, couldn't he? He wouldn't know what they were going to do with them.'

'I *told* you. He never even met Karolina and James.'

'So he says. Look, Evan, you did really well today, but you have to understand that people lie. *All* the time. You're too trusting.'

My laugh is bitter. 'I stopped trusting people a long time ago.'

I don't have to explain; he gets it. The silence between us is filled with laughter and shouts from the street below. A chant starts up, urging some poor woman to get her tits out for the lads. Harry gets up and slams all three windows shut. 'This fucking town,' he mutters.

'I don't think Lewis was into classic cars,' I say, partly to change the subject, partly because it's been bugging me since I spoke to Conrad. 'There's nothing in his room – no books or posters or anything.'

Harry leans on the windowsill and crosses his arms. 'So? It could have been a recent thing.'

My brain refuses to accept the idea, and I don't even know why. 'He just doesn't seem like the type.'

'You said it yourself – you didn't really know him that well.'

I didn't. I *don't*. What am I not seeing? I've been projecting all sorts of feelings on to him, but what do I really know? A vague idea pushes its way into my brain. Something that Conrad said earlier. 'Can you find out the licence plate number of the Saab?'

'Why?' he asks, but he pulls his phone from his back pocket.

'I'm not sure yet.'

'Hold on, I think I have it here somewhere . . .' he says, frowning at the screen as he scrolls. 'It's E472 XYB.'

I'm tapping away at my phone. Google rewards me rapidly. 'E registration . . . so the car was made between August '87 and July '88.'

'So . . .?' Harry's struggling to follow my train of thought, which is fair enough, because right now the train feels like it's missing a driver.

'*1987* to *1988*. Remember what Lewis wrote under Conrad's phone number?'

More frowning from Harry. 'But that was 1989.'

'Close, though, right? What if he wrote the date *before* he called Conrad? Conrad said Lewis wanted an old car.'

'I'm not sure what you're getting at.' Harry's sigh is almost as heavy as his footsteps as he trudges across the room. 'We're still none the wiser about so many things. We don't even know where they were going that night. Maybe they *were* headed to the warehouse party after all. Sometimes the simplest explanation is the truth, you know?' He picks up our empty mugs. 'Another cuppa?'

I nod, even though tea is the last thing on my mind.

The four of them in the car, headed to the party. Lewis in the front next to Phoebe, Karolina and James

243

in the back. Music blaring, Phoebe and Lewis – and maybe the others too – high as a fucking kite. And I *can* picture it. The laughter turning to terror as the car loses control. I don't want to picture it, but I can.

Except. Except. Except.

Harry was right about me not knowing Lewis. Even though I've lived in the same house as him and snooped through his stuff and sat next to his hospital bed, staring at his face so hard I'm familiar with every contour. But what do I actually *know*?

I make a mental list of the things I knew – or thought I knew – about Lewis before the accident. He's not big on personal hygiene. Or leaving his room. He loves our dog (and she loves him). He's selfish enough not to attend his father's wedding.

And the things I've found out about him since the accident. He likes books with elves and wizards in them. He misses his mother. He bought a car without his dad knowing about it.

It's not much. Nowhere near enough. Random snippets. But maybe . . . What if there's a bigger picture that I'm not seeing? It's there, if only I can join the dots.

I keep coming back to what Conrad said. That Lewis didn't even want to see the car before he bought it. The only thing he was interested in was the licence plate number, and for some reason that crappy old

Saab 900 fit the bill. Even though he could have gone for a better car. A newer one.

Crawling coldness in my stomach when I realise that the dots were there all along, but no one cared enough to join them.

Fingers numb as I search on Google. A few tries to get the right search, and there it is.

The answer.

I'm standing in the kitchen doorway when Harry turns round with two mugs of tea. My sudden appearance startles him. Tea splashes on the floor, and he laughs. 'Jesus, Evan, you scared me!' He puts the mugs back on the worktop and starts mopping up the spilled tea.

'This floor is filthy,' he says, on hands and knees, wad of kitchen roll in hand. 'I need to get a new mop.'

'I think I know what happened.' My voice doesn't sound like my own.

'Or maybe new lino? I'm sure I could get a cheap enough off-cut from somewhere.' Harry's knees crack when he gets up. 'Sorry, what were you saying?'

'It wasn't an accident.'

'The police said there were no other vehicles involved, so——'

'Harry . . .' When it comes to it, the words feel

impossible to say. But they have to be said out loud. I don't think I'll believe them until I hear them myself.

'They crashed the car on purpose.'

THIRTY-FIVE

Harry's eyes narrow as if he thinks he'll be able to see into my brain if he squints hard enough. 'What makes you think that?'

I start to speak but he shakes his head and ushers me back through to the living room. We sit at the tiny fold-out table with our mugs of tea in front of us. Harry places his hands flat on the table on either side of his mug. 'Tell me.'

I lay it out the best I can, even though I haven't had time to think it all through myself yet. I start with the car.

'Lewis doesn't give a fuck about classic cars – he just wanted to make sure the car was *old*. I looked it up online – airbags started being fitted in the early nineties, so he needed a car older than that. 1989 or earlier. The E registration Saab was perfect.'

'It's a bit of a leap . . .' Harry says doubtfully. 'It

makes more sense that they went to a party high on ketamine.'

'That's what they wanted people to think. And maybe they thought taking ketamine would make it easier to go through with it. But the drugs aren't the point.'

He stares out of the window. The sky is streaked with orange and pink in yet another picture-perfect sunset. He clears his throat before he speaks. 'According to the police report, there were no tyre marks at the scene. Nothing to indicate that Phoebe tried to brake.'

'You've seen the police report? *How?* Why didn't you tell me?'

'The less you know about how, the better. And I didn't tell you because . . .' He swipes his fingers across his eyes.

'Harry? What are you not saying?'

'I saw . . . There were photographs.'

'So?' I say, wondering what's the big deal about a smashed-up car. Then my brain engages. 'The bodies. You saw photos of the bodies.'

A swift nod. 'When I think of Karolina . . . You remember when the Zabeks would come round for dinner? The two of you would sneak downstairs and try to get past the dining table without anyone seeing you.'

'Ninja Dinner Challenge,' I whisper, before the memory has fully come back to me.

'And you were both terrible at it.'

'We were not! We made it to the kitchen loads of times without being spotted.'

'We *pretended* not to see you.' Harry shakes his head as if this is obvious, and of course it is – now. 'And you two would come strolling out of the kitchen with whatever snacks you could carry, looking so damn pleased with yourselves. That's what I used to remember, when I thought of Karolina Zabek. That look of absolute glee, like she'd got the better of us.' He almost manages a smile, but it falters. 'But when I think of her now all I can see is those police photos . . . She must have . . . she was sitting in the middle seat when the car . . .'

I don't want him to say any more, and thankfully he doesn't. But can it really be worse than what I'm picturing? One look at Harry's face tells me it can.

'You know I'm right, don't you? That they planned the crash.' And still there's a part of me that wants Harry to say no. To present me with some proof that this idea of mine is ridiculous.

'A suicide pact. Planned to look like an accident,' he says slowly, as if testing the words for weak spots. 'Talk me through your theory. I'm not saying I'm buying it, mind.'

'They weren't wearing seatbelts, for one thing.'

He bats that away with ease. 'Lewis was.'

I try again. 'James's boyfriend, Matthieu. He said

something at the memorial thing on the beach. That James made him promise he could have a Viking funeral.'

Harry shrugs. 'Lots of people talk about stuff like that. It doesn't necessarily mean they're planning on killing themselves.'

'Phoebe gave Ruth – her little sister – her favourite necklace and said she could look after it for her. That's exactly the kind of thing you'd do if you were planning on killing yourself.'

'Maybe, maybe not.' Harry tilts his head, then nods for me to continue.

'It bugged me from the start – it didn't look like they were friends, the four of them. That didn't seem to bother the police or the press – they were teenagers, and that was that. As if being in the same age group explains everything. People just jumped on the explanation about the warehouse party because they think that's what we do: we drink and take drugs and do illegal shit.'

Harry ignores my rant and focuses on what's important. 'How did they arrange it, then? If they weren't friends?'

'We know Phoebe and Lewis *were* friends, even if he was secretive about it. And Phoebe used to hang out at the Beach Hut where Karolina worked. So maybe she's the one who came up with the idea . . . There could be a connection between her and James and we just don't know about it yet. Or between James and one of the others. Matthieu might have a better idea. I'll talk to him . . .'

'And say what? That you're looking for proof that his boyfriend killed himself? What are you actually planning to do here, Evan?'

'What do you mean? I'm trying to find out what happened.'

'Then what? Even if you're right about this, have you considered that maybe it would be better if people keep thinking it *was* an accident? This is people's lives we're talking about here.'

'You think I don't *know* that?'

'No, Evan, that's not what I—'

'How can you sit there and say it's better if people don't know the truth? It's your fucking *job*, Harry. This is what you do. Telling the truth about that MP's expenses, or the abuse in the care home, or . . .'

'Or what?' he asks quietly.

I remember one of Harry's little crusades. That's what Mum calls them. 'What was that story from last year? Something about a helpline?'

Harry's brain isn't like mine. He remembers right away.

'Online chat service for young people with mental health issues. The council withdrew funding.' His face is grim, but there's a hint of something else. 'You read that?'

I'm not going to tell him I read every one of his stories. 'Look, I'm not saying there's a connection. I'm not naïve enough to think that Phoebe and Karolina and James would still be alive if a service like that hadn't been shut down. But maybe if people woke up and realised that being a teenager is actually pretty fucking hard and it's not because we're always on our phones or don't know the meaning of hard work or any of those other bullshit things that people say. And maybe things *were* better in the "good old days" because guess what? The world has gone to *fuck* and politicians are pissing away our future and no one fucking cares.'

My mouth snaps shut, the sudden rage surprising me almost as much as it's surprised Harry. These are things I've never articulated before. No, it's more than that. These are things I've never even thought about.

I get up from my chair, and push it back under the table.

I choose my next words carefully; my voice is taut, ready to snap. 'Maybe people would be better off believing it was an accident. Ignorance is bliss, right? But it's *not* right. If no one knows the truth, how can we ever expect anything to change? What happened is awful and upsetting and confusing, and I get that. Of course I do. But that doesn't mean we should keep quiet about it. The truth hurts, but it *matters*.'

I leave the room, and the flat, before Harry can respond. But when I reach the bus stop I take out my phone and there's a message from Harry:

What do you need me to do?

THIRTY-SIX

I go on Twitter as soon as I get on the bus. It doesn't take long to find him, with a name like that around here. I keep my message short and try not to overthink it. Send it before I change my mind.

The reply arrives five minutes later. It's short – nothing more than a time and a place. I say I'll be there.

The hall light is on when I get home. Mum leaves it on when she knows I'm coming back late. I glance into the living room, half-expecting Tim to be sitting in the darkness like something out of a nightmare.

There's a note from Mum on my pillow: *I love you* xxx

The note makes my heart ache. I wish I could tell her the truth about Tim, even if it meant I had to tell her about Marcus too. I could cope with the shame and embarrassment, but I couldn't cope with the thought of breaking her heart. She was so sure that things were going to be better with Tim. And maybe they still can be better, for her, at least, as long as I keep my mouth shut.

I stay in bed the next morning, listening to the shower going on and off, doors opening and closing, the kettle, the radio. Normal, everyday sounds. At one point footsteps approach my bedroom door, and I close my eyes but no one comes in. Mum must be listening at the door to check if I'm up. At least, I hope it's her. A few seconds later, the footsteps recede. Finally, after what feels like an age, the front door slams shut, Indy barks, car doors thunk and the engine starts up. Billy's spending the day at Norah's again, which makes me feel slightly less guilty for abandoning him last night. She always spoils him rotten – pizza for lunch and three different flavours of ice cream in the freezer.

There's an hour before I have to get up for work, if I don't bother to wash my hair. An hour of sleep would go a long way towards making me feel more human after the worst night's sleep I can remember. But thinking about my inability to sleep means – inevitably – that it's impossible to fall asleep. Every last thought and worry from last night returns with a vengeance.

Why? Why did they do it? The one question we avoided last night. Deliberately or subconsciously, I'm not sure. It's pointless to speculate why they did it. I know that, and Harry knows that. But it's impossible not to wonder.

Three lives destroyed, one irrevocably changed. Thinking about why feels like looking at the sun. It hurts too much to look straight at it, but I keep being drawn back. Over and over again until . . .

Fuck it. I haul myself out of bed and into the shower. My hair gets washed after all.

The morning has two welcome surprises in store for me. The first is blood in my knickers. The grim inevitability of my period manages to piss me off every single month. I can't seem to accept the unfairness of it – the pain and the discomfort and the inconvenience. But today is different. Because today, my period means I am definitely, categorically, absolutely not pregnant with Marcus Bloom's baby. The relief makes me light-headed, which is strange, because I'd somehow managed to forget to be worried that the morning-after pill might not work its magic. Now I just have to wait a month and get tested for every STD from A to Z. It's always nice to have something to look forward to.

The second surprise greets me when I open my bedroom curtains: clouds. Serious, proper clouds instead of fluffy white candyfloss. These clouds mean business. I stick my head out of the window and breathe in deeply. It's still hot, but the air smells different — almost zingy.

At work, Eddie keeps sauntering over to the window to check the sky. 'There's a storm coming,' he says in an ominous, horror-movie voice. Finally the excitement gets too much for him and he grabs a Fender Stratocaster from the wall and plugs it into the amp. It takes me a few seconds to recognise the song. Hendrix, of course. 'In From the Storm'. Customers gather round to listen, and Eddie puts on a real show for them. It's rare for him to do this, but the grey skies have cheered him up no end. The skies gradually darken with every passing hour, and by six o'clock it's clear that Eddie was right about that storm.

Instead of locking up the shop, Eddie props open the door, grabs a folding chair from the stockroom and sits in the doorway with a cup of coffee.

'Try not to get struck by lightning,' I say, slinging my bag over my shoulder.

'What a way to go, though, eh?' He smiles at me, then goes back to staring up at the sky. 'What a way to go,' he mutters again, almost wistfully.

The first fat drops of rain hit the pavement the moment I get off the bus. I stop and stare at the ground, trying to predict where the next raindrop will fall. Then there's a cough behind me and I realise I'm blocking the pavement; a bald man on a mobility scooter is waiting for me to get out of the way. He says, 'Toot toot,' as he passes me.

Belmont Hall sits proudly – smugly – on a hill, looking like a cross between Hogwarts and the Tower of London. I can't even begin to imagine going to a school like this, walking through these gates every day like it's normal. It's hard to picture Lewis here. He doesn't fit. I asked Mum about it the other day. She said that Lewis's grandfather – Imogen's father – went to Belmont Hall. When he died, he left money to Imogen to make sure Lewis was enrolled there too.

The path I take cuts diagonally across the front of the main building. Every ten steps or so there are small white rectangular signs saying, 'Polite notice: please keep off the grass'. I have the strongest urge to steal one of the signs for Sid, knowing that he'd get a kick out of it. Instead I take a picture and send it to him before I can change my mind. It reminds me of when he sent me a link to a YouTube video two days after we broke up. It was this cheesy eighties guy teaching a dance routine called Double Dream Feet. Pretty funny, but I wasn't much in the mood for laughing. Still, I understood the gesture for what it was: a peace offering, of sorts. I replied with a laughing emoji back then, but there's no reply from Sid today. I was a fool to expect one.

The rain gets steadily heavier as I pass the tennis courts and the cricket pitch until it's a proper downpour. I don't have an umbrella or a coat, but I don't care because it feels amazing. Delicious coolness after weeks of stifling heat.

The running track is nothing like the one at my school. Ours is cracked, the white lines so faded you can hardly see them. This track is like something you'd see in the Olympics. Does it make them run any faster, a track like this? It looks that way, when I stop to watch the boy sprinting down the opposite side. Arms pumping like pistons. Hair slicked back from sweat or rain. Eyes straight ahead. Grey vest, baggy black shorts, a pair of grubby Nikes. Regular clothes but his body is anything but. He looks superhuman.

Matthieu glances at me as he passes, acknowledging me with a nod. After two more laps he slows down and stops, leaning over with his hands on his thighs. Then he raises his face to the sky and closes his eyes. I walk towards him, slowly, not wanting to interrupt whatever it is he's doing – communing with nature or God or something. The springiness of the orange track under my feet surprises me. Maybe I'd have enjoyed athletics a bit more if I'd been able to run on a track like this. Probably not, though.

He opens his eyes when I'm a few feet away and watches me approach. 'This is better,' he says, putting his hands out, palms facing up. '*This* is what a British summer should be like.' He laughs and shakes his head like a dog, before slicking his hair back again.

I don't know what to say to this boy. I'd come here expecting hostility, or at the very least, suspicion. But this guy is holding out his hand for me to shake, saying it's nice to meet me. It's a better start than I could have hoped for, but weirdly it makes me more anxious.

'You're wet,' he says, looking me up and down. And then he blushes and winces. 'From the rain, I mean . . .' It's just as well he goes to Belmont, because the girls at my school would eat him alive. They wouldn't *let* him be gay.

'It's fine, honestly.'

'You're shivering.'

I realise he's right, but it's nothing to do with the rain.

'I left my stuff over there,' he says, pointing to a white wooden building next to the cricket pitch. 'You said you wanted to talk, yes?'

The cricket building (*Pavilion?* The word pops into my head from nowhere) has a covered porch. Matthieu's things are neatly piled up on a bench to the right of the door. He gives me a towel and I half-heartedly dry my hair and face before handing it back. He takes off his vest and now I'm the one blushing, which is so stupid I can't even. I look away as he towels himself down and only look back as he pulls a sweatshirt over his head.

He picks up a watch from the bench and pauses before wrapping it round his wrist. Something about his expression makes me look at the watch more closely. It's not a flashy watch. It's simple, classic. Black leather strap, white face. He notices me staring. 'Eighteenth birthday present. From James.' He rests the fingers of his right hand on the watch face for a moment.

'I'm sorry.'

Matthieu smiles as he sits down next to me. 'I've heard these words so many times over the past few weeks.'

'I'm sorry. I mean . . . sorry.' I'm really crap at this.

He laughs. 'Don't be. I get it. No one knows what to say. I wouldn't know what to say either.'

We sit in silence, listening to the rain drumming on the roof. The air smells green and fresh for the first time in a month. The sky is even darker. A low rumble of thunder in the distance. A blackbird lands on the cricket pitch and pulls a worm from the ground.

'That was a lovely thing you did,' I begin. 'With the memorial.'

He wrinkles his nose, and shakes his head. 'It was selfish, really.'

'*Selfish?*'

'It was for James, yes, and the others. But it was also for me. It gave me something to do, organising it. Buying the drinks and sorting out the sound system. I had something to focus on. A task that I could make sense of, instead of . . .' He exhales through his nostrils. 'I'd been saving up to go away with James, you know. We were meant to go travelling for a month. The whole point was we would not plan *anything* – which went against everything James believed in.' Matthieu stops with a sharp intake of breath. 'I'm still getting used to the past tense.'

I bite my lip to stop another 'sorry' escaping.

'We should be there now. Somewhere in Europe. Turin or Krakow or Dubrovnik, then back here to celebrate our exam results.' I wonder what it's like, to be so sure that your results will be worth celebrating. 'I thought I might as well use the money I saved and do something for James. But it wasn't for him, was it? It was for me. Silly, really.'

'Not at all. It helped people.'

'How?' He sees that I don't have an easy answer, but he doesn't push it. 'Anyway. It's over. And now the only thing that can distract me is running. Pushing my body harder and harder until it all just . . . disappears. But you can't run for ever, can you?'

There's nothing I can say to that; we both know the answer.

Matthieu puts his hand to his chest. 'Forgive me. I should have asked about Lewis.'

I shouldn't be surprised that he cares, because I'm starting to get an idea of the kind of person he is. I tell him about Lewis's physiotherapy and how he's slowly getting stronger.

'But how *is* he?' His voice is low, hardly louder than a whisper.

I stare at Matthieu for a beat or two, and he stares right back. 'I'm not sure.'

He goes back to looking at the rain.

I have to do this now. 'What was James like? If you don't mind me asking. All I know is what I read online.'

'Star athlete? Star football player? What's the word . . . *Jock*, I think?' His smile is hard to read. 'That was James. One side of him, at least. Sport made him happy. Not because he was so good at it – although maybe this had something to do with it – but because he liked to test himself. It was the same with school. He liked to be the best.' He pauses, shakes his head. 'But he had another side. He loved reading. He would spend hours online on these forums of his, arguing about the economics of Middle-earth or the quickest route to Mordor . . . he was *such* a nerd.'

Matthieu's eyes meet mine. 'James was a lot of things, but to me he was everything.' The pain in his eyes makes me want to look away, but I don't. I see the burden of his grief, even if I can't share it. I wish I were here to comfort him instead of hurt him even more.

Instead of offering sympathy, I forge ahead before I can change my mind. 'What about partying? Drinking?' I have to force out the next word. 'Drugs?'

A long pause. 'Why are you here?' There's a new coolness to his voice, but he doesn't look angry. He's gone very still, as if I pressed the pause button.

'Did you know that Phoebe was on ketamine that night?' I watch his reaction closely, which is pointless because there doesn't seem to be one. 'He didn't do drugs, did he?'

Matthieu hesitates. 'Never. He was very . . . particular about what he put into his body.' It's an odd sort of answer.

'I was wondering whether had he been acting strangely, leading up to the accident.'

'These words – *acting strangely*. He asked the same thing.'

'Who? Who asked you?' My heart is beating fast suddenly. Is it possible that Harry's already talked to him behind my back? But Matthieu is shaking his head. 'Evan, I would really appreciate it if you would be honest with me now. What is it you are trying to say?'

I open my mouth but I can't speak. This was a terrible idea. I should have left him alone.

'Just say it. *Please.*'

'I think – I think it might have been a suicide pact.' I say the words fast, as if it will hurt him less. Like ripping off a plaster. 'Those four weren't friends, so why were they in the car together? And why weren't they wearing seatbelts?' *Except Lewis*, I think. 'The police report showed that Phoebe didn't even try to brake before hitting that wall.' I take a deep breath. 'I keep thinking – it's the only explanation that makes sense to me.'

Matthieu doesn't wince or flinch or grimace. He doesn't do or say any of the things I'd braced myself for.

He closes his eyes and just sits there for a second or two. When his eyes open, there's emptiness. His voice is flat and oddly detached when he says, 'I think you might be right.'

THIRTY-SEVEN

I let Matthieu talk.

'When I heard that he was with the others – new friends, I thought – and on the way to that party . . . it was a small comfort, because I was able to tell myself that he must have been happy when he died. If the person you love has to die, at least you want their last moments to have been happy ones. Now I see that this was the lie I told myself, because it was easier than seeing the truth.'

'What is the truth?'

The thunder is louder, longer. Almost a drum roll. 'The truth is that I was fooling myself. I thought he was doing better – that things were going to be different.' His laughter is joyless. 'I was right about that. Things are definitely different.'

'What was wrong with James?' I ask.

Matthieu seems lost for words. He stares at his hands as if the answer is written there. Finally, he looks up. 'He thought he wasn't good enough.'

It's not what I was expecting to hear. I had the impression James was one of those super-cocky high achievers – a golden boy. 'Not good enough at what?'

'*Everything*. At schoolwork and sport and being a son and a boyfriend. He wanted to be better, always.'

'Why?'

'How can we ever know why someone's brain works a certain way? I suppose there was pressure, from his father. Donovan wanted James to succeed.'

I remember the picture of Donovan Gayle, surrounded by the countless trophies his dead son had won in pursuit of something he could never achieve. Perfection. Self-acceptance.

'James had trouble sleeping; he could never relax, never switch off. But when he was with me, he said it was better. He said I kept him sane. It felt like . . . it was a lot of pressure, for him to think that of me. He got particularly bad in January, when we had exams. Afterwards, I suggested he get help, go to the doctor or even the school counsellor, but he just laughed and said I worried too much. He said everyone gets stressed in their final year at school – that it would be stranger if he was *not* stressed. But I knew it was not normal, the way he acted.'

'What do you mean?'

'I knew he weighed himself every day. I saw the

numbers in the notes on his phone. He became obsessed with what he ate, and he would only ever drink water – he wouldn't even have tea and that boy loved his tea . . . so very English.' His face softens, but only for a second. 'But because he wasn't too thin, I told myself it was nothing to worry about. How stupid could I be? When I think that he could have taken drugs that night . . . He wouldn't put something like that into his body – and he wouldn't want to be around people who were on drugs either. Unless . . . unless he knew it wouldn't matter.'

Matthieu's face is desolate. Beyond sadness, beyond grief.

I reach for his hand. It feels natural, the right thing to do. We sit like that – saying nothing – for I don't know how long. Long enough for the storm to rage around us. For lightning to flash and the branches of trees to whip this way and that in the wind.

I think about James Gayle and how unhappy he must have been. It's hard to fathom. But we all say we're fine when we're really not. We all slap a smile on our face to avoid an argument or a conversation we don't want to have or to spare the people we care about. So why is it still a struggle to imagine James Gayle would want to die? Is it really just because he looks so healthy and happy and strong in the photos? Am I that stupid?

The truth is we have no idea what anyone else is going through, no matter how close we are to them. You can never really know. That's the problem.

All you can do is hold your loved ones close. And hope.

The storm has blown itself out, leaving a drizzly rain in its wake. The air smells green, as if it contains more oxygen. If I knew anything about science I'd probably know whether that could possibly be true.

It's hard to say goodbye at the school gates; I don't want to be the first to walk away.

'I'm sorry, Matthieu.'

'For what?'

'You don't deserve this.'

'Does anyone?' He has a point. 'I'm grateful to you for helping me see the truth.' Matthieu takes a deep breath and straightens his shoulders. 'I *love* James, and I always will. But now I get to hate him too, for doing what he did. Isn't that supposed to be one of the stages of grief?'

'I think it might be anger.'

'Well, I'm angry too. It might sound strange, but it's actually a relief. To feel something.'

I think I understand. 'Are you going to be OK? Do you have someone? Someone you can talk to, I mean.'

His shoulders drop slightly. 'He was my someone.'

I hug him. After a second or two, he puts his arms around me and hugs me back.

I look up the stages of grief when I'm waiting for the bus. The last stage is acceptance, apparently.

What a fucking joke.

THIRTY-EIGHT

I know it's not urgent, but after talking to Matthieu it suddenly feels like it. Things are not OK with Sid and I need them to be OK. I need to know he's all right. So I set up the group chat again and write a message:

> *You're not getting rid of me that easily. We're a team . . . a fucked-up, dysfunctional team, but still. Here's the deal: I love you both and I miss you and I'm sorry and there's stuff I need to talk to you about and where the fuck have the commas disappeared to in this sentence? Can we meet up? Pretty please with a massive dose of sorry on top?*

It doesn't feel like enough, so I send a separate message to Sid.

> *I really am sorry. Will you let me fix this?*

I expect no response, or a long wait. But Sid never

was one for playing games. His reply consists of a single word, but it's a word that gives me hope: *Yes.*

He follows up a few minutes later: *Am at Cassie's cos Mum said she was sick of me moping around the house. Now Cassie's sick of me moping around the house. Back tomorrow.*

Sid's older sister is at uni in London; this is the first summer she hasn't come home. I'm glad he's with her. It's practically impossible to be miserable around Cassie. She's one of those glass-half-full people who could somehow manage to look on the bright side even during the nuclear apocalypse.

Sid and I message back and forth a few times, and it gets easier with each message, because we're talking about nothing important. We both know that the bigger conversations will have to wait until we're face to face. We both know things aren't OK between us, but hopefully he trusts – like I'm trying so desperately to – that they *will* be.

I call Harry as soon as I get off the bus, but he doesn't pick up. Maybe he's still with them, doing what I asked. Or perhaps he bottled it. I can't really blame him if he has. Talking to Matthieu was hard, but at least he was a stranger to me.

Mum won't be home yet, but I don't want to hang around the streets just to avoid Tim. I keep my headphones on when I enter the house – the international symbol for 'do not fucking talk to me'.

The sight that greets me when I walk into the kitchen is a surprise, to say the least. Tim, sitting at the kitchen table with a mug of tea in front of him. Harry, sitting opposite, an untouched mug of coffee next to his phone on the table. Harry looks up when I enter, but Tim doesn't react. I take off my headphones and sling them round my neck to hear Tim say, '. . . must have dropped ten degrees, at least. Give it a few days and people will be moaning about it. We're never happy, are we?' The weather. My father and this monstrous man are talking about the fucking weather. Finally, Tim looks at me. 'Some storm, wasn't it? I hope you didn't get caught in it? We don't want you coming down with a cold now, do we?'

Who is this 'we' he keeps going on about? I ignore Tim and address Harry. 'What are you doing here?'

'Harry doesn't need a reason to be here, Evan. He's part of the family, after all,' says Tim, raising his mug to his lips.

I stare at him, amazed that he didn't even try to disguise the sarcasm in his voice. Either Harry doesn't notice, or he doesn't care.

'Why don't you sit down, Ev?' Harry gestures to the seat between him and Tim. I sit, against my better judgement.

Harry sees the question in my eyes, but instead of answering with a nod, he says the words out loud, addressing Tim instead of me. 'I went to visit the Zabeks.' He sounds like I feel – drained.

Tim makes an odd sort of tutting noise. 'How are they managing? What are their names again? Friends of yours, aren't they?'

'Nik and Agata.' Harry places his hands flat on the table. 'Tim, there's something I need to talk to you about. It's good that Evan's here, actually, because she was the one who realised . . .'

'What has she told you?' There's a slight sourness to Tim's voice. A squeeze of lemon on his words. Harry doesn't catch it – too busy running through what he's going to say in his head.

I watch Tim closely as Harry says, 'It's about the accident,' and I swear Tim's shoulders drop slightly. That's when I figure it out: he thought I'd told Harry what happened at the radio station. Probably thought Harry was going to punch his lights out.

'I didn't want to come to you until I was a hundred per cent sure, but after this afternoon I really don't think there's much room for doubt.'

Tim raises his eyebrows in expectation, and I feel a flicker of sympathy. Harry glances at me, as if there's anything I can do to help, but he's on his own here. He chose to do this. He didn't give me a say in it. If he *had*, I'd have told him to talk to Mum first. Let her be the one to talk to Tim. Knowing Harry, he probably thinks this is the Right Thing to Do.

'There's no easy way to say this, Tim, but it looks like the kids planned to crash the car that night.'

Tim's grimace is almost comical. 'What?'

'I'm sorry. I know it's a hard thing to get your head around.'

'Nonsense. The police have already been through this. That girl – Phoebe – she was on drugs. Lost control of the car.'

Harry lays it all out for Tim, step by step, starting with the car. He explains that the four of them weren't friends. They weren't on their way to a party together – they just wanted it to *look* that way. To protect their families, most likely.

Tim seems to be listening, head tilted to one side, seemingly staring at a postcard pinned to the fridge.

Harry sighs. 'I went to see Agata and Nik this afternoon, to ask them—'

'Lewis was wearing a seatbelt!' Tim's face lights up as if he's just solved an impossible equation.

Harry nods in concession. 'Maybe he changed his mind at the last minute. If that's the case, he was lucky. A car going at that speed straight into a brick wall, the chances were—'

'*Lucky*? You think my son is lucky?'

'He's alive, isn't he?' There's an edge to Harry's voice.

Tim exhales noisily. 'This is absurd. When I was that age all I cared about was chasing girls . . . They were *teenagers* . . . you seriously expect me to believe that they wanted to die?'

'I hear what you're saying, Tim, although things weren't so rosy for all of us back in the day. The truth is that there's a mental health crisis affecting young people today, and nowhere near enough is being done to combat it.'

I wince. Why can't Harry see that this is exactly the wrong way to play this?

Tim sits back and crosses his arms. 'Oh, I get it.'

'Get what?'

'This is some crusade for you, isn't it? Some political agenda you've concocted to try to reboot your career? I bet you started planning it as soon as you heard about the accident.'

'*What?* I'm not the enemy here, Tim. I came to you because I want to—'

'And roping your daughter in to help? I can't say I'm surprised, but I am disappointed.' Tim's eyes meet mine and I have an idea what he's going to say before he says it. 'Maybe you should take a look a little closer to home before you start trashing my son's reputation.'

Harry holds his hands up in a pointless gesture of

peace. 'You're dead wrong, mate. If anything, I want to make people see that Lewis—'

Tim cuts right across him – again. 'I'd be more worried about your daughter's reputation, if I were you.'

Harry stops, alert. 'Do you have something you want to say, Tim?' he asks, and his voice is dangerous.

It feels like the walls are closing in on me. I stand up, desperate to escape. 'We're wasting our time here, Harry. Come on, let's go.'

'No, I want to know what the hell he's talking about.' Harry's face is flushed with anger.

'It's nothing,' says Tim, with an awkward half-laugh. He looks nervous, I realise. 'I didn't mean anything by it.'

Suddenly I feel tired. So this is how he thinks things are going to go. He reckons he can taunt me with what happened at the wedding reception whenever he wants. He thinks he can leave it hanging over me, the threat ever-present. Well, fuck that. I feel none of the shame or worry Tim wants me to feel. I almost pity him, unable to accept the truth, lashing out at whoever he can.

I've had enough.

'What Tim's trying to imply,' I say loudly, 'is that you should be worried about *my* reputation, because he saw me having sex with a waiter at the wedding reception. I appreciate your concern, Tim, I really do. But I'm perfectly happy with my life choices . . . can you really say the same?'

The two men look up at me. Harry's jaw gaping slightly more than Tim's. 'Is it OK if I stay the night at yours, Harry?' Instead of waiting for an answer, I tell him I'll pack a bag and meet him outside.

I take the stairs two at a time, feeling like I could fly up them if I chose to. It's an unfamiliar feeling, but I'm able to recognise it for what it is. It's *power*.

THIRTY-NINE

By unspoken agreement, Harry and I put off talking about what we really need to talk about until after dinner. Neither of us eats much, even though the stir-fry he whipped up is pretty tasty.

We settle on the sofa with cups of tea and two muffins left over from last night. Harry takes a sip of tea and sighs. 'What a day.' Then he puts his tea down and looks at me, waiting.

I can't avoid it any longer. 'He blackmailed me. At the radio station. I didn't want to play, but he implied he'd tell Mum about me and that boy if I didn't.'

Harry's jaw tightens. 'I should have punched him when I had the chance.' His voice softens. 'Don't you worry about him, OK? I'll talk to your mother tomorrow.'

I should tell him not to say anything, but part of me wants him to. I want Harry to make everything OK, just like he did when I was little and scared of the monster under the bed. Every night he would make a big show of checking under there with his torch. But now the monster isn't under the bed, and now the monster is all too real.

Instead of asking Harry not to say anything to Mum, I thank him. Then I ask him how it went with the Zabeks.

Harry's wry smile is replaced with a grimace. 'It was bad.'

'You asked them if they thought Karolina might have been suicidal?'

'I did. Nik told me to get the hell out of their house. That his daughter would never do such a thing. I thought he was going to deck me. Then his anger just . . . collapsed. He broke down, sobbing, and told me that Karolina was diagnosed with bipolar disorder last year.

'For a while they thought it was just teenage mood swings. They desperately wanted that to be the case, because it turns out that Agata's sister has bipolar disorder. She was committed eighteen months ago. That was what finally made Agata march Karolina to see her GP, because bipolar disorder often runs in families. I think there was more – something Karolina did – but they wouldn't tell me.'

I tell Harry what Jaime said about Karolina climbing out of a car's sunroof while it sped down the motorway.

'Risk-taking behaviour is one of the symptoms of a manic episode,' Harry confirms. 'Stuff like gambling, over-spending, unprotected sex.' He doesn't look at me when he says that last one, but that doesn't stop my cheeks from flushing.

'Karolina was prescribed medication and went for regular CBT sessions. Things were better until she stopped taking her meds a couple of months ago. Said she didn't need them any more. She spiralled into depression, and there were manic episodes too.'

'Was she depressed the day of the crash? Is that why she went through with it?'

'They said she seemed fine that day. Cheerful, even. But we'll never know for sure. Agata and Nik are a mess. Blaming themselves, of course.'

I give that some thought. 'It's *partly* their fault, though, isn't it? If they hadn't been in denial, Karolina could have got help sooner. It could have made a difference. And they definitely shouldn't have let her stop taking her medication.'

Harry's eyebrows shoot up. 'That's not fair, Evan. They did what they could.'

But I'm not really listening. 'Matthieu said something about James's dad putting a lot of pressure on him. I'm not saying it was his fault, but it could have been a factor.' I tell Harry the rest, the painful truth beneath the surface of golden boy James Gayle.

'Evan. Can I ask you something?'

I don't like the sound of this, but I nod, and take a muffin from the plate to give me something to focus on.

'You've never thought about . . . I mean, you would never . . . ?'

'Are you asking if I've ever wanted to kill myself, Harry?' I shouldn't smile but I can't help it. 'The answer is no. Why? Have you?'

I regret my flippancy when he looks away and starts picking imaginary dust from the arm of the sofa. 'No,' he says quietly. 'But I can understand it.' Harry cricks his neck to the left, then to the right, like he's gearing up for something. 'I've made a lot of mistakes in my life . . .'

'You don't have to do this, Harry.'

He purses his lips together and his nostrils flare. 'I wish you wouldn't call me that.'

He's never complained about it before. Maybe he felt he never had the right to. 'I don't see why it's such a big deal.' The words come out sounding sulkier than I intended.

'I feel like things have been different between us, these past few weeks. And maybe this seems awful – probably because it is – I mean, I'm not saying I'm glad the crash happened, of course I'm not. But I'm . . .' Harry shakes his head, then looks to the ceiling in search of the right words, 'I'm grateful, I suppose. That I've been able to spend this time with you. Fucking hell, I'm useless at this. What I'm trying to say is that I'm glad you're here. So, to summarise, I don't want to be Harry to you. I want to be Dad. If you'll let me.'

The silence when he finishes speaking is worse than awkward. I could tell Harry what he wants to hear, but I don't want to give him false hope. This is still new to me. I'm in the dark, trying to feel my way towards a new kind of relationship with him. One that isn't based on disappointment and shame.

'Should we talk to the police about what we know?' Harry shakes his head at the change of subject, but I continue, 'I thought, maybe, you could have a word with them so they tread more carefully with Lewis . . . He's been through enough.'

'It's not my place, Evan,' he says.

And I know he's right, but that doesn't stop me pushing. 'Since when has that ever bothered you before? You're a journalist, Harry, it's your life's mission to stick your nose where it's not wanted. And if you don't do it, who will? *Tim*?'

Harry doesn't rise to the bait. 'Lewis will need to answer their questions sooner or later. At the coroner's inquest hearing, if not before. Lewis will be called as a witness.'

'What's the hearing for?'

'It's standard practice to hold an inquest to establish the cause of death after an accident like this. It probably won't be for another few months yet.'

I'm surprised they're even bothering with an inquest. The police don't seem to care about what happened. They've made a couple of half-hearted attempts to talk to Lewis, but Mum reckons it's just a formality for them – to confirm their theory about the crash. If another car had been involved it would have been a whole different ball game.

I think of Lewis having to sit in court, deciding whether to admit that he wanted to die . . .

They didn't want anyone to know. James and the others went to great lengths to make sure people thought it was an accident, even down to the timing of the crash, on the same night as the warehouse party. They were trying to protect the people they cared about.

It's not my decision to make. It's Lewis's.

FORTY

I've never stayed over before; neither of us knows how this is supposed to go. Harry offers me his bed and says he'd be more than happy to sleep on the sofa, but there's no way I'd agree to that, and he doesn't insist.

I brush my teeth in the tiny bathroom, and leave my toothbrush in the mug next to Harry's instead of putting it back in my sponge bag.

When I get back to the living room, there's a fresh cup of tea on the coffee table, and a pale blue sleeping bag neatly laid out on the sofa. That sleeping bag. Memories come flooding back, making me dizzy. Billy's best birthday ever, and the time we went camping in Yorkshire. Him yelling, 'Snap!' a split-second before I registered the card he'd slapped down on top of mine. Me trying to convince Harry that the raindrops falling on the tent sounded like applause. Planning what I would do – how I would protect Billy – if a wild animal tore through the tent in the middle of the night.

If I'd ever thought about this sleeping bag in the years since Billy's birthday camping trip, I would have guessed it must have been bagged up with the rest of the camping stuff and delivered to the charity shop. But here it is, laid out for me like some kind of offering.

I sit down and unzip it, just to double-check it's the same one. There's the proof: 'EVAN'S BAG OF SLEEPING. KEEP OUT!' written in permanent marker around the inside. Mum was furious when she saw I'd done that; Harry thought it was hilarious. *Dad* thought it was hilarious.

When I hear him pass the living room on his way to the bathroom, I say, 'Night, Dad.' Too quiet. Clear my throat and try again. 'Night, Dad!' Then I worry that it sounds fake and forced.

His footsteps come to a halt, and there's a long pause. Then, in a perfectly normal voice, he says, 'Night, Evan.' The footsteps continue towards the bathroom.

If we can both manage to act like this is normal for us, hopefully it will start to *feel* normal.

I cocoon myself in the sleeping bag. Another memory. One of the last sleepovers at Karolina's house, aged twelve. Me wriggling across the floor, sleeping bag pulled up over my head. 'Look! Look! I'm a caterpillar!'

I should have known the end of our friendship was near when I peeked out from my sleeping bag to see her engrossed in a magazine. 'Why are you such a *baby*?' she asked, without looking up. And even then, I knew the question was rhetorical. I understood that Karolina had out-paced me, even if she hadn't meant to: she was ten years old when she got her first period and by eleven she was wearing a proper bra. How could I possibly begin to understand, with my vest and flat chest and hazy understanding of what would happen to my body over the next few years?

I dream of an alternate reality in which I am the best friend that Karolina Zabek could ever wish for. The kind of friend who marches you to the doctor and supports you through a difficult diagnosis, and is there for you when your thoughts are dark and all seems hopeless.

After rubbing my eyes and struggling to bring my sleep-addled brain into focus the next morning, I still can't make sense of the message Mum sent at 11.22 last night. *Everything ok there? xxx.* There were four missed calls from her too.

I reply with a question mark, but the message remains unread.

There's a note from Harry in the kitchen, written on the back of an envelope: *Off to see a man about a dog. Lock the door behind you. Keep the key. Dad x. P.S. Not an actual dog.*

The key in question is carefully placed to underline the message. It looks brand new.

There are two thick slices of bread in the toaster, and a plate and knife set out on the worktop next to a butter dish and a jar of jam. In front of the kettle there's a mug with a teabag in it. The kettle is full.

I've never been in Harry's flat without him. The obvious temptation is to snoop, to search for bottles. So it's a miracle that I eat my breakfast and take a shower and roll up the sleeping bag and leave the flat without opening a single drawer or looking in a single cupboard.

I add Harry's key to my key ring like it's no big deal. It sits between the back door key that takes several attempts to work properly, and the old brass key Sid found on the beach last Christmas. He chucked it to me and said, 'Key to my heart, right there,' with a cheesy wink. I brought the key home and washed it and dried it and decided I needed to keep it with me at all times. I could have given it back to him when we broke up at Easter, but that would have shown that I'd taken him seriously.

I didn't plan to come to the Beach Hut, but it's where I end up. I peer through the window to check that Alice isn't working today. In her place, there's a short Italian boy with nice forearms. He grabs a menu from the stack by the door and tries to usher me towards the back of the café, but I ask to be seated at the table next to the window. Phoebe's table.

This is next-level procrastination. I'm not hungry or thirsty. There is no good reason for me not to go straight to the hospital. It's fear, pure and simple, of how Lewis will react and what he'll say. That's assuming he will talk to me at all. He could blank me, keep spinning the amnesia line, and there's not a thing I can do about it.

Lewis may not have all the answers, anyway. It depends how close he and Phoebe really were. Because something tells me that she's the key to this. After all, someone had to be the first to suggest the idea to the others. The youngest of the lot, and yet she was the one behind the wheel. That has to mean something. The kind of girl you could pass in the corridors without giving her a second glance. Phoebe was the one who knew Lewis and Karolina. And James too, probably, even if I haven't quite figured out how yet.

I picture her sitting where I sit now, scribbling in her notebook. What was she writing? A list of names? People who felt like she did, or who she suspected might feel the same way. People who had given up on life, for one reason or another.

I wonder, about this need to place the blame on someone. For some people, that someone is Lewis, because of how he looks and what they think they know about him. For me, right now, that someone is Phoebe, even though I know it's unfair.

Four people got into that car of their own volition. They didn't fasten their seatbelts and did nothing to stop Phoebe driving straight into a brick wall.

But one of those people *did* fasten his seatbelt. The question is, why?

FORTY-ONE

He's sitting in a chair next to an open window. It's the first time I've seen him wearing his normal clothes — black jeans and his Che Guevara T-shirt. The sight of his stripy socks brings a lump to my throat, which is weird. I've never found feet particularly poignant before. His face looks much better — almost back to normal.

Lewis glances at me, but says nothing. There's a pillow on his lap, and on the pillow is a book. *Our* book. The book is held open by a plastic device, so that he can turn the pages using one hand. It makes me wonder how many other things I haven't thought about — things Lewis is going to have to learn to do differently.

I pull up a plastic chair, and wait.

'Turns out there's an epilogue.'

'You've finished? What happened?'

He tells me, stripping all interest and emotion from the story, just giving me the bare bones.

'Happily ever after, then?'

'I'll only know if I read the epilogue, and I fucking hate epilogues. Wrapping everything up with a big bow as if life is actually like that. No, thanks.' He takes the plastic holder off the book and chucks the book on to the bed.

He asks me about Indy, and I tell him she's fine.

Lewis nods. 'My dad was here this morning.'

'Yeah?' Mouth suddenly dry.

'He's not very happy with you right now.'

No shit. 'Why's that, then?' I ask.

'You shouldn't have told him. You don't know what he's like.'

'What do you mean?'

His face transforms – I don't even know how – and I can suddenly see the family resemblance. '*On your way to a party, weren't you, son? That Karolina was a bit of a looker, wasn't she? Bet she was the one you had your eye on.*'

'He actually said that?' Lewis nods. 'And what did you say to him?'

'That I don't remember.' His eyes bore into mine, and it feels like they contain a challenge. Then they soften, and all that's left is a plea. He *wants* me to ask, I realise. I get up to close the door, even though

I'm scared – suddenly terrified – to hear what he has to say.

I pull my chair a little closer to him and sit down. 'Tell me what happened, Lewis.'

Now he's the one looking like he wants to make a run for it. His gaze flicks between the door and the window, before finally resting on me. 'I shouldn't be here. I'm not supposed to be here.'

'Well, you *are* here.' There are shades of my mother in my tone of voice, so I adjust it. 'I'm glad you're here.'

If there's a halfway point between astonishment and disgust, Lewis's face nails it. 'You don't even know me.'

'But I'd like to. I have it on good authority that you're worth knowing. Indy speaks very highly of you.'

'Indy's a *dog*.'

'A discerning dog, though, right?'

'Has anyone ever told you that you're kind of weird?'

'You're the first today.'

He doesn't smile, but there's a loosening of the tension in the room. It's as good a time as any to start. 'Why were you wearing a seatbelt?'

If he's surprised at the question he doesn't show it. 'Because I'm a fucking coward, that's why.' He glances at me, but I say nothing. He sighs heavily, turns

293

his head to look out of the window. There's not much to see out there – a half-empty car park, an overflowing bin. 'She said it'd look better, if at least one of us was wearing a seatbelt. Not as suspicious. She told me not to worry, that it wouldn't make a difference – she'd done her research and the car would be a fireball. But I knew – I *knew* – it was bullshit, even with the ket scrambling my brain. I think . . . maybe she wanted me to have a chance.' He pauses and searches for the words he needs. 'It was like I was watching myself from a distance, as if I was in the middle of a video game. I was in control, but there was a disconnect, you know?'

It's just as well his question is rhetorical, because I'm too stunned to speak. Hearing him talk like this, so matter of fact about something so terrible, is more horrible than I could ever have imagined.

'She was whispering in my ear and the other two were laughing in the back seat – *laughing*, for fuck's sake. And she said, "Do this for me. Please." And who the fuck am I to deny someone their dying wish? And I can tell myself that all day long – that I did it for her – but I didn't. I did it because I was scared.'

'You'd changed your mind?'

'No!' A fierce whisper. 'No.'

I don't believe him, but it doesn't matter.

'It's not that simple. It was like . . . letting the

294

gods decide.' Lewis raises the stump of his right arm. 'Looks like the gods decided to fuck with me, didn't they?'

There's a lie nestled in there somewhere, I'm sure of it. 'Tell me what happened.'

'What's to tell? Phoebe asked if we were ready. We said yes. She floored the accelerator. She'd even worked out the distance she needed to get the car up to speed. She'd thought of everything, right down to the last detail.' And he actually sounds impressed. 'Karolina started screaming,' he says, and sees the horror on my face, 'No, not that like that. Like she was on a rollercoaster or something.' His eyes lose focus for a second, then he nods decisively. 'Yeah, like that.'

All I can think is, *How can you be so sure? How can you know for sure what type of scream it was?*

'What about James?'

'I don't know. He was quiet, I guess.'

'So that was it? Phoebe just drove into the wall.'

Lewis nods, a second too late.

'What are you not telling me?' I lean forward in my seat and reach out for his hand, and he doesn't shy away. He grips my fingers, and when I look up, tears are streaming down his face.

'I let her down. She trusted me and I let her down. I can't even . . . I wasn't thinking.' He closes his eyes, wincing. 'I tried to grab the wheel. But Phoebe was strong. Her arms were locked at the elbows and there was no way I could . . .'

'That's why you lost your arm,' I say, shocked, as the truth dawns on me.

'I betrayed her. Every time I close my eyes I see the look on her face the moment before we hit the wall. She wasn't angry, she was *hurt*. She was looking right at me. I could see it in her eyes. I stole those last few seconds from her.'

'You did the right thing.'

'They're still dead, aren't they? And I'm still here.' Lewis lets go of my hand and stretches his fingers a couple of times, as if my grip had been constricting the blood flow. 'Phoebe was desperate to get it right this time.'

'She's tried before?'

'Last year, just before I met her. But her brother found her before she could do it. She was fucking *raging* – blackmailed him so he wouldn't tell their parents. She threatened to tell them he was dealing.' What Conrad told me suddenly makes sense – that Phoebe had barely spoken to him in the last year.

'Have you? Tried before, I mean?'

'I thought about chucking myself off the pier,' he says dully. I think back to the article I found in his room. It wasn't pride over Tim's charity work – it was *research.* 'That's where I met Phoebe, actually. She was . . . intense. It was her who told me about the wreckage down there . . . mangled metal and shit. You hit the right spot and the chances of surviving are zilch.' He smiles at me – a strange, gleeful sort of smile. 'She was a bit of an expert on ways to die. The car thing was her idea – getting one without airbags. The rest of us would never have come up with a plan like that. It was sort of genius.'

I have to look away. It's awful, hearing this. I realise something's still bothering me. A missing piece of the puzzle. 'I know she used to hang out at the café where Karolina worked, but how did she get to know James?'

'Through me,' he says, and there's something defiant in his tone, as if he's expecting me to challenge him.

'At Belmont Hall?'

Lewis shakes his head. 'We got talking online – a forum. Chatting about books and shit. Then we started talking about other stuff. Deeper stuff. I didn't even know who he was for ages. His username was Boromir.' Lewis almost smiles, but his face contorts.

Is it guilt he's feeling? For getting James involved in this? Or simple grief for the loss of a friend? 'I'm trying to understand, Lewis. But I can't get my head around it – I just *can't*.' James and Karolina, I can just about get, now that I know more about them. But

Phoebe is still a mystery to me. And Lewis . . . I've been trying so hard not to think about it. My voice shakes slightly as I ask a question that's long overdue. 'Why did you do it, Lewis? Why did you get in that car?'

His smile slips away and he starts to talk.

He tells me why.

FORTY-TWO

I can hear shouting as I turn down my road. The walk back from the hospital has done nothing to clear my head, and it takes a few seconds for me to realise that it is coming from my house.

My hands are shaking as I try to fit the key into the lock. When I finally get inside, Billy almost knocks me over when he rushes past, his face red and shiny with tears. He stomps up the stairs, stopping halfway to scream, 'I HATE YOU!' in the direction of the living room. It's as if he doesn't even see me. Indy slinks up the stairs after him, staying close to the wall like she does when she's scared.

Mum and Tim are in the living room. She's crying and he has his arm around her. 'He doesn't mean it, darling,' Tim says, and I realise that Mum was right when she said his voice sounded like caramel. Sickly sweet, will rot your teeth.

'What have you done?' I spit the words at Tim and wish each one were a poison dart.

'Evan!' Mum's eyes widen in shock.

'What? It's a simple question.'

Tim says nothing, carrying on rubbing my mother's back. Mum takes a tissue from her bag and starts dabbing under her eyes. 'This is nothing to do with Tim. Billy's upset because I told him he can't see his father tonight.'

Billy and Harry are meant to be going bowling; Billy's crap at bowling but he really likes the shoes. 'And why did you do that?'

Tim starts to speak, but I cut him off. 'I wasn't talking to you.'

Mum says another outraged, 'Evan!' but I just stand there, arms crossed. 'Why can't Billy see Dad?'

Mum's expression is incredulous. At first I think it's because I said 'Dad', but then she says, 'After what happened last night?'

Tim's watching me, with this sad, empathetic look on his face. But I see right through him like a piece of clingfilm. I try to pretend he's not looking at me. That he's not here. I focus on Mum instead. 'What did Tim say happened last night?'

'What was he was thinking, coming round here and spouting his stupid theories? As if Tim hasn't been through enough without having to listen to that.'

'*Stupid theories*? Harry was just trying to—'

Tim talks over me, but his words are aimed at Mum. 'We can't blame him, Di.' He shakes his head sadly. 'It's an illness. Harry needs help.'

'What are you *talking* about?'

Mum sighs. 'It's OK, Evan, you don't need to cover for your father.'

Tim puts his arm around my mother again, his expression sad and serious and dripping with faux concern. 'I knew straight away something was up.' His eyes meet mine. 'Even before I smelled the alcohol on his breath.'

Two hours ago, I might have stood there, stunned into silence. But two hours can change everything. And I lose my fucking mind.

I lunge at him, and my flailing punch lands, cracking his glasses and knocking him back on to the sofa. And Mum's screaming at me and grabbing at my arms and I'm shaking her off and Tim is looking up at me and the mask slips slightly. It's not a smile – he's not stupid enough to be caught smiling. It's in his eyes, though. The look in his eyes isn't what you'd expect from someone who's just been punched. It's a look you'd expect to see from someone who's just got exactly what they wanted.

I want to pound his face into a bloody pulp, till there's no Tim left. But Billy's scrambling down the stairs and Indy is barking her fucking head off and Mum's yelling and pushing me pushing me pushing me. 'Out! Get out! Get out of my house!'

He's won.

FORTY-THREE

They're both in the garage when I arrive, Daze plumping cushions and Sid sweeping the floor. Sid mutters, 'Dusty as fuck in here.' Then Daze nudges him and they both turn to look at me.

Sid doesn't look great. The dark circles under his eyes are even darker and he could do with a shave. His T-shirt seems to be hanging off him. His expression is guarded.

Daze must have thrown on the nearest clothes and raced out of the house. Ripped jeans and a faded red sweatshirt is about as far away from her usual look as it's possible to get. She looks completely different without the lipstick. Without the quirky fifties clothes and the hair styled just so. The last time I saw her looking like this was the last time we slept together.

'All right, Page?' Daze's casual tone is betrayed by the kindness shining from her face. 'So who do we need to kill?'

Her words break the dam inside of me. There's a mess of crying (me) and hugging (all three of us) and sorries (me again) until Daze put a stop to proceedings. 'Seriously, guys, we need to park the us stuff to one side for a bit. Evan, tell us what happened.'

We sit down, and the words come tumbling out of my mouth. The wedding and Marcus Bloom and what happened at the radio station, finishing up with Tim's face getting punched.

'I'll rip his throat out,' declares Daze.

Sid mutters, 'Get in line.'

'You do realise I'm not talking about Marcus Bloom, right?' Daze elbows Sid in the side and laughs.

'Ha.' Sid's withering look isn't particularly withering. He reaches across and touches my arm. 'Are you OK, though?'

Daze slow-claps. 'Why wouldn't Ev be OK? It's not as if her stepfather's a fucking psychopath or anything. Oh, wait . . .'

I attempt a smile for Sid's sake. 'I'll be fine, thank you.'

I don't think I'll be fine. There's a monster in my home and my mother can't even see it. But it's what you say when people ask if you're OK. And one part of my life – a huge part – is now on its way to being fine. They're here. I said I needed them, and they were

304

here for me. No questions asked, grudges and anger forgotten. For now.

Sid's not buying my pathetic attempt at smiling. 'There's more, isn't there? Is it about Lewis?'

I nod, and the words come slower this time. I trace the story from the first suspicions about the crash to my visit to Lewis this afternoon. Stripped bare of emotion, just the facts.

When I'm finished, Daze sits there in stunned silence. But Sid . . . Sid's gone deathly pale, his hand on his stomach. 'I think I'm going to throw up.'

Daze rubs his back, but says, 'All right, drama queen. This isn't *about* you.'

A strange sound escapes his mouth – a sort of strangled moan. Daze flashes me a what-the-fuck look, but I'm too busy staring at Sid as he starts to cry.

'What the *fuck*, Sidders?' says Daze, but there's sympathy in her voice.

'Oh God oh God oh God,' he mumbles, his clenched fist pressed against his mouth.

I scoot across and put my arm around him. Daze does the same on the other side – flashing me another what-the-fuck look behind his head. I shake my head, because I have no idea what this is about either.

After a few minutes, Sid sniffs a couple of times and his breathing returns to normal. 'OK. OK.'

'Do you want to talk about it?' I ask.

'This is a safe space, Sidney. You're amongst friends. Sharing is caring.' I glare at Daze, but Sid does this sort of hiccupy laugh even as he tells her she's not funny.

'OK. OK,' he says again. 'There's something I need to tell you. I should have said something before, but my head was all over the place. I didn't know what to think. Can you two, please . . . can you stop looking at me?' I don't know about Daze, but I oblige, staring at the stickers on the fridge. 'I slept with Karolina the night before she died.'

Daze starts to speak, but Sid talks over her. 'We swapped numbers at George Fearnley's party, but I didn't call her or anything. She was . . . she kind of scared me, if I'm honest. Anyway, I forgot all about it until she called me that night and asked if I wanted to hook up.'

Daze pats his hand. 'And of course you had no option but to say yes. To get back on the horse after this one.'

'Can you just *not*, Daze? Please. She messaged me after . . . but I . . . I didn't reply.' He closes his eyes and covers his face with his hand, but I still see the grimace.

'Then I heard about the crash. And I thought, what if there was something I could have done? What if I'd replied, arranged to meet her that night? Then she wouldn't have been in that car, would she?'

Sid's eyes are imploring when he finally brings himself to make eye contact with me. 'But now you're telling me that she killed herself and it's all my fault.' He bows his head and presses his fingers to his eyes.

There's silence in the garage, except from the low hum of the fridge and Sid's too-loud breathing.

Daze bursts out laughing, and the sheer inappropriateness of it makes me laugh too. I can't help myself.

Sid's head snaps up and the horror on his face makes us laugh even more.

'Oh my *God*, Sid! This is too much . . . I can't . . .' Daze collapses and covers her face with a cushion. 'You are a sweet, sweet boy,' says Daze, wiping tears from her eyes.

'This isn't funny, guys.' He's scowling now, and of course he's right. None of this is funny.

Daze shakes herself down like Indy after a rainy walk. She takes Sid's hand in hers and looks in his eyes. 'Are you trying to tell us that you honestly think Karolina Zabek killed herself because of *you*?'

'No . . . I mean, yes. Maybe! I don't know . . . how the fuck am I supposed to know?'

Daze shakes her head in wonderment. 'The ego of this boy . . .'

I take pity on Sid. 'She had a mental illness, Sid. She'd been off her meds for months and they'd been planning the car crash for weeks. This was *not* about you. You have to know that.'

I can practically see the cogs in his brain, working to push against my words. 'But I . . . ?'

'It's not.'

I keep saying the words, and variations of them, until I see the truth of them start to dawn on his face.

The truth dawns on me too. What happened is no one's fault.

It's nowhere near that simple. But while Sid and Matthieu and the Zabeks have all been busy blaming themselves, there's someone else who hasn't shown the slightest sign of guilt or remorse. Maybe there's something I can do about that.

FORTY-FOUR

Daze pulls a face at me in the mirror as we brush our teeth. She takes her oral hygiene very seriously — mouthwash and flossing twice a day.

I thank her for letting me stay the night, and she rolls her eyes and bumps me with her hip. 'What are friends for, if not impromptu sleepovers when your nutso mother kicks you out of the house?'

I try to ignore the punch-in-the-gut feeling of the f-word. 'She hasn't kicked me out of the house. She . . . ejected me from the premises. Temporarily.'

'Riiiight. You know I knew there was something fishy about Breakfast Tim. It's not normal to be cheerful at that time in the morning. So what are we going to do to him? I vote public humiliation.'

'You don't get a vote,' I say as we make our way back to her room. I flop down on the bed with a sigh. 'First thing's first. I want him out of the house.'

Daze pretends to consider that for a moment. She

sticks up her hand like we're in a classroom, and I swat her hand away. 'You're going to ask how the hell I can do that when he's in the house and I'm not, aren't you?'

'You know me so well,' she says, and her smile makes me feel things I really shouldn't be feeling right now. But I just want to pretend that the world isn't awful and Lewis will be OK and Mum will come to her senses. I want to remember happiness.

We get under the covers and turn out the lights. Daze always sleeps on her side facing the door, so that she'll be ready for the bad guys. But tonight she's facing me.

My eyes adjust to the darkness, and I look at her and she looks at me.

'You weren't surprised, were you? When I said about Karolina being bipolar.' There's no need to whisper, but I can't help it.

The slightest shake of her head.

'Alice told you.'

She nods.

'You like her.'

'She likes me.'

'What's that supposed to mean?'

'That I've got some mad lady-loving skills?'

'Stop it.'

'Stop what?' But she knows. She always knows. 'She likes me. We have fun together. It's nothing serious.'

The words she doesn't say seem to float in front of my eyes. *Not like us.* Or maybe she doesn't say the words because they're not true. We were never serious either, not really. We never officially put a name on the thing we had.

'Evan? You're being weird. Which is fine – and totally understandable with everything that's going on. I like Weird Evan.' Her face turns serious. 'But if there's something you want to say to me, you can just say it.'

I look at her face – really look at it – for the first time in ages. I always liked her eyebrows. They're slightly evil-looking, but in a good way. I like everything about her face, actually. As if it was created to my exact specifications. But the truth is that I like everything about her face because I like everything about *her*.

'OK, now you're going slightly cross-eyed,' Daze cracks, and sticks her tongue out at me.

I even like *that* about her. Her complete inability to be serious for longer than a minute at a time.

I reach out and touch her cheek. *Now* she's serious. Eyes wide, lips slightly parted.

Darkness amplifies every little sound. My breathing. Hers . . .

And the ringing of my phone.

Harry sounds exhausted. 'Your mum just called. Wanted to know if you were with me.'

'What did you tell her?'

'I said I hadn't the foggiest where you were.'

'I'm at Daze's place.' I cast a look over my shoulder and Daze flashes me a reassuring smile.

'Right. Well, you should probably tell your mother that.'

'She chucked me out of the house.'

'Because you attacked Tim.'

'Because he told her you'd been drinking!'

'Yeah, funnily enough, your mum mentioned that. I don't need you to fight my battles for me, Evan.' He clears his throat. 'But thanks.'

'You told her, though? That he's full of shit?'

'I said he must have been mistaken . . .'

'What the fuck, Dad? He wasn't *mistaken*. He's trying to turn her against you!'

'I managed to do that all on my own a long time ago.'

'Why are you being like this? Why don't you care?'

'Of course I care!' He pauses and his breath huffs down the line. 'I want Tim out of your lives, but I have to tread carefully, OK? Anyway, that's not why I'm calling. Conrad Mackintosh is in hospital.'

A wave of dizziness hits and I have to grip the mattress to steady myself. I remember Conrad's hard, angry face at the cemetery. What did that guilt and anger drive him to do? I'm vaguely aware of Daze sitting up, a hand on my back. 'Is he . . . ?'

'Oh God, no – he's all right. He'll be home in the morning. He got roughed up by one of Lacey's boys. Apparently he turned up at Lacey's house to return the drugs he'd been supposed to sell. Lacey was fine with that – Conrad's small fry to him – but the ketamine had been cut . . . with *sugar*, if you can believe it.'

I don't even want to know how Harry found all this out; he's obviously got mates in some very dodgy places. But I'm glad I know that Conrad told me the truth, about not dealing any more. That can be added to the very short column of good things that have come out of this fucked-up mess.

'Phoebe must have cut the ketamine after she nicked what she needed. Conrad swore that he didn't give her the drugs, and he'd have sussed it if she'd just swiped the whole lot.'

'Well, she got her brother some broken ribs and a concussion for her efforts,' says Harry.

'She got herself dead,' I say flatly, and Daze's hand squeezes my shoulder.

Harry and I agree to talk in the morning and I hang up.

I realise Daze is staring at me. 'You called him *Dad*!'

'Apparently that's a thing I do now. Sometimes.'

'I'm glad.'

'I'm knackered.'

She holds one side of the duvet up for me to snuggle under. I relay Harry's side of the conversation, and we talk for a while. But my eyelids keep drooping shut, so Daze tells me to shut the hell up and go to sleep.

'But . . . but . . . ?'

'Don't force me to make a butt joke at this time of night.' She strokes my hair and kisses me on the forehead as my eyes close.

The words, 'Sweet dreams, you,' are the last thing I hear before I sleep.

FORTY-FIVE

The smell of frying bacon wakes me up, and I follow
my nose to the kitchen where Daze is flipping pancakes
with one hand and taking a frying pan off the hob with
the other.

'Grab the maple syrup from the cupboard, would
you?'

She's even set the table. Kitchen roll instead of
napkins. She serves up the pancakes while I pour the
OJ. I turn on the little DAB radio on the breakfast
bar because something about the silence makes me
tense. I should have known better, because it's tuned
to Claybourne FM. Daze groans when she hears his
voice.

'Sorry,' she says. 'I hate-listen to it sometimes.'

Breakfast Tim is wishing the very best of mornings
to any listeners just waking up. I tell him to fuck off
and die.

My finger is on the power button when I hear what's coming up next. A segment on parenting and 'blended' families.

'Oh, boy,' Daze mutters.

'It can be tricky, can't it?' Tim is saying. 'When one or both of you has kids from a previous marriage. But it can also be the most wonderful thing. Forgive me for getting personal for a moment, but it's been such a *privilege* for me to get to know my stepdaughter and stepson. I'm not saying it's always easy, but we're getting there. And all you can do is try your best. Be the best dad you can be.'

'Amen to that,' says the woman who reads the news.

'Was it a privilege to get punched in the face by your stepdaughter too? Wanker.' Daze comes over and unplugs the radio at the wall, because I seem to have turned to stone, finger still on the power button.

'Evan. Sit. Eat,' she says, taking me by the shoulders and guiding me to my seat.

Daze is an excellent cook, but I can't seem to taste much. Is that a thing? Can rage destroy your tastebuds?

There's a loud knock, then a face appears at the patio door. Jaime has her open mouth against the glass, cheeks puffed out. 'Lost my keys!' she yells. Daze rolls her eyes at me and pushes her chair back.

316

'Don't tell her about any of this,' I whisper, and Daze nods and goes to open the door.

The Jaime Show begins. I'm grateful for the distraction as she tells us about her night. It was wild, apparently. It always is. When she finally runs out of stories to tell, she nicks a pancake from Daze's plate and heads upstairs to bed.

After breakfast I take a long shower while Daze clears up in the kitchen.

I linger at the front door. What I really want to do is get back in Daze's bed and pull the covers over my head and stay there until things are fine again. She hugs me for a long time. 'You call me, OK? You're not alone in this. I'm here.' There's a pause before she adds, 'Sid too. We're here for you no matter what.'

I thank her, and tell her that I might need her help later – her and Sid – and that makes her happy; Daze likes to feel useful. I hug her again, because sometimes one hug isn't enough. Then I head out into the real world, where monsters lurk.

The missed calls and messages from Mum should make me feel guilty, but they don't. She's the one who chucked her own daughter out of the house. But if today is going to go to plan, I have to make peace. I sit on a wall and message her. *Sorry about yesterday. Can we talk later? Please?*

317

She replies straight away, saying that she'd booked the afternoon off for a haircut, but she'll move the appointment. It's all very civil.

I swing by the hospital, but stop in the doorway of Lewis's room. It's the first time I've seen his arm without the compression dressing. The wound looks surprisingly neat, the surrounding skin smooth and bone-white. The nurse is rubbing cream on the stump when Lewis looks up – and smiles.

I wasn't planning to stay long, but I need his blessing for what I'm about to do. I make him a promise – a promise that isn't really in my power to keep. It all depends on someone else; I just have to trust that they'll do the right thing when the time comes.

FORTY-SIX

Three hours and several cups of tea later, I'm sitting in the living room at home, waiting, when I hear a key in the lock.

Tim is whistling a tune — one of the jingles from his show — but he stops when he sees me sitting there. 'Ah,' he says, with a smirk. 'The wanderer returns.'

His glasses are held together with sticky tape; a bruise has blossomed next to his eye.

He glances up the stairs. 'Where's your mother?'

'How should I know?'

'There's really no need to be so combative, Evan. I'm not the enemy here. Did I call the police yesterday, after being assaulted in my own home?' He waits a beat. Dickhead. 'No, I did not. Because this is a family matter, and family matters are *private*. Look, Evan . . . I'm the first to admit I haven't got everything right.' He sits down on the sofa and picks at some of Indy's fur on a cushion. 'But this has been a learning curve for me too. I wanted everything to be perfect – for us to be the perfect family – and I may have got a bit carried away.'

I stare at him. He's good – really good.

'So tell me – how can we work together to get past this little . . . bump in the road? Speaking of bumps, that's some right hook you've got there!' He laughs; I don't. 'Evan? Look, I'm *trying* here.'

'Like you tried with Lewis after his mum died?'

The only reaction is a slight tightening around his eyes. 'What are you talking about?' Ostensibly still friendly, but a slight coolness in his voice.

'She was leaving you, wasn't she?' I watch for a reaction but still there's nothing. 'Been planning it for months. Because you made her life a living hell. Controlling her, always wanting to know where she was going, checking up on her every minute of the day. And then she went and died and you got to play the grieving widower while you made life hell for your son instead.'

He takes his broken glasses off and cleans them with his handkerchief. 'That's quite some story,' he says, putting his glasses back on. 'Is that what he told you? And you believed him? Really, Evan, I expected better of you. Lewis is a very angry young man, who has a tendency to blame other people for his problems. But tell me, if I'm really such a terrible father, why

320

didn't he just move out? He's an adult. He's free to live wherever he pleases.'

I asked Lewis the same question, and he struggled to answer, but I don't. 'Maybe it's got something to do with the years you spent making him feel worthless. Telling him to pull himself together the day after his mother died, and then implying she'd still be alive if he hadn't caused her so much stress. You're *despicable*. You undermined his confidence at every opportunity and gaslit the fuck out of him so he didn't even know what was real any more. He had no one else. You were *it*. And you failed him.'

He snorts. 'This is utter nonsense. I worked hard to provide for him. That boy never wanted for anything.'

'Lewis may have had the latest games console and phone and laptop, but that's not what he needed. He needed love.'

'Who the hell do you think you are, telling me I don't love my own son? He's all . . . he's all I have left of Imogen.' He has tears in his eyes. Another person might feel sympathy. But I know better. 'She wasn't serious – about leaving me. It was just a . . . phase she was going through . . . a mid-life crisis. She *loved* me. We were happy.'

'*Happy*? So happy that on her birthday, you forced her to stay sitting at the table until she'd finished every last bite of the meal you'd cooked for her, even though she told you she felt unwell. Lewis said she was still there at midnight, face wet with tears, begging you to let her go to bed.' I hold his eye until he looks away. 'So happy you wouldn't even let her go clothes shopping on her own in case she got something you didn't approve of? And Lewis saw it all. He had to grow up watching you treat his mother like shit. And when she wasn't around any more for you to torment, you started on him.'

Tim's tears don't last long. He can clearly turn them on and off at will. 'This is nonsense,' he says coldly.

'So it's not true, then? That the only time you ever hugged him or told him you loved him was when there were other people around to see you do it?'

'He's a grown man! He doesn't need me holding his hand and kissing him goodnight after a bedtime story. This really is . . . I've had enough of this.'

The muscles in his neck are taut as steel cables as his jaw clenches. He makes a visible effort to slow his breathing. 'I see what's happening here. Lewis has been spinning you some sob story, trying to blame me for the bad decisions he's made.'

'He tried to kill himself, Tim,' I say, almost gently.

I'm not prepared for the transformation in Tim's face as he jumps to his feet. He's a snarling puce-faced demon. I pushed him further than I realised. 'Because he's *weak*!'

It occurs to me that this man could hurt me. But somehow I don't feel scared. I'm in control – and he knows it.

I stay seated, keeping my face impassive. Waiting for the inevitable.

'And as for you, you jumped-up little bitch . . . I won't have you ruining my marriage with your lies and bullshit theories, so you'd better keep your mouth *shut*.' He's towering over me now, eyes bulging. 'You really, really don't want to make an enemy out of me, Evan. I can make your life hell.'

'You already have.'

'Oh, you think so, do you? Because you have no idea what I can do to you. Your mother already thinks you're dangerously unstable. Wait till I tell her about your little performance at the wedding. I watched the whole show, you know. I saw how much you liked it . . . moaning and gasping while he fucked you hard.' I break eye contact for the first time, and look down in horror to see an erection straining at the front of his chinos. 'How do you think she's going to react when she finds out you're a filthy little slut?'

I want to escape, but I can't. Not yet.

Somehow I manage to shrug and clear my throat. 'Let's find out, shall we? *Mum*?'

The kitchen door swings open.

FORTY-SEVEN

My mother is not a tall woman, but standing in that doorway she looks like a fucking Amazon. She is Ripley and Sarah Connor and Wonder Woman. She is spectacular.

The look on Tim's face is spectacular in a different way. He's aghast.

Mum has him by the front of his shirt before he can move. 'Don't you ever EVER call my daughter a slut again, you disgusting piece of shit.'

Tim takes two steps backwards, hands up. 'Whoa, there. Hang on a second, I can explain.' He attempts to smooth down his shirt. 'I'm glad you're back, Di. I think Evan needs help.'

Mum crosses her arms and raises her eyebrows. 'Go on . . .'

And stupid fucker that Tim is, he doesn't even realise she's just giving him more rope to hang himself. He looks over at me and shakes his head. 'She . . . this is embarrassing, and I'm so sorry. I don't quite know how to tell you this, but . . . Evan made a pass at me.'

My mother laughs – hard. 'Oh, she did, did she? Let me tell you this. My daughter wouldn't touch you with someone *else's* barge pole. Just. Stop. Lying.' He opens his mouth to speak but she holds up a hand that doesn't shake. 'I don't want to hear another word from you.' And his mouth actually shuts!

Mum turns round to look at me. 'Your father's on his way.'

'You called *Harry*?' I ask, with a mixture of happiness and disbelief.

'I did.' She turns back to Tim, makes a big show of checking her watch. 'So I reckon that gives you . . . ooh, about ten minutes to pack your shit and get the fuck out of our house.' Mum hasn't sworn this much in ages, and it's fucking glorious to witness.

But Tim seems to puff up again, shoulders back, defiant chin. He's given up all pretence of being the wronged party here. 'You think I'm scared of him?' He snorts, and a little bit of snot shoots out of his nose, which he angrily wipes away with the back of his hand. He advances on Mum, but I'm right there by her side. We stand firm. 'You honestly think I'm scared of a washed-up alcoholic?'

Mum stares at Tim as if she's seeing him for the first time. And I suppose she is, in a way. 'Harry may be a washed-up alcoholic, but he's twice the man you'll ever be.'

'Aw, Mum, that's not fair . . .' I say. 'Harry's at least *three* times better than Tim. Maybe even four.' I'm having fun now, standing tall with my mother by my side. A fierce, dickhead-fighting duo.

Mum cracks a brief smile, then looks back at her watch. 'Nine minutes. Better get a move on.'

Tim stands there for another thirty seconds or so, fists clenched at his side. The heat of his anger is almost enough to warm your hands on. Trouble is, it doesn't touch us. It doesn't touch Mum, because she sees him for who he really is. The nice-guy mask lies shattered on the floor.

Breakfast Tim tries one last glare on for size before slinking up the stairs. I squeeze Mum's hand and realise she's shaking now. I put my arms around her and hold her tight.

He struggles down a few minutes later with a huge wheelie case and a bulging rucksack. He picks up his keys.

'My lawyer will be in touch,' he says coldly. It's supposed to sound threatening, but instead it sounds comical.

'Keys.' Mum holds out her hand, and the shaking is back under control.

His mouth twitches and he swallows down whatever

it was he was going to say. It takes him so long to get the house keys off his Harry Potter key ring that the tension drops a little. Mum rolls her eyes at me and I stifle a laugh.

He drops the keys in Mum's hand, and I'm ready for him to say something vile. He doesn't, though. He stares at her, his eyes flicking from feature to feature, like he's trying to memorise it. It's creepy as hell.

Mum clears her throat. 'You stay away from us all. And that includes Lewis. Stay away from the hospital.'

'You can't keep me away from my own son.'

'You said it yourself – he's a grown man. Evan says he doesn't want to see you.'

He doesn't argue with that, even though he clearly wants to. Harry will be here soon, and no matter what he says, a man like Tim is always going to be intimidated by a loose cannon like Harry.

We follow him to the door, and neither of us helps when one of the rucksack straps gets caught on the handle.

And then he's out of our house. He's officially off the premises. He pauses for a moment on the bottom step; his shoulders rise and fall. Then he trundles his case over to the car.

'Tim?' I call, as he's lowering himself into the driver's seat. 'I just want you to know . . . your lasagne tastes like shit.'

FORTY-EIGHT

I know she's crying up there, but I also know she doesn't want me to know she's crying.

It's simple for me, black and white. The tumour has been removed, the wicked witch is dead, the good guys have won. It isn't like that for her. She loved him. Only a few weeks ago, she stood up in front of her friends and family and promised to love and cherish him until the day she dies. She believed in those vows. She thought she'd found her happily ever after.

It must have been unfathomably hard for her to stand on the other side of that kitchen door and listen to Tim. She didn't like my plan, not one little bit. Especially not the last part – making her promise she wouldn't enter the living room until I asked her to. But she went along with it because she needed to hear for herself.

When we sat down at the kitchen table earlier today, the first thing I asked her was: *'Do you trust me?'*

She didn't answer for a long while; she sat there with her head down. When she looked up, she had tears in her eyes. *'Of course I trust you.'* There was something fearful in the way she said it, though, as if on some level she already knew she wasn't going to like what I had to say.

She didn't like any of it, but she listened. She listened as I explained that Harry wasn't drunk yesterday. She cried when I told her about the suicide pact, and my conversation with Lewis. Not once did she say that she didn't believe me, or that I was exaggerating or must have got the wrong end of the stick. My mother took everything I threw at her. All in all, it amounted to a grenade lobbed into the middle of her marriage. Why didn't she try to argue? Did she already know – or suspect – that Tim wasn't what he seemed?

'Are you OK?' Harry asks, and I nod. He's not convinced, but he pretends to be. 'Where's the cumin? You can't make a decent chilli without cumin.'

'Middle shelf, behind the peppercorns.'

It was Harry's idea that we make dinner. It was my idea to turn the ingredients Tim had bought for lasagne into chilli con carne. 'She won't mind me sticking around, will she?' He nods up to the ceiling.

'She called you, Harry. She wants you here.'

'Well. I'll just get this started and leave you to it.'

We settle into a companionable silence of chopping and measuring out spices. I used to do this all the time with Mum, but I've barely cooked anything more than a cheese toastie since Tim moved in. Weird, though, that I didn't notice until now. He took over the kitchen, cooking most nights, and Mum thought it was brilliant. He insisted on making packed lunches for her to take to work, even though she said she liked the food in the canteen. After all, food is love, isn't it? But it wasn't, with him. Food was control. The kitchen became his territory, and we gave it up without a fight.

'So when are you going to write the story?' I ask, when Harry's browning the meat in a huge pan on the stove.

'About Breakfast Tim being a terrible human?' Harry allows himself a tiny smile.

'I would read the *shit* out of that story, but I meant the car crash.'

Harry stares into the saucepan. 'I'm not writing the story.'

'Is it that conflict of interest bullshit that Jane was going on about? Is she giving the story to someone else?'

'No. I talked to her this morning, went through everything I have.'

'*And?*'

'We both agreed . . . we're not running the story.'

'But people should know the truth – that this wasn't a bunch of partying, drug-guzzling kids and that Lewis isn't some shady dealer.' I sigh. 'Come on, Harry. You're the one who keeps banging on about this mental health crisis or whatever. A story like this might actually make people pay attention. Might make them *do* something.'

'I know,' he says softly. 'Believe me, I know. But it's not that simple. A story like this . . . it would probably do more harm than good. There are guidelines, when it comes to reporting suicides. Most suicides aren't reported at all. Often it's to spare the families, but you also have to weigh up the public health issue against the risk of vulnerable people latching on to the story . . . using it as inspiration.'

I stop chopping the peppers. 'But . . .' But what? I never even questioned that Harry would write the story. It's what we've been working towards this whole time: the truth. I thought that was more important than anything else, but what if I was wrong? 'What about Lewis?'

Harry looks at me for a second, weighing something up in his mind. 'I went to see him. He doesn't want me to write the story either.'

'What? You talked to him behind my back?'

'This isn't about you, Evan.' It's a gut punch, and Harry knows it. He gives the pan one last stir and places his hands on my shoulders. 'I don't mean it like that, I'm sorry. None of this would have come out if it weren't for you.'

Tears prickle in my eyes. 'What a fucking waste of time *that* was.'

'*No*, it wasn't.' He lowers his head, forcing me to meet his eyes. 'The people who matter know the truth – that's what counts. Lewis will get the help he needs. And Tim is out of this house. All because of you.' Now there are tears in Harry's eyes, as well as mine. 'I want you to listen to me, OK? You did a *good* thing. You did a good thing for all the right reasons. It may not have turned out quite the way you thought it would, but things rarely do.'

I let him hug me. I want to believe him, but the truth is that Karolina and James and Phoebe are still gone. What if there'd been some big public outcry about the lack of mental health resources last year, or five years ago, or ten? If people actually bothered to look beneath the surface, to find out what was really going on with them. If they'd got the help they needed, would they still be alive?

There's no way of knowing. That's an even harder truth to accept than the fact that everyone else can go about their lives believing that the car crash was nothing more than a stupid accident.

I know the truth; I can't unknow it. The question is whether I *do* something with that knowledge.

The story of Karolina and James and Phoebe and Lewis may never be written, but that doesn't have to mean they died for nothing.

FORTY-NINE

I don't get much of a chance to explain everything to Daze when she brings Billy and Indy back, but, 'Ding dong, the witch is dead,' gets the message across nicely. Her smile is even bigger than mine.

'You're unstoppable,' she whispers into my ear as we hug.

'I wouldn't go that far,' I mumble, which earns me an eye roll. Daze has no time for my inability to take a compliment.

'Thanks for keeping Billy out of the way.' I look over my shoulder into the house, where Billy's subjecting Harry and Mum to a full-on barrage of chat. Mum's been down ten minutes; her face is only slightly puffy from crying. Billy would never notice anyway – he didn't even stop to wonder why Harry's here, cooking dinner in our kitchen.

'It was no bother at all. Sid kept Billy entertained while Indy and I did some serious strolling up and

down the promenade. Turns out people *really* like dogs
. . . who knew?'

I promise to call her tonight and tell her everything,
and she makes me promise to call Sid too. 'I know we
took the piss yesterday, but it really messed with his
head – the Karolina thing.'

I know she's right. 'Maybe he should talk to his
doctor about counselling or something?'

'Why don't you suggest it? He's much more likely
to listen to you. He never takes me seriously.'

I tap my finger against my lips and pretend to
look thoughtful. 'Hmm . . . I wonder why that could
be.'

Daze gives me the finger as she backs away down
the path, then blows me a kiss before skipping down
the road.

Billy scoops chilli and rice into his mouth with alarming
speed. 'He was a bad man,' he says, like he's stating
the bleeding obvious. The sky is blue, the grass is green
and Tim Rossi is a bad man.

'What do you mean, Bill? Why was he a bad man?'
Harry asks.

'He just *was*. Can I have some more cheese, please?'

I pass the bowl and Billy sprinkles a small mountain
of grated cheddar on to his plate, then mashes it all
together with the chilli and rice.

'What makes you say that, Billy?' It's my turn, trying to keep my voice casual.

'He said things that made me feel not good.' He talks with his mouth full but no one tells him off.

'What sort of things?'

'I dunno . . . He said I shouldn't cry, because crying is for girls. But that's not true, is it? And he said drawing is a waste of time.' Billy looks across the table and puts down his fork. 'Mum? Are you OK? Did I say something wrong?'

'No, sweetheart, not at all! Don't ever think that. I'm just . . . I wish you'd come to me. You know you can tell me anything.' She's doing her best to smile, but there's no hiding the tears in her eyes.

'I know. But you were happy and I wanted you to stay happy.' He shrugs and dives back into his food. 'This is very tasty, Dad. Nice-y and spicy. Can we go bowling tomorrow?'

Mum pushes back her chair, turning her head away so that Billy can't see her crying. 'I'll just need to . . . I'd better get the washing in.' She hurries out of the back door, and Harry shoots me a helpless look before following her, leaving the door ajar for a grateful Indy. I'm not sure he's the right person to comfort her, but I'm also not sure it's my place to interfere.

Billy shakes his head and says, 'Weird!'

I manage a smile, despite the guilt twisting my

guts. I knew Billy hadn't been himself lately, but I did fuck all about it. The thought of that man whispering poison into my brother's ear is too much to bear. I should have punched him harder, kept punching and never stopped.

Billy's busy talking about Sid and how cool he is and how he said this really funny thing that made Billy laugh so hard he peed himself a little. I listen and smile and choke down a couple of mouthfuls of food. He's going to be OK, I think. But then after a few minutes he stops in the middle of a sentence, eyes wide. 'Hold on a second . . . if Mum and Tim aren't going to be married any more, does that mean Lewis won't be my stepbrother?'

What the hell am I supposed to say to him? He doesn't understand. He shouldn't have to understand something like this at his age.

I feel a pair of hands on my shoulders, and Mum rests her chin on my head like she used to do when I was little. 'That's a good question, Billy, but I'm afraid I can't answer it.' I feel her words through my skull as well as hearing them. Billy's face falls, and he pouts down at his empty plate. 'So how about we pay a visit to the hospital tomorrow to ask someone who can?'

FIFTY

Later, Billy goes off to bed without a fight, but then he knocks on my bedroom door an hour later. He comes in and puts a large box down on the rug next to my bed. The console Tim bought for his birthday, still in the box with the packaging intact. 'I thought Sid might like it. He's got the old version.'

'You don't have to give it away, Bill. Why don't you set it up and we can play on it tomorrow?'

He crosses his arms, far too serious in his SpongeBob pyjamas. 'Why don't you play your new guitar?'

Outwitted by an eleven-year-old.

After I call Daze to give her the lowdown, I call Sid. It's much quicker, telling him, because he doesn't interrupt as much. I mention Billy's offer of a brand-new games console and he turns me down flat, as I knew he would. 'You should put it on eBay. You'd get four hundred quid for it, easy.'

Tim spent a small fortune trying to buy us. He

must be regretting it now, wasting more than two grand. *Two grand.* You could actually do something useful with that kind of money . . . which gives me an idea.

I tell Sid what I'm thinking, searching on my laptop as we talk; it doesn't take long to find the article.

'Will you help me? You and Daze?'

'I can't speak for Daze – well, I probably can, since she'd go to the fucking moon and back if you asked her to – but I'm in. Definitely.'

'It might help, a bit . . . which gives me an idea.'

Silence for a few seconds and then, 'Maybe.'

'I know I've been a terrible friend lately, but you do know I'm here for you, don't you? I don't ever want you to feel like you can't talk to me.'

He sniffs and says a hoarse, 'I know.' Then he says he's going to see the doctor in the morning, about not being able to sleep. Sid clearly doesn't need me and Daze to stage some sort of intervention. He knows that he needs help and is prepared to seek it out. I can't help thinking that he's always been better than I've given him credit for. The song he wrote was a perfect example; never in a million years would I have thought he could come up with a song that beautiful. It makes me wonder.

Mum insists on talking to Lewis on her own first, so

Billy and I kill time by mooching around the hospital gift shop. He's brought his own money with him to buy Lewis a present but can't decide whether to get a jumbo bag of Skittles or M&Ms. It really bothers him, that he doesn't know which Lewis would prefer, so I chip in a couple of quid so he can buy both.

It's nearly an hour before Mum messages to say we can join her in Lewis's room. When we get there, she's kneeling down to tie the laces of his Docs. She looks up and her eyes are red from crying, but the smile on her face reassures me. 'There you are!' she says, as if they'd been the ones waiting for *us*. 'We thought we'd wander down to the canteen, see what delicacies are on offer.'

Billy's lurking behind me, so I give him a gentle shove in Lewis's direction. 'I got these . . . for you. I hope you like them.'

'Are you kidding? They're my favourites!' Lewis grins as Mum helps him to his feet.

'Which ones?' asks Billy, suspicious.

'Both. Skittles in the morning, M&Ms after dinner. Thank you, Billy. That's really kind of you.'

Billy blushes and Lewis coughs and it's all kinds of adorable.

We make our way to the canteen, Billy and me trailing behind Mum and Lewis even though they're walking really slowly. Lewis walks like an old man, stooped and shuffling. It will take him months to regain the strength he lost, but it's a big deal just to see him on his feet.

The canteen is busy, but we find an empty table in a corner. Mum and I leave Billy to fill Lewis in on Indy's latest antics while we queue up for food.

'He talked to the police after you left yesterday . . . Shall I just get a selection of pastries?'

The switch from police to pastries makes me do a double-take. 'What did he tell them?'

'The truth. He'll have to do it all over again at the coroner's inquest, but that won't be for months yet. I told him we'd cross that bridge when we come to it. Two croissants, two Danishes and a pain au chocolat should do it, don't you think? Actually, what am I thinking? *Two* pains au chocolat.'

I stand there, stunned, as Mum pushes our tray along the counter and starts loading up the pastries. I can't believe Lewis had to do that all by himself. Someone should have been with him – been *there* for him.

We settle down at the table and Billy nabs one of the pains au chocolat straight away. Mum gives him a warning look, but he's already taken a huge bite. Lewis takes a Danish and nibbles at the edge of it.

'Would you like me to cut that up for you, love?' asks Mum, already brandishing a knife.

'No,' says Lewis, following it up a little too late with, 'Thank you'.

'Are you going to get an arm with different attachments?' asks Billy between bites. 'You should get a hook . . . that would be amazing.'

'Billy!'

'It's fine, Diane. I'm not sure what type of prosthetic I'm going to get yet.'

'You can get ones that look really real, can't you?' Billy persists. 'I saw this chef on the telly and I didn't realise for ages.'

'Yeah, but you can't actually use them for anything. The ones you can use properly don't look real.' Lewis sounds and looks neutral enough. There's no way of telling if it's an act or if he's managing to come to terms with his injury.

'It'll be a few months yet. Plenty of time to explore the options. First things first, though . . . we've got some good news, haven't we, Lewis?' Mum smiles encouragingly.

Lewis's face doesn't seem to be quite sure about that, but he nods.

'They're discharging him on Monday! Isn't that wonderful?'

'That's brilliant, Lewis,' I say. 'Bet you can't wait to get out of this place.'

'At least here no one stares at me. Well, not much, anyway.'

I thought – hoped – he didn't notice the two kids

we passed in the main corridor. They weren't laughing or pointing or anything, but they were definitely staring.

'Mum always says it's rude to stare,' Billy says. 'If someone stares at you and you don't like it, you should tell me and I'll . . . I'll . . .'

Lewis glances over at me, a smile twitching at the corners of his mouth. 'What will you do, Billy?'

'I'll tell them to . . .' His face scrunches up as he thinks hard. 'I'll tell them to . . . stop staring?'

'Thanks, Billy. I'll bear that in mind.'

Billy's face unscrunches in relief, and he nods, like his job here is done.

'Now that's settled,' says Mum with a wry smile, 'there's something Lewis wants to ask the two of you.'

A flicker of panic crosses Lewis's face. 'Actually, can we . . . ? We don't have to do this now, do we?'

Mum's eyebrows shoot up and she purses her lips as she nods. It's her *yes, you* do *have to do your homework* look, which is exactly the same as her *thank you cards for birthday presents* must *be written and posted less than a month after said presents are received* look. There's no arguing with it.

Lewis wipes his fingers on a paper napkin and stares down at the remaining pastries. 'I was wondering . . .' he starts, then shakes his head. 'If it's OK with you both – really OK, I mean, not just because you feel sorry for me . . .' His gaze is still fixed on the plate of pastries. 'God, I'm not very good at this. When they let me out of here, I was hoping that I could come and stay . . . *live* . . . with you. Your mum said it would be fine, but I didn't want to assume, especially with my dad being a—'

'Where else would you live?' Billy interrupts in the nick of time.

'I don't know . . . I hadn't really thought that far ahead,' says Lewis sheepishly. He finally manages to tear his eyes away from the plate, and when his eyes meet mine, the raw hope is almost too much. The weight of it could sink me, but I won't let it.

'Of course you're coming home.'

FIFTY-ONE

Lewis stands in the doorway, staring, while Mum fusses about. 'I hope you don't mind, I had a little tidy-up. I wanted it to be nice for you.'

Little tidy-up is the understatement of the fucking century. Lewis's room is barely recognisable. Brand-new sheets on the bed, still with the creases from the packaging, a new rug to replace the old one with all its stains and fag burns. He seems stunned as he looks around. 'You didn't need to do this. I'd have sorted it myself.' His left hand hangs by his side, where Indy's looking up at him with total adoration. She nudges his hand with her head and he scratches behind her ears.

Mum stops her fussing. 'I'm sorry. I didn't mean to overstep . . . I'm so sorry.' She's been like this all day, jumpy and anxious and unsure of herself. It's been good for her, though, having this to focus on between tense phone calls with Tim and letting friends and family know that the marriage is over. She even baked a cake.

Lewis makes his way over to the bed and sits down. Indy hops up next to him and props her chin on his knee. 'I'm the one who should be apologising. I don't know how you put up with it, the way it was before.'

'It wasn't that bad,' Mum says with a laugh.

'It *was*,' I chip in, to put a stop to this walking-on-eggshells politeness more than anything else.

Mum sticks her tongue out at me. 'I'll get the kettle on. I'll warn you now, the cake's a bit . . . wrong. More of a large biscuit than a cake, really. Should taste fine, though.' She leaves the room, pausing to pick a piece of fluff from the lampshade on the bedside light.

'She'll start acting normally soon, don't worry,' I say.

Lewis is still in some sort of daze, and then I realise. The last time he was in this room, he wanted to die.

Mum's been reading up about depression, and about the best options for Lewis's treatment. In the past forty-eight hours she's become something of an expert on mental health. She sat me down last night and said we'd have to keep an eye on Lewis – look out for the warning signs. *Not like spying or anything.* I'm not stupid enough to think that everything's going to be rosy now, just because Tim's gone. Mum's working her way through a list of counsellors; she's determined to find someone Lewis can feel comfortable with.

'Listen, I can't stay long. I have to get back to work. I just wanted to be here when you got back.'

Lewis is frowning at the pile of books on the bedside table. He shuffles over, earning an annoyed *hmph* from Indy who then stretches and curls up next to his pillow.

He picks up the book on the top of the pile. It's a fat paperback with a sword on the front. Every book in the pile has a sword on the front, or a man in a cape, or both. 'These aren't mine,' Lewis says.

'They are now.'

'Where did they . . . ? Did *you* get these?'

I shrug. 'Trawled through a few charity stops on Saturday. I hope you don't mind that they're not brand-new, but I'm . . . sort of saving for something.'

'I like second-hand books. It's like getting a dog from a shelter instead of buying a puppy.' I'm starting to realise that Lewis has a weird way of looking at things. Good weird. 'You didn't have to do this, Evan.'

'Well, I did.'

'Why?'

I sit down next to him on the bed and Indy shuffles again so that she's in between us. She's never happier than when she's in the middle, sandwiched between humans who love her.

There are so many possible answers to his question, but only one that feels true. 'We're family.'

He buries his hand in Indy's fur while the battle inside his brain plays out on his face. Hope versus doubt. When it looks like doubt is winning, I say the words again. 'We're *family*.'

He turns to look at me, his eyes searching for the truth in mine. 'Even though . . . ?'

'Even though.'

Lewis moves his hand, haltingly, to rest on top of mine. The smallest gesture, the biggest leap of faith.

We'll muddle along, this fledgling family of ours. Sometimes we'll make mistakes. Arguments will be won and lost, tears will be shed and sorries will be said.

But we will make it work.

Even though.

ONE MONTH LATER

'Do you think it's possible to throw up and shit yourself at the exact same time?' asks Sid as he wipes a cold sweat from his forehead.

'What a delightful mental image. Thanks for that, Sidders.' Daze ruffles his hair, which means he has to get his phone out to check it for the fifth time in as many minutes.

Daze is nervous too, but she's better at hiding it. She keeps surreptitiously wiping her hands on the back of her dress. Sweaty hands are not ideal for playing drums.

An odd sort of calm has descended on me in the past half an hour or so. There's nothing more to organise or think about. No more begging phone calls trying to wheedle donations out of people. The last of the last-minute problems has been solved.

Ticket sales picked up after Harry's latest article in the *Courier* about teenage mental health, and as of yesterday the Mind Your Head gig is officially sold out. Between ticket sales and the online auction, the total raised so far stands at a little over thirty-one thousand pounds.

The success of the auction surprised me – it took on a life of its own, with people contacting us to donate items quicker than I could load them on to the site. Sid ended up bidding for, and winning, the games console that he could have had for free. His bid came with the proviso that Billy comes over for a gaming session at least once a week, which Billy is more than OK with.

My guitar attracted a few bids – some of them downright cheeky – before going to the not so mysterious Jim E. Hendricks. It turns out that Eddie has paid three grand to buy back a guitar he sold to Tim for eighteen hundred and fifty quid.

The biggest surprise was the football shirt signed by the local team. I thought it would go for a hundred quid, maybe two hundred tops; bidding stalled at seventy-five for a couple of days. Then, two days ago, and a couple of hours before the auction closed, I checked the site and found a bid for ten grand. Donovan Gayle must have made the connection, even though there's no mention anywhere about his son and the others. It must have been the police who told him they were treating it as suicide, because Lewis definitely hasn't talked to him.

Lewis did talk to Matthieu and Conrad, and even paid a visit to the Zabeks. No one asked him to do that. Mum even tried to talk him out of it, but he was adamant that they deserved to know the truth from someone who was there. It's seems like a kind of penance for him. The guilt overwhelms him at times. Guilt that he changed his mind at the last minute, guilt that he survived, guilt that he went along with Phoebe's plan in the first place. He's going to therapy twice a week, and it's helping, I think. He talks to me too, late at night after Mum and Billy have gone to bed. We sit in the kitchen, we drink tea, Lewis talks, I listen.

I peek out from backstage. Five hundred people doesn't sound like a lot but it sure looks like it. Lewis is there, sitting on the sand at the front with Indy on one side, Billy on the other. Mum and Harry are behind them on deckchairs.

The crowd is quiet and respectful as the woman on stage explains why we're doing this, and where the money's going. Susila talks about the mental health charity she's been running for the past ten years, and the issues facing young people today. I know the stats by heart now — the escalating rates of depression, self-harm, anxiety, eating disorders — but that doesn't make them any easier to hear.

Everyone cheers when she says that so far we've raised enough money to get the online chat service back up and running by the end of September, and to keep it running for a year. That gives us plenty of time to figure out how to raise enough money to keep it running permanently.

The service will be staffed by trained volunteers; Sid, Daze and I have already signed up for the training. Lewis wanted to sign up too, but Mum thinks he needs some time to focus on his own mental health first. I thought he'd fight her on that one, but he just nodded and said that sounded sensible. They're still very polite with each other, Mum and Lewis, but they're gradually getting there. There are positive signs, like Mum shouting at him about the state of his room yesterday. You could see it in his eyes, when he apologised, that he was glad she cared.

A tap on the shoulder brings me back. Daze and Sid are staring at me and I realise this is it. We're up next.

The nerves hit me like a tidal wave, and I start to babble. 'I don't think I can do this. We're not ready. We're nowhere near ready. I think I've forgotten the words . . . what are the words again? My fingers are numb. Are your fingers numb?'

'Hold these, Sid,' says Daze as she hands him her drumsticks. 'And could you maybe turn around for a few seconds? You won't want to see this.' Sid rolls his eyes but he does as he's told, turning his back on us.

She's smiling that mischievous smile of hers — the one that means she's up to no good. 'Daze, what are you . . . ?'

My unfinished question is answered when her lips meet mine. It's unexpected and inevitable and so absolutely, fundamentally *right*. I can't help sinking into the moment, kissing her back.

It's over much too soon and Daze is wiping her lipstick from my mouth with her thumb. 'OK, then,' she says cheerily, 'Let's do this thing.'

'But . . . ?' I glance over at Sid who's fiddling with his guitar strap and blushing.

'Don't mind me, I'll just be over here. Alone.' But he gives me a nod and a smile, and that means everything.

'What about Alice?' I whisper.

'What *about* her?' Daze whispers back. I glare at her; she's enjoying this far too much. 'OK, OK! Alice and I aren't even a thing. We haven't seen each other for weeks.'

'Why didn't you tell me?'

'I was waiting for the right moment.'

'And this is what you call the right moment? Five seconds before our first-ever gig?'

That smile again. 'It took your mind off the stage fright, didn't it?'

'I hate you.'

'You *love* me.' She's serious now, her eyes locked on mine. 'And I love you. Obviously.'

I open my mouth to speak, but she stops me with another kiss. 'I know,' she whispers in my ear. 'Tell me later.'

I don't know how I'm going to get through the next twenty minutes, but I'm really, *really* looking forward to later.

My legs are shaking as I adjust the height of the microphone. Lewis and Billy are cheering the loudest, but Mum and Harry are giving them a run for their money.

I manage to focus on a few faces in the crowd. I spot Matthieu standing amongst a group of Belmont boys. Conrad with his little sister, Ruth, balanced on his shoulders, her necklace glinting in the sunshine. Both of them are smiling.

Alice stands off to one side, alone. Nik and Agata are near the front. Knowing they support what we're trying to do gives me strength.

I turn to Sid, who manages to nod even though he looks like he wants to run and hide in a hole. I glance over my shoulder at Daze, her back straight and her drumsticks poised. She winks at me.

I play the first couple of chords, closing my eyes to conjure up their faces. Karolina, James and Phoebe. This is for them.

When I open my eyes again, my gaze lands on Lewis. This is for him.

But it's also for the rest of us. For anyone who's ever felt voiceless and hopeless. Because we *do* have a voice, and there *is* hope. Even — maybe especially — when it doesn't feel that way.

I open my mouth and start to sing.

HELP AND ADVICE

If you need help or advice, please think about reaching out to one of the organisations below.

Childline

A private and confidential service for young people up to age 19. Contact a Childline counsellor about anything – no problem is too big or small. Available 24hrs.

Call free on **0800 1111** or talk online at **www.childline.org.uk**

LGBT Youth Scotland

From questioning your sexual identity, coming out, relationship issues, bullying to sexual health – this is a private place designed for you to comfortably chat online with a youth worker.

Find them at **www.lgbtyouth.org.uk**

The Mix

Offers counselling to those under 25. Open 24/7 and 365 days a year.

Call free on **0808 808 4994** ot talk online at **www.themix.org.uk**

Samaritans

Confidential and emotional support for people who are experiencing feelings of distress, despair or suicidal thoughts. Lines open 24/7 and 365 days a year. If you need a response immediately, it's best to call on the phone.

Call free on **116 123** or find them at **www.samaritans.org**

Hope Again

Offers confidential help to young bereaved people. Mon-Fri 9.30am-5pm.

Call free on **0870 808 1677** or find them at **www.hopeagain.org.uk**

Papyrus

Young suicide prevention society. Mon-Fri 10am-5pm & 7pm-10pm. Weekends 2-5pm.

Call **0800 068 4141** or find them at **www.papyrus-uk.org**

Beat

Offers support and information about eating disorders. Helplines are open 365 days a year: 4pm-10pm.

Call free on **0808 801 0711** or find them at **www.b-eat.co.uk**

ACKNOWLEDGEMENTS

The making of a book is a team effort. My heartfelt thanks to . . .

Julia Churchill. It's a pleasure to fight the good fight alongside you.

Emma Goldhawk, an exceptional editor brimming with insight, understanding and humour. I couldn't have done it without you.

Hélène Ferey, Prema Raj, Alexandra McNicoll, Vickie Dillon and Hana Murrell at A.M. Heath.

The Hachette Children's Book gang: Sarah Lambert, Emily Thomas, Becky Logan, Ruth Girmatsion, Sarah Baldwin, Naomi Berwin, Jenny Glencross, Kelly Llewellyn, Anne McNeil and Hilary Murray Hill.

Sinem Erkas, for the stunning new cover look.

Two very helpful (anonymous) police officers, for answering my bizarre questions.

Ciara Daly, Anna Frame, Isobel & Graham Fisher, Victoria Schwab, Cate James, Sarah Crossan, Alan McDonald, Rob Clarke, the Sisters and my merry band of writer pals. You lovely folk have fed my mind, soul and body in all kinds of different ways. I'm lucky to know each and every one of you.

As ever, my biggest debt is to Caro Clarke, for steering me through tricky times with stellar ideas, an endless supply of homemade pickles and Very Strong Feelings about Breakfast Tim.